Inside our National Parks and Monuments

—*A Perilous Fight*—

WES WOLFE

PAGE PUBLISHING, INC.
New York, NY

First originally published by Page Publishing, Inc. 2019

ISBN 978-1-64462-048-9 (Paperback)
ISBN 978-1-64462-049-6 (Digital)

Printed in the United States of America

To my loving wife, Ginny, who lived through
many of the perilous fights.

Her encouragement and guidance made this story possible.

In appreciation of my special daughter, Jennifer, her
husband, Keith (my best friend) and my grandsons
Carson and Collin who keep me young.

CONTENTS

PREFACE

This book is a historical novel about our national parks and monuments. The major purpose in writing the narrative was provocation, although the reader may find the stories entertaining, humorous, even outrageous. The author has attempted to use humor and embellishments to reveal how our national treasures are being exploited by anti-environment, anti-conservation public officials in the White House. Each episode is fictionalized although it happened or should have happened. The author was aware of many illegal, damaging and irreversible actions by political appointees. He shares little-known footnotes in American history and rare insights into the history and management of national parks.

The law creating the National Park Service was an unworkable compromise that stated that the new federal agency was "to provide for the enjoyment" and "leave them unimpaired." In the ensuing almost one hundred years, it is questionable if visitors found Alcatraz, Grant's Tomb, or Custer Battlefield enjoyable. But there is no question that our historical and natural resources have been severely impaired. Witness melting and soon-to-disappear glaciers at Glacier National Park; obnoxious noise and sickening carbon dioxide from snowmobiles at Yellowstone; acres and miles of concrete at Yosemite; the exclusion of Native Americans (the victors) at the Battle of Little Bighorn, the selling of religious fundamentalism at the Grand Canyon, the sandbagging of the King family at the Martin Luther King National Historic Site; objectionable government history at the Statue of Liberty; and the accusations of a First Lady stealing silverware from the Executive Mansion.

The federal courts and the US Congress seem reluctant to take up arms to protect and preserve the national parks. Their effective actions usually follow a public outcry after the damage has been done. The private conservation groups and organizations keep the issues alive in the public mind but do not have the resources or the daredevil audacity to sabotage the powerful politicos.

The past, present, and continuing struggle between the career park people and the political opportunists is told through two bands of brotherhood: the Peyote Society (no, they do not use drugs) and the Spoilers (who relish their role as self-serving evildoers). The two chief protagonists are Cool-Head Fred, a former and future ping-pong champion, and Gotcha Butcher, a daddy's boy bred to crush any obstacle or foe. They are opposites in every way except in their commitment to their cause. Gotcha rewards only blind loyalty; Cool-Head Fred encourages and leads guerilla warfare. The battle continues even today.

CHAPTER ONE

COOL-HEAD FRED

No one ever had to hunt him down on the tournament floor. He was six feet five and one hundred and sixty pounds. On his head he sported an old Smoky Bear hat that was over sixty years old. The hat had a hole in the top where a battery-operated propeller had been inserted, which blew cool air over his sweaty face. He wore black short pants and a red polo shirt with the collar turned up so the refreshing breeze could pass down his body to his toes. He wore no socks. The white sneakers on his feet were tongueless and had ventilating holes cut into the sides. Fred had suffered a lifelong battle with athlete's foot. He didn't try to hide the varicose veins that webbed upward from his ankles to the back of his knees.

His hands were humongous. The fingers were almost an inch longer than most men. Grasping the handle of the racket was difficult and more than inconvenient—too much hand and not enough handle. It bothered him when he played and affected his concentration. So he wrapped a whole roll of black electrical tape around the handle to get a better and more comfortable grip. When the handle increased to the size of the hitting end of a baseball bat, it felt just right, and he no longer thought about it when receiving an opponent's serve.

The sound of the ball hitting the blade of his racket made a strange noise like the ticktock of a grandfather's clock. It distracted and irritated the other players, as he thought it would. But what really exasperated them was his laborious process of retrieving the battered balls. Because of his arthritic knees and recurring spasms from spinal stenosis, he had difficulty bending over. As he grew older, it became increasingly worse. To ease the effort of picking up a ball from the floor, he made a simple contraption that he called a "getter." It was constructed from a metal coat hanger and an empty cat food tin can.

Both the top and the bottom of the tin can were cut out, and two wide rubber bands were glued to the bottom of it, forming four equal squares. One end of the coat hanger was attached to two small holes on equal sides of the can. The other end of the three-foot hanger was bent to form a handle. Fred would then shuffle over to the ball, and without bending over, he would place his getter over the ball and then slowly push the cat food can over the ball, which would pop up through one of the openings. He would then lift up the can with his left hand and remove the ball with his right. It saved him from bending over at least thirty times during a single match. His wife, Ginny, often said that the most frightening thing in her life, next to opening a can of cat food in front of five hungry cats, was watching him play.

His friends and admirers called him Cool-Head Fred, and he was in good physical shape except for the arthritis. It was ping-pong that got him there and ping-pong that kept him there. He was an inspiration to his fellow seniors, who marveled at his extraordinary efforts to succeed and wondered why he gave a damn. It was a puzzle to them why he drove to Seattle every Sunday to play with the Chinese players when he could play against them in the local senior center. Fred was grateful that he had the game of table tennis, and he put much time, most of his energy, and a slice of his income into the game. Fred and Ginny had won numerous mixed doubles championships, and she had beat him on occasion. The game rewarded him with lifelong friends, recognition, and a mountain of tournament trophies and medals.

Table tennis was something to give a damn about since he had long ago given up on the government and believed that the only salvation for the country was to elect a "do nothing" president! How things had changed since that victorious day in June 1945. Fred was a World War II veteran who almost paid the ultimate price. He felt that the present bunch of politicians got the nation into stupid, unnecessary, and endless wars fighting guerilla ghosts, losing innocent lives, and wasting billions of dollars.

Most men Fred's age were in nursing homes, many in wheelchairs, some bedridden. The genes in Fred's family had been a special gift—mother, father, grandfather, grandmother—all living into their nineties. And Fred had something else, a secret desire to be the national table tennis champion, age ninety and over. He almost became the national champion age eighty and over, but there was one Chinese American whom he could not beat. Fred and Ginny would continue to practice, practice, practice and play in the major table tennis tournaments all over the country.

Fred started playing the ping-pong game in 1930 at Moultrie playground in Charleston, South Carolina. It rained and rained in Charleston, and it drove the playground kids off the baseball and football fields, the outdoor tennis and basketball courts into the playground clubhouse. The rain also got rid of the bugs, gnats as big as ping-pong balls and mosquitoes larger than tennis balls. There was a ping-pong table and a basket of bats and balls. Most of the balls were cracked. The paddles were also cheap, and the sandpaper on both sides was split and torn. The top surface of the nine-foot table was a mosaic of chips, dents, scratches, peeled paint, and no paint. It sloped on the right end because the thirty-inch metal leg was bent. The six-inch net drooped in the middle and didn't quite cover the five-foot width of the table.

The ping-pong–playing kids didn't complain, and they would kick the table when they lost a point. Fred was able to beat all the other boys, even those who were older and taller. He collected playground ping-pong trophies and became the Charleston Junior Champion. His success continued in high school, college, and he began hustling other players while stationed inland during the war. After the war, he finished college, taught school for two years, and got married. He later joined the National Parks Service, and the work became all-consuming.

The national parks and monuments, next to his wife and daughter, Jennifer, became the most important mission in his life. He no longer thought about or played ping-pong, a.k.a. table tennis, and his return to the game would have to wait for thirty-five years.

Being tall, Fred stood out in any group, and you could tell by the way he wore the Ranger uniform that it stood for something larger than life. The Ranger uniform was a deep forest green, and his was always neatly pressed. His gold-plated Ranger badge and US Park insignia were polished to brilliance. His shoes were highly polished—a carryover over from his military service. The dark leather hat band with silver acorns highlighted the distinguished and easily recognizable Smoky Bear felt hat. No one presented a better image. It was also true that he was ambitious and was willing to take on any assignment—even serving in New York City and Washington DC. On these assignments, he gained valuable experience and was exposed to the inner workings of top management and the hidden political agenda at the highest levels.

But it was his earlier service in the Southwestern parks and monuments where his beliefs and philosophy about life were changed forever. He became a spiritual person and began viewing the government and its policies in a different way. The Parks Department was not only yielding to political pressure, but also it was becoming politicized at almost every level. The White House was exploiting the natural resources for personal gain, beyond anything one could imagine. Would the parks be there unimpaired for the next generation and the next? Who would make sure that it happened? It was at this time that Fred became a founding member of the Peyote Society.

CHAPTER TWO

THE PEYOTE PEOPLE

The Peyote People were a small group of unselfish, dedicated career federal Parks Department employees whose mission was to protect and preserve the natural, historical, and archeological treasures set aside by the laws of the United States Congress. There were a few concerned and influential individuals outside the parks who were also members. The mandate of the Peyote Society was to ensure and safeguard the 1872, 1906, and 1916 congressional legislation that established the National Parks and Monuments and the government agency to enforce the laws.

None of the members of the Peyote Society ate, drank, or smoked the ritualistic drug Peyote. But they maintained the spirituality of those First Americans who used the Peyote in their healing ceremonies. There were ten tenants of spirituality that guided the mind, heart, and soul of the society:

1. Spirituality is a state of mind that frees us to be in harmony with all elements of the universe.
2. Our spirituality is a connection to the truth.
3. Our spirituality gives us the strength to face adversity and injustice and to right those wrongs.
4. We strive to be free of selfishness.
5. Our spirituality is the force that puts our passion into play.
6. Our spirituality gives us a feeling of inner peace.

7. Our spirituality provides us complete confidence.
8. Our spirituality demands total honesty.
9. Our spirituality is an invisible, unpredictable, and uncontrollable force.
10. Our spirituality makes the ride worthwhile.

There were no secret handshakes, no esoteric passwords, no membership cards, no dues, no laws, no rules, no dogmas. The only requirement for membership was a good heart and to do the right thing to save Mother Earth. But it did require the members to take action, when necessary. One member could only recognize another by the decisions made, the actions taken, and the results of one's commitment. The original brothers and sisters all served in the Southwestern parks where they gained an understanding of the connection between spirituality and the earth. As the society grew, its singular purpose became fighting those who would do damage to the parks for nothing more than selfish reasons.

So there would be no misunderstanding about the Peyote Society and the extent to which it would go to protect the national parks, individual members were willing to sacrifice their careers for their beliefs.

The society would not tolerate any legislative, judicial, or executive political actions that threatened its goals. They would not be intimidated by anyone. The members would take whatever means that were necessary, which would include intervention, hindrance, disrupting, embarrassment, leaking to the media, obstruction, resistance, subversion, and sabotage to stop the mindless, greedy, mean-spirited, self-serving, immoral, illegal actions of any group, organization, or individual.

CHAPTER THREE

THE SPOILERS

The Spoilers were the sons and daughters, brothers, and sisters, friends, and financial supporters of the right-wing, conservative, anti-environment, big business administration. They were also known as the Bully Boy Bastards. Some were young, recent college graduates whose parents had contributed heavy dollars to the Conservative Party. The payoff was a job in the most glamorous agency in the federal government.

They were bright, eager, and most importantly, willing to infiltrate the Parks Department. They were carefully placed under park career supervisors whose loyalty was in question. These nasty little people—the Spoiler Spies—were looked upon by the park people as SS Troopers. They ruined the careers of many good men and women, who were banished to Death Valley and Grant's Tomb. They were eventually driven out of the National Park Service by career employees who feigned loyalty.

The mantra of the Spoilers was "to the victor go the spoils." Most of the Spoilers were political appointees to high-level management positions such as assistant this and deputy that. They were from the business and media world, and their mission was "to turn it around," meaning that they would circumvent laws established by the United States Congress. To them the parks were there for the pickings.

The US Congress on August 25, 1916, established the National Park Service as the federal agency whose responsibility was to "to conserve the scenery and the natural and historic objects and the wildlife therein and to provide for the enjoyment of the same in such manner and by such means as will leave them unimpaired for the enjoyment of future generations." Only a bunch of lawyers could write something so vague, so indefinable, so meaningless, something impossible to accomplish. How could anyone reconcile two separate, divergent missions—"conserve" and "enjoyment." "Conserve" means to protect from loss or depletion, to use carefully, to avoid waste. "Enjoyment" means to receive pleasure from, to relish, to make happy. "Unimpaired"—not to diminish in strength, value, quantity, or quality. This could mean "use it, but don't abuse it." But does it?

One could say the dedicated scientist would like to build a wall around the national parks to keep people out. The parks would be a living-study area, a laboratory to research and produce scientific treatises. The parks would be like the Bible of ancient times, and the scientists, like the high priests, would tell the people the meaning of the parks and what the experience was like. But the people would not be allowed to see the parks for themselves. One could only hope that one day the research would be completed and the people's grandchildren would be able to experience the great unknown.

And at the other extreme, the parks would be a fun-loving place where one could pick the flowers and the kids would be entertained, like Disneyland. One could use, abuse, and the devil may care. Parks are for the people, and the dog-and-pony shows would amuse, and everyone would have the time of their lives. Leaving them unimpaired would not be a consideration.

The middle ground would be "wise use" provided by the Parks Department education/interpretive programs. The staff would teach and show the people how to experience and enjoy the parks so they were there for others to explore. The pendulum swings away from this wise-use approach when an administration is set on exploiting the parks for political purposes and personal gain.

Where is the oversight? Who are the watchdogs? Where are the private conservation organizations? Where is academia? Why can't they stop the ruinous policies and not just pay lip service to the problems? The Spoilers' plan had always been to buy loyalty within the ranks of the career employees. They dangled bigger budgets, promotions, and park developments to the park superintendents. They would target African Americans, women, and other minorities who would support their political assault on the natural resources and the destruction of conservation programs. Some of the Parks people sold out, some caved in, and a few pretended to go along.

In the business world, success is measured by increased revenues and earnings. In the parks, it is numbers—the numbers of visitors. So the visitation numbers were inflated at the park level, at the regional office level, and mostly by the number crushers in the Capital City headquarters. Maintenance needs were exaggerated, questionable new developments proposed, and always terrorist threats would require greater security. All these requests would be approved by the Spoilers, and the taxpayers would just keep on giving, mostly those who never visited a national park or monument. Serving the parks became a big, big, profitable business.

CHAPTER FOUR

GOTCHA

The presidential policy makers appointed Bennett "Gotcha" Butcher as the assistant secretary in the Interior Department to spread their destructive exploitation. Gotcha was five feet five, going bald, with a bulging belly in an advanced stage. He was thirty-eight years old, and there was a certain meanness about him. No one liked him, especially his wife, but his blind loyalty is what the White House Spoilers admired. His nickname, Gotcha, came from those who knew him and his attitude about people and life in general. He usually got what he wanted, and if he couldn't, his daddy would get it for him.

His old man had raised millions for the Conservative Party as chairman of fund-raising in the Southern states. He was considered nouveau riche, having made a fortune in the construction business using illegal Mexican labor. Senior Butcher often said, "The wetbacks are hard workers, unlike that other bunch, who just sit on their fat asses and draw welfare. Well, damn it, if they want a job, I'll give them one." His company dominated the public works sector of the economy in the South. He built roads, parking lots, highways, bridges, tunnels, office buildings, jails, schools, and city, county, and state park recreational facilities.

The Butcher Construction Company used inferior building materials, rebuilt machinery, and the lowest grade of electrical and plumbing parts and fixtures. The workmanship was hurried and was the worst in the industry. They were par excellent in circumventing public safety and contract requirements. Gotcha's specialty when he worked for his daddy was paying off building inspectors, local politicians and judges, and contributing to tax-deductible but questionable charities. He was also the enforcer who would intimidate, threaten, and destroy anyone who got in his way. Not surprising, Gotcha was named the Young Man of the Year by the Georgia Junior Chamber of Commerce when he was only twenty-three.

The first decision that Gotcha made as the new assistant secretary overseeing the Parks Department was to select a former Secret Service guard as the director of the Parks Department. Tyrone Browne had a reputation as the best White House tour guide during his three years guarding the president's daughter.

Recently, Tyrone had been the acting assistant coordinator for the president's advance team. He was at his best in arranging photo ops at the parks and monuments. Yet he would seldom be seen because Gotcha would micromanage the Parks Department.

The second decision was a major organizational change that would establish twenty district offices. Each office would tightly control about twenty park areas. Gotcha would select only political appointees as district directors. They would smother the local park operations and leave the park superintendents with little authority. The directors would hire and promote, issue all contracts, approve all overtime, control all expenditures, and make all contacts with the concessioners. The Butcher company dreamed of replacing all the concessioners.

There was a Peyote in the Capital City Parks Department who would direct the Peyote actions at the park level. He was sixty years old and would be the last person that Gotcha would ever suspect as being disloyal. This man acted like a Spoiler, talked like a Spoiler, walked like a Spoiler, so Gotcha concluded he must be a Spoiler.

The battle was joined—Fred against Gotcha (and he didn't even know it) and the Peyotes versus the Spoilers. The Spoilers had the money, the power, and the political clout to grab all they could from the parks. They had a Gestapo mentality—ruthless, punishing, and always made an overwhelming frontal assault. The Peyotes possessed a strong spirituality and an undying commitment! They were almost invisible and employed guerrilla tactics. They moved with lightning speed—masters of the hit-and-run. Their prayer was "rest assured my children, the parks will be there for you—unimpaired."

HURRY, HURRY, HURRY

Long ago, before Fred and Gotcha and Peyotes and Spoilers, before fossil fuels, concrete parking lots, golf courses, swimming pools, hot dog stands and bubble gum wrappers, the stewards of this most beautiful plot in the world were the Miwoks, "The People." They called the most beautiful plot on earth "Ahwanee," deep grassy place.

Other First Americans had lived there for thousands of years before, where they hunted, fished, and gathered plants and fruits, in harmony with the land. It was their Sacred Place. One clan, the Uzumati, the Grizzlies, were living there in 1850 when the California Gold Rush pushed onto their sacred place. The Uzumatis tried to live in peace with the invaders, but the gold miners formed the Mariposa Battalion to force them off their land. The miners accused the Uzumati Indians of raiding their mining camps. The Mariposa Battalion were merciless in pursing the Uzumatis and killing them— women, children, and the old ones. In less than three years, "the deep grassy place" was theirs to exploit, populate, and desecrate. They stole all the gold.

After the gold miners took away the gold, a few adventurers trickled in and reported that, indeed, it was the most spectacular site in California. Curious sightseers came to Uzumati, as it was known, by foot, horseback, wagon, stagecoach, and eventually by railroad. An entrepreneur, James Rustler, who had missed out on the gold rush, settled in and built the first accommodations. The artists, writers, photographers, the curious, and the dreamers soon followed.

In 1864, the Civil War president ceded the federal land to the state of California. But no meaningful conservation, protection, or administration were established. One dreamer, a Scot by the name of John Puir, first saw the beautiful place in 1868 and called it the most "Incomparable Valley." Puir became the soul and savior of Uzumati. He lived, worked, hiked, and climbed the mountains and studied the rocks, plants, and animals for the next forty-five years. He was captivated by the magnificent scenery and wrote "no temple made with hands can compare—it is the grandest of all special temples of nature." Puir believed that nature was God revealed, and he exclaimed that hunting animals was murder.

He was the first to publish research that glaciers had sculpted the peaks and valleys, which was contrary to the prevailing scientific theory that they were the result of earthquakes. He was recognized by the literary and scientific communities for his conservation efforts and prolific writings, especially "The Treasure of Uzumati." Puir wrote about how the hoofed locusts, the large herds of sheep, were devastating the meadows. He was successful in persuading the US Congress to establish Uzumati as a national park in 1890. But the divine masterpiece was still under California authority. He fought against those who wanted to use the resources for personal gain, and he formed the Sierra Club to terminate the state's management.

Puir invited President Teddy Bear to Uzumati, and the conservation-minded president was mesmerized by the storytelling and devotion of the Scotsman. Finally, in 1916, California receded Puir's precious preserve back to the federal government. No one had done more to ensure that the establishment, preservation, and protection of Uzumati become a reality. His words, "Climb the mountains and get their good tidings. Nature's peace will flow into you as sunshine flows into the trees; The winds will blow their own freshness into you and the storms their energy, while cares will drop off like autumn leaves," are immortal.

He died in 1914, many say from a broken heart because the nearby valley, Fetch Fetchy, was destroyed when the Toulumne river was dammed to provide the coastal city with drinking water and electricity. The miners had gouged out the gold, the big city stole the water, but the worst devastation was on the way—mobs of city folks with creature comfort habits. Two years after Puir's death, Congress finally established Uzumati a national park. Today the park is an outstanding example of the continuing imbalance between conservation and public misuse, which does not leave the natural resources unimpaired.

For centuries, the First Americans humbled themselves in spiritual silence as they looked up from the valley floor and viewed the great monolith, "tis-sa-ack" or cleft rock, their spoken word for "half dome." They believed the stories that their grandfathers told about how the Great Spirit, angry at the chief for neglecting his people, split the chief's throne in half. Their name for "el capitan" was "to-to-kon," and they never thought about climbing straight up the four-thousand-foot vertical granite wall.

Modern-day scientists have a different interpretation on how the cliffs were formed. They say a million years ago a great glacier, about a mile thick, gouged, ripped, sliced, and carved two spectacular monuments. Ice, water, and wind joined to sculpt the rocks into unique shapes and created pillars, columns, and spires in the Uzumati Valley. The water keeps giving, forming Yosemite Falls, 2,425 feet deep, one of the tallest anywhere. Bridalveil Falls, 620 feet, flows all year and is often the first seen by those entering the park. Vernal Falls, 317 feet, flows all year round and is best seen from Glacier Point, and the other Falls Nevada, Ribbon, and Illouette.

Added to the grandeur are the wildlife of Uzumati, their home for thousands of years. The black bear, gray fox, mountain coyote, California mule deer, and the big mountain lion are still there, somewhere. But not the great grizzly bear or bighorn sheep—gone forever due to indiscriminate hunting. The gnawing animals are still scampering around too—the Alpine chipmunk, golden ground squirrel, Sierra chickaree, mountain beaver, and the flying squirrel can sometimes be seen against a moonlit sky. The toe-walking deer are seemingly unafraid of man, but ever watchful for a mountain lion. The mountain coyotes are common and often seen on the hunt for mice, rabbits, and an occasional fawn. If one spots a fox, it is probably a gray, since the red fox is a rare find.

All the bears in Uzumati are black bears, but sometimes light brown in color, and they usually dine on berries, grass, nuts, and roots. They can run and climb a tree faster than any gawking photographer. They do hibernate in the winter, neither eating nor drinking. About a dozen black bears can usually be seen in the overcrowded valley, eating potato chips, candy bars, popcorn, and ice cream gratis of unthinking tourists. They usually weigh about 250 pounds, but one garbage bear dented the scales at over six hundred. They are not cute, not warm or fuzzy. The black bear is a dangerous animal, and it is against the law to feed, tease, or molest any wildlife in Uzumati.

Bird watching is mostly rewarding near the rivers, the Tuolumne, an Indian word for cave, and the Merced (mercy) where one is likely to see the Stellar's jay, American robin, woodpecker, black-headed grosbeak, and the ravens. There are twenty-seven varieties of trees. The most distinctive—California black oak, incense cedar, ponderosa pine, and the giant sequoias—the largest trees on earth. They grow in Uzumati in the groves of Mariposa, Tuolumne, Merced, and some are over one thousand years old. In the valley and at Wawona are the park's most visible flowers—dogwood, mariposa lily, redbud lupine, sierra onion. In the Toulumne meadows, there are little elephant's head, gentian, yarrow, and shooting stars. The most spectacular view is from Glacier Point, the most awesome panoramic overlook in the world.

All this magnificence to protect and preserve for posterity and beyond, with the newly established National Park Service, the public was assured that past exploitation and destruction of the park's geology, flora, and wildlife was over forever. But the stagecoach travelers of old soon arrived by train and then in automobile caravans. The Parks people were a Johnny-come-lately bunch, since poachers like Rustler had already broken ground, built facilities, and gained political support. The question was asked, Who is going to manage Uzumati National Park? Didn't President Teddy Bear say about another great national park, "Leave it as it is, you can't improve on it." But the poachers would surely ignore that advice. Their greed for profit would supersede all attempts by conservation groups to effect protective park management.

Only a few days after the park rangers moved in, the chief poacher, a man named Murray, wrote a letter to the Capital City Spoilers: "Uzumati concessioners can only make money for about two months in the season, and for the rest of the time, they might as well take money from one pocket and put it in another and allege that this was a money-making process." It was always about money. To keep the attention of 28,823 curiosity seekers, 14,572 who came by automobile, Murray proposed, "Please allow me to suggest further attractions that would absolutely extend the season to six months: a golf course would be a big hit, and a fire fall show—the best advertising stunt ever conceived for bringing business to the park." Hurry, hurry, hurry—see the bears dance for Murray."

The Fire Fall attraction was produced by a low-paid Murray employee who at nine every night would let it rip when he heard the cry from below, "Let the fire fall!" A great bonfire of red fir bark would descend from Glacier Point, three thousand feet of eye-popping red ribbon. Great care was always taken to ensure that the embers were pushed off the edge to simulate a steady flow of flaming red and create the illusion of a waterfall of fire. The Fire Fall was always enhanced by the singing of the "Indian Love Call," accompanied by two violins. The whole show lasted about thirty seconds, and the crowd would cheer.

A special event was the Indian Field Days. A three-day full-fledged rodeo with real horse bucking, cowboy, and Indian games, all-day pony rides, and best of all, a horse mounted tug of war. It was a show the early visitors didn't want to miss. Hurry, hurry, hurry—see the bears dance for Murray. The Princely Poacher continued to bombard the Spoilers with proposals. How about a bowling alley, billiard tables, horse shoes, square dances, a beauty contest? "We should provide the same amenities," exclaimed Murray, "that the good folks are used to having at home." Coke machines, hairdressers, the ever-popular beer parlors, and gift shops that would sell fresh flowers, rocks and pebbles, and cute little black bears were high on the list. After all it was what the people wanted. "Just the other day, Murray wrote, a guest requested a masseur."

The Big Tent Show, one that would attract the city folk for sure, was Guess Who's Coming to Dinner—an obese, hungry black bear. The poachers would charge fifty cents for the bus ride to the river's edge to view the bears' dining table. The bears had been cajoled to show up on time for the feast on cue. The Parks Department had been assured that the "bears would only be fed clean and sanitary garbage." Once the invited guests mooched around the outdoor cafeteria, a giant floodlight would heighten the drama, and the ringsiders would be entertained for the next fifteen minutes. The most frequent response was "Ain't that something to see, I gotta get a picture of this." P. T. Barnum would have applauded.

The first rule of a successful poacher was "Never take no for an answer." Sometimes other people can get it done for you. An English lad horrified at the primitive nature of the facilities greased the skids for the building of a first-class, five-star hotel in a national park. Lady Caster, the first of her gender in the British parliament, complained to the president of her "unheated room, lack of proper bath facilities, tasteless food unfit for even an Australian, and the whole place just a bore." She left in a huff, never to return to any national park again. The unfortunate episode cinched the approval from the early Capital City Spoilers. A grand hotel—elegant, majestic—a granite facade, a striking beamed ceiling, lavish bedrooms and baths, a football-size ornate dining room, resplendent with First American art and artifacts, a smoking parlor, a huge lounge with a nude painting of some French floozy on the wall behind a massive stone hearth. It would be a one-of-a-kind experience for the rich and powerful—all in the great outdoors.

An outdoor swimming pool with live music to entertain the swimmers was only a minor success. If Murray could only get approval for a cable car he dreamed of, but it was only a dream. All the creature comforts—hotels, restaurants, gift shops, transportation—were approved by the Spoilers in Capital City. The on-site park managers went along for the ride because more and more tourists were coming, and that meant bigger budgets, bigger staffs, and a higher pay grade. A win-win situation for everyone except the natural resources in the park. And even if they didn't go along, they would be replaced by those who did. Any protection and preservation for the flora and fauna would have to come from outside the government. One member of the Sierra Club cried, "Nibble, nibble, nibble, they are nibbling away our national parks."

One Uzumati park ranger exclaimed that "we can't keep on killing the black bears just because some stupid people are getting hurt. What do these people think is going to happen when they hug a wild animal for a picture?" The postmaster wrote that "Uzumati is getting to be an awful place. We have crowds all season, and the air is filled with dust and the smell of gasoline. I'm tired of the constant whiz of automobiles. I thought I'd have some rest and peace in Uzumati, that's why I came here, but there's no solitude." (This letter was written on July 5, 1927.)

Because the park sported the largest ice-skating rink in North America, Murray pushed hard to grab the 1932 Winter Olympics. But it didn't happen. But the Great Depression offered a boon to development and construction. The Civil Conservation Corps built many roads, trails, picnic shelters, restrooms, sheds, campgrounds, drilled tunnels through mountains, concession facilities for Murray, and numerous concrete parking lots. The ecological damage was ignored, most often not even considered.

Murray was a tour de force in ingratiating himself and winning the backing from the politicians, both local and national. He contributed the tourists' money to the public office holders' political campaigns, and all the amenities in the park were always available to them for the asking, family and friends included. In return, Murray got exclusive rights to hawk all the wares to the general public—hotel rooms, gasoline, food, souvenirs, and liquor and beer at outrageous prices. He had to pay the government an annual fee, three cents on each dollar gouged from the unsuspecting public. When Murray heard the Spoilers say that now that the war is over and gasoline rationing is over we'll see a deluge of automobiles and people, it was Eureka—the gift that keeps on giving.

But when the government announced a new and massive development program, called Mission 66, Murray began to salivate. The big bucks would spruce up the parks and provide for the oncoming multitudes. Millions would be spent and misspent on new and wider concrete roads, Murray's buildings and facilities, visitor facilities, and more and more concrete parking lots. The new mantra was "Nothing is too good for our guests." Visitation doubled, so they say, over two million trounced through Uzumati in 1976. One-way traffic and more and more concrete parking lots. The park superintendents came and went, but Murray and his successors stayed on and on and continued to poach through it all. Some Capital City Park executives retired and joined the Poachers and guided them on how to refine their methods of poaching.

Conservation groups started to pressure the government to do something about saving Uzumati so it wouldn't become citified. They lamented that you don't have to go to a big city to find a five-star hotel; just go to your national parks. The majority of the Uzumati visitors were Californians, and it was a rare occasion to see an African American, Hispanic American, or First American in Uzumati National Park.

Hurry, hurry, hurry—see the bears dance for Murray. Twenty-five things made in China for sale in Uzumati National Park: rubber duck rangers, rubber mountain lions, rubber black snakes, coffee mugs, beer mugs, key chains, red fire trucks, plastic bow and arrows, rhinestone necklaces, brass-plated deer, toy plastic pistols, raccoon charm bracelets, black bear booties, rubber clogs, fake Indian dolls, plastic salt-and-pepper shakers, silver-plated commemorative spoons, fake Indian feather headsets, stuffed black bears, plastic deer antlers, imitation leather cowboy belts, jigsaw puzzles, crossword puzzles, pine cone–shaped plastic earrings, and shot glasses. There are thirty-two outlets in Uzumati National Park that sell beer, wine, or liquor. Twenty of them are in the Sacred Valley.

As advertised in the slick Murray brochure, ten wonderful things to do in Uzumati: play video games, attend a wine seminar, have your teeth cleaned, massage and manicure, play golf, play tennis, go bowling, play ping-pong, see the latest movie, get a divorce.

Enough already. Fifteen thousand trespassers ripping up Mother Nature every day. Enough already. The miners got the gold; the poachers just sold, sold, and sold; and what is the government's role? The garden of Eden has lost its soul. Enough already.

The Parks Department heard from over twenty thousand interested citizens on what to do about it. This resulted in an in-depth, farsighted document by the best professional planners in the government. It was touted as brilliant, innovating, state-of-the-art. What was it? A diesel engine busing plan. The sightseers would now have the drive-through experience of a lifetime. A thirty-minute ride through Uzumati's God's Little Green Acre. Hurry, hurry, hurry—see the bears dance for Murray. Enough already. The conservation groups, Academia, the global warming fuzzies, all cried out, "A national park should be a vignette of primitive America." A world-renowned artist wrote, "We have been duped by the government." The Poachers had heard it all before, and they knew from experience that "this too will pass."

Except that the rains poured down in buckets and the mountain snow melted. The dam weakened then exploded, the rivers rose, and every man-made thing in Uzumati was washed away. And when the deluge was over, a beautiful one-hundred-foot-deep lake filled the valley floor, and it was more beautiful than ever. And as the wildlife returned from the high country, someone said they saw John Puir on Glacier Point looking down on Lake Peyote. And he had a smile on his face or it could have been "Cool Head Fred."

"You cannot improve on it— man can only mar it." — Teddy Roosevelt

CHAPTER SIX

ADOPT A PRAIRIE DOG

"Adopt a what?" Bill laughed, the superintendent of Devil's Power National Monument. "That's the dumbest damn thing I've ever heard of." Seymour Hudson, the Parks Department's Chief Flack, replied, "Well, we think it's a most humane concept, and Gotcha Butcher is expecting your full support." It was Molly Butcher, Gotcha's wife, who actually had the idea. She had a pet white rat who slept on her pillow, so caring for a prairie dog was understandably the next step. At the Parks Advisory Board meeting in New Orleans the previous week, Molly got drunk and dragged the chairman into the hotel's kitchen freezer and seduced him. The next morning, with his support, she announced before the members her innovative program: "Adopt A Prairie Dog."

The prairie dog adoption campaign would be kicked off to celebrate the establishment of Devil's Power as the nation's first national monument. The fluted monolith, the remains of some past volcanic eruption, is 867 feet high and 1,267 feet above the meandering Belle Fourche River. The First Americans called it Bear Lodge, to them a place of worship. Their legend tells of some Sioux maidens who were picking flowers when they were chased by three big bad bears. To rescue them, the Great Spirit raised the ground beneath the girls, forming a high tower. The bears fell off the top, leaving scratch marks on the sides. The landmark is the most dominant site in the Northern Great Plains.

On the entrance to Devil's Power is a thirty-four-acre Prairie Dog Town on both sides of the road. It is composed of a large number of closely spaced burrows, each comprising an elaborate network of interconnecting tunnels and multiple entrance holes. It was the French who gave them the name "Petites Chiens," or little dogs. These rodents weigh about two pounds with eyes and ears set back on their light-brown furry heads. They have short, muscular legs and long-nailed toes on their front and rear feet.

The prairie dog is much more like a squirrel than Molly's white rat. They are very social animals and recognize one another by a sniff and a kiss. They were called dogs because of their squeaky cry, which some thought sounded like a dog's. With their extremely sharp claws, they can dig much deeper than any gray squirrel—as far as fifteen feet down. The dogs live in colonies, and one male services three females. The female can produce a litter of six pups in thirty days. They can eat up to a pound of weeds a day, which the ranchers need for their cattle. They have a propensity for obesity, and their life span is seven years, which is remarkable since the cow folks have shot, poisoned, trapped, and gassed the little buggers with the help and approval of the government. But the dogs keep finding new digs and keep stealing the ranchers' cow food.

One unsuccessful method used for prairie dog control was to spray coyote pee around the boundaries of the grasslands. It was believed that the prairie dogs wouldn't cross this odorous perimeter. The dogs simply did the obvious—they tunneled under the pee boundary, decimating the grass. But when the prairie dog population began to dwindle, this same government, being pressured by "people for the preservation of the cute little critters," began to protect the noisy diggers from the cattle clutches. The ranchers vehemently opposed the lifesaving program, screaming that the dogs were nothing but a costly nuisance, robbing them of millions of dollars every year.

Only the government would support a program that was as likely to succeed as protecting rats in London. Molly presented a ten-point program, highlighting the advantages of adopting a prairie dog:

1. You would receive a tax deduction equal to those received by foster parents.
2. A one year's supply of grass and grass seeds.

3. The dogs will keep your front and backyard trim.
4. Two six-foot leases will be mailed to you the day you take delivery.
5. The doggies have been a proven companion for shut-ins and senior citizens who don't like cats.
6. You will receive two bumper stickers for your automobile, designating you as a member in good standing of the Friends of Homeless Prairie Dogs.
7. Next to grass, the dogs love insects. This should resolve your bug problem.
8. Once a year, you will be invited to attend the Thank God for Prairie Dogs National Convention. All expenses paid.
9. A list of veterinarians (if we can find any) who will be willing to administer flea and rabies shots.
10. Molly the Magnificent will send you a gold-plated framed certificate for your thoughtfulness.

The Save the Prairie Dog bunch were well aware of the unhealthy and unsafe conditions of the Prairie Dog Town at Devil's Power. They blamed the unruly mobs who had been feeding their little darlings potato chips, peanut butter cookies, popcorn, french fries, and M&Ms. Some of the young ones had been run over by automobiles, buses, and motorcycles. Worst of all were the undisciplined children who chased, trapped, and played catch with the funny furry fellows. Molly Butcher was furious. This travesty of justice must stop immediately. She sweet-talked her husband, Gotcha, to have the best lawyers in the department to formulate a legally binding contract for the adoption program:

Ten Conditions for Prairie Dog Adoptions

1. No household that houses any children under the age of eighteen will be considered.
2. Only homes that agree to adopt at least one male and three females.

3. Only grass, weeds, and insects will be allowed for the doggie diet.
4. Eliminating obesity is the responsibility of the caregiver.
5. Contract is for six months, and performance will be evaluated before an extension.
6. The prairie dogs will have the run of the house.
7. Caregiver will maintain a clean and sanitary litter box, changing it twice daily.
8. No fraternization with other animals will be allowed.
9. All dogs will be examined every three months.
10. All radios, computers, and television sets will be turned off at 7:00 p.m.

Three hundred households were properly investigated, personally screened by Molly, and passed a one-hundred-question exam. The participants were basically good-natured folk, fair and balanced fundamentalists, warmhearted Great Plains people who were looking for something in their lives that was fulfilling. After one year, a management review and operations evaluation was conducted, and the program was deemed to be a national disaster. It would cost the taxpayers millions of dollars to resolve all the issues. All three hundred families filed lawsuits against the government. A class action lawsuit, handled by the law firm of Chase, Katch, and Payup, presented fifteen complaints:

1. The dogs turned over the litter box and kicked smelly litter all over the house.
2. They ate every plant in the house.
3. We started with four dogs and now have fifty-seven. The average was fifty-one.
4. Our cats left and have not returned.
5. Our house is filled with fleas.
6. The government never did deliver any grass or grass seeds.
7. Could not find a vet willing to be bitten.
8. The dogs dug deep holes in our sofa and mattresses.
9. They destroyed the pantry looking for insects.

10. They bark all night, and we haven't had a good night's sleep since they moved in.
11. Our drapes are in shreds.
12. They never keep still and built mounds of fiber from our carpet.
13. One of the dogs bit the mailman, who is suing us.
14. They tunneled through the sewer pipes and stopped up the toilets.
15. Our house smells to high heaven.

The sexy Molly divorced her husband because he blamed her to save his career. The federal government, to escape the embarrassment of the class action lawsuit, made a settlement between two and five million dollars for each of the participating prairie dog caregivers. All the prairie dogs, estimated at 16,232, were transported back to their original homes at Devil's Power National Monument where they sniffed and kissed their way back into the burrows.

CHAPTER SEVEN

WHO DAT STOLE THE FISHUN BUS

The presidential palace people and the Big Robber Titans, who helped them get there, were having a major political strategy gathering to ensure that they held the palace. It was held at the People's Park, just outside the Capital City. And that's all the Parks Department needed, another Conservative Party function that would tie them up, take them away from normal park operations, and waste more taxpayers' money.

Arrangements had been made by Seymour for the Poobahs to use the lodge at the People's Park. The park had long served as an Environmental Education Center for the poor, disadvantaged, inner-city youth. It provided them a rare opportunity to enjoy and learn about the great outdoors.

The park lake had been stocked with rainbow trout so that all the kids would catch at least one fish. Seymour had contracted for a special city bus to take the party faithful to the lake, about one mile away from the lodge, for lunch. It was a nice touch that would relieve tensions that resulted from these "who gets what confabs." The lunch included the necessary cocktails and a scrumptious buffet spread. When the political bunch were well fed and half boozed up, they would return by the same bus to the lodge. How it happened and who was responsible was only known by a Peyote faithful. The bus driver couldn't get the bus started because the battery was missing. The bus company never did tell Seymour what happened. But Seymour moved quickly. He saw another bus driver sleeping in an empty bus and offered him two hundred dollars if he could borrow the bus for ten minutes. The bus driver accepted the bribe, and the great hijacking was under way. The unaware lunching bunch started boarding a bus that belonged to someone else.

She was eighty one and a product of the festering ghetto in the Nations Capital—little education, poor paying jobs, but she had a big heart. And then Georgia Mae appeared. She weighed over three hundred pounds and was dressed in a short-sleeve white shirt, oversized Levi pants, and dirty blue tennis shoes. Her biceps measured twenty-two inches. She had been wearing glasses since she was a teenager, and the latest pair came from the Salvation Army. One of the lens was cracked, and the left arm piece was held together by duct tape.

Her husband had joined the Army, and she hadn't heard from him for seventeen years. She had been at Martin Luther King's Dream speech, but she never did see any little black girls holding hands with little white boys. Georgia Mae had been taking ghetto kids on the fishing trip for many years, because she wasn't so busy with no job to go to. No need to work. She got US Army checks and them welfare checks every month. But this fishing trip would be her last. One of the kids, Calhoun, had forgotten and left his lunch bag on the bus, and when Georgia Mae went back to the bus to get it, what happened would change her life forever.

As Georgia Mae faced some thirty well-dressed white bureaucrats and businessmen, she gave them her best black panther stare, and with her hands on her overly developed hips, she screamed, "Jesus be in the heavens for he ain't be here. Ain't yawl done enough to my poh childrens—now you gonna steal duh fishun bus." This was the first time she had ever let white people know how black folks felt. "Little Calhoun be hungry and leave he lunch bag on duh fishun bus. He done axe me how many fish in dat ocean, so maybe he gonna eat a raw trout fish or something. He ain't but seven years old—ain't got no momma or daddy to take care of him, and now you white cracker people steal he only lunch. Jesus be in the heavens—yawl be lyen', cheatin', stealin' black people stuff all the time. Schools ain't no equal, can't get no job except sweepin' something from here to over there. We be wash your clothes, cooks yawl food, take good care of your bratty ass kids and what you say. We is lazy, late, and just no count. Don't get no socials security 'cause you don't pay no money for us. The brothers and sisters get tired of this shit and try to get some schoolin' and minimum wage job and you won't even let them flip burgers. Got some tall white boy with pimples on the face at the McDonald's."

She took a deep breath and let it all out.

"When dat white man, Jefferson, take a good-lookin' black girl into the big house, nobody say nothing. The slave people be scared though. They know what he gonna do wit her. And when that white man Jahns Braun tried to get them guns at the Barber's Ferry and free the slaves, you say he be crazy and hung em from a cherry tree. Look what's you done to the Negroes people, shackle em to a boat, take dem from the home to pick your white cotton. You lie to the corner street kids, tell em he gonna go to college, gets money and what you do, send him to the Vietnams to get shot up.

"And nobody care. Always be lyen, cheatin. stealin from us poor peoples. Now you be stealun the fishun bus. Jesus, Jesus, be in in them heavens, please help us from the mean, bully white man. You knows you ain't nothun but a bunch of mother—I ain't say the word for I be a churchgoing lady, but you know what you is, and the Lord gonna get you."

Hell, Georgia Mae was just getting started.

"Once in deh lifetime, my neighborhood children's gets away from the stinkin' tenements wit rats as big as basketballs and grabs some fresh air and catches them a trout fish and you steal little Calhoun's bologna sandwich wit no mayonnaise on it and take all the seats on the fishun bus. I seen yawl over at the lake eaten dat fancy food and drinkin dat Dowaz scotch whiskey. I seen yah.

"You gots you a broken down ole bus so you just be stealin our fishun bus. Just like when that hardworkin black lady Miss Rosie Sparks gives her money to the busman and sits down. And then she gotta move to the back of the bus so some big ass white man can take her paid for seat."

And on and on she nagged and bullied the belching bunch of bureaucrats and business biggies. Georgia Mae didn't know what came over her, but she liked it and felt good about it and couldn't stop herself.

"Yeah, I know who you be 'cause I seen your picture in the throwaway newspaper. You be the salt man—name be Gus or something. Makes all that money from the salt the negro man dug out for you, and now you got dat big gov'ment job after you donates the Negro sweat money to the palace peoples. You ain't care nothing about little Calhoun being hungry and he daddy be put in jail for smoking dat crack, trying to forget what the white man done to him.

"We ain't axe to come to no America in the first place. Yawl comes to our homes in Africa, hits us in deb head with deh gun butts. Kidnaps us on those slavery ships. We never come through no Alice Island, but we be in chains before you put us in the cotton fields. Always we be pickin', pickin', pickin' that damn cotton. Never lets us learn to read and writes, just keep 'em pickin' all the time. It ain't make no difference now whether we reads or writes, we still gonna' get the same old broom. Never care about nobody but yourselves. Be stealin' Calhoun's bologna sandwich wit no mayonnaise on it. And now you be sittin' on ours fishun bus and what's my children's pose to do, grow some wings and fly back to the stinkin' tenements. Jesus be in the heavens."

The Poobah flack Seymour tried to play nice and told Georgia Mae that it was all one big mistake and that he was sorry as hell about little Calhoun's daddy and his lunch bag. He promised that all the inner-city kids would get new Sears, Roebuck bicycles and wouldn't have to steal them anymore, and brand-new Wilson basketballs and nylon nets for the rusty hoops on the sides of the tenement buildings.

Georgia Mae exploded.

"I ain't care about no basketballs from Mr. Wilsons. I just wants to get the bologna sandwich and gets yawl off deb fishun bus. Now don't be g'tting Georgia Mae mad, 'cause I be breakin' white man bones."

A local TV cameraman had captured all of it on tape with sound. That night on television, all the major networks carried the story. Georgia Mae became a national sensation and appeared on all the talk shows rapping her number one hit, "Who Dat Stole the Fishun Bus."

Who dat stole the fishun bus
Makes Georgia Mae cus and fus
Who dat stole the fishun bus
Fat ass white man—name be Gus

CHAPTER EIGHT

THE WILDLIFE CONFERENCE

This vast and divergent land was formed over six hundred thousand years ago by a gigantic volcanic eruption. Legend has it that the First Americans named the river that rushes through the Great Canyon, Yellowstone, but the gorge is also red and orange. There is no place like it in the world, and in 1872, it became the first national park. There are over six hundred species of plants and trees, some of which are found nowhere else. And over two hundred geysers, including Old Reliable, that blasts about every hour. Boiling hot pools, bubbling mud pots reveal that magna lies beneath. Mountains, meadows, valleys, rivers, canyons, lakes, waterfalls, and petrified forests form the natural phenomenon.

There is a feeling of wildness and strangeness in this place, which is often frightening. The Dashburn Range is 10,240 feet high, and the Continental Divide crosses the southern end of the park. The largest lake, formed by the Swilling River, is some twenty miles long, and in the canyon the Upper Falls drop a hundred feet and the Lower Falls three hundred. There are acres of petrified forests. Wildflowers, some of them hidden, are the wild aster, the pink monkey, lupine, Indian paintbrush, kinnikinnick, and the harebell are abundant. Trees that you don't have to hunt for—aspen, Douglas fir, Engelmann spruce, and the lodgepole pine—the king of the forests.

The birds that one might see are pelicans, bald eagle, trumpeter swan, gulls, ospreys, geese, blue herons, goldeneye, and mallard. In the winter, when there are few visitors, the ten-point elk move closer to the steam-heated geysers and hot springs. About a thousand buffaloes swing their huge heads from side to side to sweep away the snow to uncover the grasses below. There were once fifty million buffaloes in North America. A time when "Oh, give me home where the buffalo roam, where the deer and the antelope play."

Around the sanctuary are the black bear, moose, deer, wolf, coyote, and their smaller brothers—rabbits, marmots, beavers, tree squirrel, muskrat, and lizard. The pronghorns can run up to fifty mph, twenty miles faster than the grand grizzly. The grizzly eats both plants and animals, and it takes a ton to make him happy. He has a body of power and speed but cannot climb a limbless tree. They are solitary animals, and to see a grizzly mother and her cubs on the prowl can be an awesome sight and scary at the same time. She knows that man is her enemy, and she will attack if threatened.

The smaller black bear may look cuddly and cute, but they can weigh up to five hundred pounds and is not man's best friend. If she smells food, the black bear will beg, dance, strut, stand on her head, pose for pictures with your family and will claw to death the unthinking morons to get what she wants. But it's not the grizzly or the black bear that is a serious threat to the national park. The park protectors, the cross-country skiers, the trees, the flowers, the wildlife are all being attacked by the screeching, smelly Neanderthal Snowmobilers, a.k.a. SBS. These infidels are the enemy of all who love nature and cherish the first national park. These SBS are uncaring, unseeing, unfeeling, knuckleheads who think only of the thrill of the bouncy ride that the snowmobiles provide.

What is a snowmobile? Sometimes called a snow scooter, a sled by the easy riders is a land vehicle propelled by one or two rubber tracks with attached skis. They are designed for lazy, unathletic people to be operated on snow or ice and require no established trail or road. They are powered by a two-stroke gasoline internal combustion engine. A Ford dealer coined the term "snowmobile" to describe the Model T' automobile that he mounted on tracks and skis. Once used to deliver the rural mail, the snowmobile was made available to the public in the 1950s. Ski Doo marketed as open cockpit, which became the modern version of the original. The major makers of snowmobiles are Polaris, Ski Doo, and Yamaha.

The Polaris 600 is a "Screamer." "Best in its class for acceleration and quickness" at the Old Forge Shoot Out. It produces 19 percent more horsepower at 6,000 RPM to enhance the ride. The Polaris Predator goes for $4,500 and the 600 Ho about $8,000. The Ski Doo devotees say "There is nothing like it." The powerful 800 engine puts "one on the edge of excitement!" The Mach 2 "eats the competition for breakfast." Cost: $10,000. And the Yamaha, the motorcycle maker who tempts with the SRX 700, "the quickest top performer sled on the snow." "It has changed the rules and turned heads." "One venomous bite is all it takes." "One ride is all it takes to discover excitement." The awesome Apex Mountain Sled: $12,000.

They are all mobile, agile, and hostile, but never the threat of the empty-headed bodies who ride them in a national park. It's family fun for everyone, where the kids often fall off and break something. The choices of costumes available for the "Look, Mom, no hands" bunch include the last word in snowmobilers suits. The Blast Vegas Evo Racing suit: $1,200; Cold Wave SX boots: $150. For the Ladies Snow Boot Altima: $139. The Caberg Jusatissimo Modular snowmobile helmet from Italy, with internal dropdown sunglasses, space age crystal clear sound: only $375. Toddler jacket, $90, and gloves, $80.

The snowmobile industry sucks in $21 billion annually. They get the terrifying redneck family fully equipped for their assault on Rhinestone National Park. The cowboys, cowgirls, and their calves cannot snowshoe, cannot cross-country ski, cannot hike because they are too lazy and don't want to learn. It takes no skill, no training, no brains to jump on a make-believe bucking bronco and zoom, boom, and bring gloom to the calmness of the sane world. They sicken the park employees, harass the wildlife, and disturb the serenity of the other wintertime park visitors. The screeching, blasting noise and tons of carbon dioxide is their contribution to "for others to enjoy."

They explode down the well-groomed roads and trails, producing ear-piercing explosions and gut-wrenching fumes. They do not see because they do not wish to see, they do not hear because they do not know how to listen, and they do not smell because their nostrils are filled with nitrous oxide and hydro carbons. The park is not a destination. It simply provides a road for the ride. They are a "me first" mentality, "out of the way, here I come, look at me—whoopee!" If they ever get off their fat asses to commune with nature, it's because their wretched machines ran off the road. Their long convoy of ignorance, selfishness, and indifference is desecrating one of the most magnificent places in the world. One cross-country skier lamented that "snowmobilers are just a smokescreen for noise."

A test was developed by a conservation group to determine "what is the SBS experience in the first national park?" The SBS who took the test all chose answer D:

Snowmobilers' Experience Test

1. How was the park formed? a. Volcanic eruption b. A meteor burst c. Scientists aren't sure d. Who cares?
2. Why was the park established? a. To preserve the scenery, natural, historic objects, and wildlife therein b. Pork barrel c. Government land grab. D. For the snowmobilers, of course
3. What fowl did you see along the Big Lake? a. Trumpeter swans b. Bald eagle c. Blue herons d. Didn't see no stinkin' lake
4. Why can't a grizzly bear climb a tree? a. Claws prohibit b. Genetic knee malfunction c. Hips are too narrow d. Too fat
5. What is the view from Mount Dashburn? A. Blue lupines b. A trout stream c. Coyotes d. Hopefully a hidden snowmobile trail
6. If you encounter an elk, what would you do? a. Watch and listen b. Take a picture c. Live and let live d. Chase it on my snowmobile
7. What did you enjoy the most? a. The wildlife b. The flowers c. The geysers d. Racing other snowmobilers
8. How long did you stay in the park? a. One week b. Three days c. Two days d. About three hours

9. Why does 99 percent of the public want to ban snowmobilers in national parks? a. They produce choking smoke and deafening noise b. Protect the flora and fauna c. Protect the health of the park employees and park visitors d. They are just jealous, that's all.

The parasites that own and manage the snowmobile rental facilities in Stinkytown, USA, line their pockets with millions of dollars from SBS. These lowlife capitalists rent smoke-belching, eardrum-breaking, murderous snowmobile machines; a vast array of costumes for the whole family; provide gasoline to produce the killing gases; the junk food; low-grade beer and cheap digs. These larcenous leeches suck the serenity, the clean air, the quietude, and any possible serendipity from the pristine natural wilderness. They pride themselves on the 75,000 maddening machines they propelled into Rhinestone National Park in one winter season to pollute, pollute, pollute.

The Stinkytown mayor is a major provider of snowmobiles and all that goes with them. He cries that the tree buggers are trying to put him out of business. He laments that what will he do, where will he go, how will he send his children to college, how will he enjoy his retirement if the snowmobiles are banned? Those who want to ban them say who cares about the mayor losing his business? The sooner the better. One Smellytown snowmobile dealer when asked about his supply of machines exclaimed, "Well, we got some little ones. Don't go too fast though. We got some medium-size ones that will give you a little thrill, and we got those big beautiful bastards that go barooom, barooom, barooom, a real ball buster. And that's the one the SBS want." Somewhere, someone heard a boys' choir sing, "Oh give me a home where the buffalo roam, where the deer and the antelope play."

Only 140,000 experience Yellowstone in the wintertime. Half of them are snowmobilers. There were twenty-two public hearings where the anti-snowmobile conservationists were hassled by the loudmouth, closed-minded, coldhearted snowmobile people. They cried that the reports from the Occupational Safety and Health

Administration stated that countless park employees had suffered from nausea, dizziness, headaches, sore throat, and eye irritation were hogwash. And that the park rangers had to pump fresh air into the entrance stations to combat the poisonous fumes from the snowmobiles was more hogwash. In just a single winter, SBS emitted the equivalent of sixty-eight years of automobile pollution in the park; the study recorded. It further stated that the SBS noise had been reported to have been heard as far as twenty miles away. Two hundred buffaloes have followed the snowmobilers, on the well groomed trails, out of the park into Wyoming and Montana, and were slaughtered by recreational gunmen.

Why is all this devastation happening when Congress has passed laws to protect the national parks? In a word, money. The snowmobile manufacturers, the dealerships, national associations, the retail renters, and the machine repair shops all lobby the local and national politicians. They contribute to their political campaigns, maintain effective lobbying offices in the Capital City, and they get rewarded with favorable legislation and administration of that legislation. The park managers are intimidated, threatened, careers ruined if they don't support the administration's ruinous policies. The first national park became the battleground in the legal ping-pong game taking place in the courts. As fly-fishing shop owner in Stinkytown asked, "Why is it that five guys (the major snowmobile dealers and renters in his town) can destroy one of the most spectacular and revered places on earth?" The solution was right there in a comment by a truthful SBS, who said "it's more fun to snowmobile outside of the park because you can go faster and there's more bounce from the bumps."

The Environmental Protection Agency, the Sierra Club, the Wilderness Society, the National Conservation Foundation, the park people, the public, and the Peyote Society were all fighting to ban snowmobiles from the parks. The law is clear. The public opinion is clear. No snowmobiles in our treasured national parks. None! Never again. Period. Not even the undercover efforts of the Peyote Society could change the actions of Gotcha and the Spoilers in the presidential palace.

Cool-Head Fred said he had a dream, and in that dream the park wildlife gathered around the Big Lake and said "Enough is enough." They all agreed that the SBS were trying to kill them and that they must protect their families, especially the young ones. The Wildlife Conference included the elk, black bear, grizzly, wolf, moose, coyote, beavers, squirrel, and the deer. Fighting the snowmobilers was their cause célèbre. They bound together against the common enemy— the evil Snowmobilers. When the SBS trespassed into their natural habitats, they blocked the roads and trails, surrounded the SBS convoy, and each animal screamed out in their own special way, all in unison, "Get the hell out of our homes and stay the hell out." They harassed and chased all the SBS back into Stinkytown. They would never return, never. The mayor went broke, and Stinkytown vanished from the face of the earth. But it wasn't a dream.

It happened! It happened!

CHAPTER NINE

THE KACHINA BOY

Tad Hamilton, the new assistant superintendent at Petrified Trees National Monument, had been on the job less than three weeks before his first encounter with the First American Ropi culture. It was becoming common practice in the Parks Department to put a no talent, uncaring, anti–environment White House hack in a park service uniform, but that doesn't make him a park ranger. Tad had no law enforcement training, no experience, and no authority. But he just couldn't resist trying to prove himself so he could impress the whole park ranger staff. The misguided superintendent who supported his selection to gain favor with Gotcha was on annual leave, and Tad was the acting superintendent. He and his family had moved into the park employee housing area, but they were shunned by the other park families because he was a political appointee. But Tad would show them that he had the right stuff, and then he would gain their respect.

He was driving the official park superintendent's vehicle on a dirt road near the park boundary when he spotted someone picking up something. As he moved closer on foot, he saw a young boy picking up parts of a tree and putting them in a sack. Nearby, he observed a downed tree, and he made the assumption that the kid had cut down a tree within the park boundaries. He wasn't positive but rationalized that this must be against Parks Department regulations. Before acting, he thumbed through a copy of the Code of

Federal Regulations that he had been studying at home, out of sight of the other employees. He couldn't find the section on cutting down trees, so he continued his surveillance.

The boy was Komovi, a twelve-year-old Ropi who was picking up the broken roots of a cottonwood tree, as he done before with his father and uncles. The Ropi Indian Reservation was adjacent to the park, and the Ropis always believed that the federal government had stolen their land—because it was true. The Ropis call themselves the "peaceful people." They lived in the Southwest, at the end of Midnight Mesa. Their oldest village, Oryebu, dates from AD 1050 and is the oldest living village in America. Their pueblo homes are made of stone and mud, a few four stories high. The Ropis have always been farmers who raised maize, beans, squash, melons, pumpkins, and fruit. The women owned the land and the home. They did the cooking, weaving, and other household chores. The men planted the crops on fertile fields below the mesa and brought in the harvest. They hunted deer, antelope, elk, and smaller animals. They also performed the spiritual ceremonies, which were the centerpiece of their culture. Today most of the men work off the reservation to provide the modern appliances, supermarket food, transportation, and health care. Although they adopted many of the white man's creature comforts, they cherish and preserve their kachina spirituality. The kachinas, the people of the spiritual world, have great powers and wisdom. They dispense spiritual and material blessings, especially rain for their crops.

During the spiritual ceremonies, the adult men dress up in elaborate costumes and ornate masks that resemble the kachinas. The performers dance, pray, and honor the ones of the spiritual world. They impersonate over four hundred different kachinas, and to the Ropi people these men are intermediaries between the spiritual and life on earth. The kachina dancers are the human personification of the kachinas' spirits. The ceremonies are more than just a petition for clouds and the badly needed rain, but for long life and happiness. One of the most popular, at least for the Anglo spectators, is the snake dance. The dancers dance with real live rattlesnakes in their mouths, and after the dance, the snakes are released to carry the prayers to the kachina gods. During the ceremonies, the dancers, especially the clowns, give gifts to young girls, which are small wooden dolls created in the images of the kachinas.

The kachina dolls are symbols of spirituality of the Ropi people. They have been made for hundreds of years and are sacred, never viewed as toys. Each doll is carved from the roots of a cottonwood tree, but only after the root has eroded and broken away from the dead and downed tree. When it is thoroughly dried, the wood is porous and easily carved. It is believed by the Ropis that the roots of the cottonwood seek out water—precious water for the desert farmers. The original carving tools were a sharp stone sliver for cutting and a sandstone for smoothing. Today a saw, hammer, and chisel are used for shaping the wood. The details are then created by using a knife and sandpaper. Then the surface is coated with a layer of fine white clay to produce the basic surface. The painting with various colors and symbols is the next step. Then feathers, shells, leather, metals, and colored stones are added, which represent the actual items worn by the kachina dancers. About a thousand authentic dolls are made each year.

The little boy, Komovi, continued to fill the bag with cottonwood roots that one day would become the prized kachina dolls. He was unaware that an incompetent political appointee was watching his every move. Acting Superintendent Tad Hamilton got out of the ranger vehicle and slowly moved toward the culprit. He was very nervous as he approached the wood-gathering boy. He watched and wondered why he was stealing small pieces of wood and thought about handcuffing the young Ropi, but he had none.

He finally summoned up enough courage and yelled out, "Hey boy, why did you cut down that tree?" Komovi was confused, scared, and he froze. He asked himself who was it that yelled at him. Then he saw a white man in a funny-looking hat coming towards him. He had been taught by his father that in the face of danger remain calm; show no emotion. Tad came closer and asked him what he was doing. Komovi remained stoic and said nothing.

Tad Hamilton wasn't sure what to do next, since he had never arrested anyone before. He didn't trust anyone of the park staff to help him. And he didn't want anyone to know that he didn't know what to do. He remembered that he had met a deputy sheriff in the nearby town's only supermarket, and the deputy seemed to be impressed with his title. He told the Indian boy to get into the front seat of the vehicle, and he headed for the sheriff's office. Tad was in luck for the same deputy was alone in the office and appeared glad to see him.

Hamilton explained to the deputy sheriff that the young criminal had destroyed a living sequoia and was stealing government property. He emphasized that he had caught the boy in the act of breaking the law.

Further, he stated that the park did not have a jail and could the deputy help him out until he could transport the culprit to a federal facility. The deputy was more than agreeable to assist a federal authority and had no reason to believe that the "acting" didn't know what the hell he was doing. The redneck cop, who hated all Indians, handcuffed Komovi, roughed him up, and did a brutal body search for weapons. The deputy sheriff threatened to hit Komovi with his billy club and slammed him into a holding cell. The deputy also assumed that Hamilton had contacted Komovi's parents and informed them of the incident. Hamilton wasn't sure what he should do next, so the next morning he called the deputy and told him to release Komovi. When the school principal notified Komovi's mother that he was absent from school, the Ropi tribe began a search for the boy. When Komovi returned home after a long trek from the town, his father and mother hugged him tightly, realizing how much they loved their son.

When Komovi told his parents what had happened, they got their Kutcahon clan together to decide what to do. The Kutachon clan were famous and considered the best kachina doll carvers in the world. Kitty Domenjopi, the leader of the clan, owned the largest collection of authentic kachina dolls, which were on display in the Ropi Cultural Center. The sixty-two-year-old grandmother was barely five feet tall, and she was also a leading attorney with the American Civil Liberties Union. The Ropis had battled with the federal government many times before, and Kitty Domenjopi had never lost a case. While in college and studying for her law degree at the university, she had worked seven summers as a park ranger at Petrified Trees and was a founding member of the Peyote Society. The Ropi tribe with the ACLU sued the Parks Department over the kidnapping of Komovi, and the case would be heard by a federal judge. The judge's decision would be final, and there would be no appeals.

Kitty Domenjopi submitted her questions to the judge for the assistant superintendent to respond to. Hamilton had been cut loose by the Spoilers and was left to dangle from a cottonwood tree and defend himself. He declined to have any legal representation since he felt he had only been doing his duty. The judge had lived in the Southwest her entire life and had been appointed a federal judge by a previous administration. Her record on the bench clearly showed that she was a liberal in matters of civil rights.

JUDGE: Mr. Hamilton, how long had you been assistant superintendent at Tall Trees when you encountered the young Ropi, Komovi?

HAMILTON: About three weeks.

JUDGE: And what park did you transfer from?

HAMILTON: Tall Trees was my first park assignment.

JUDGE: And how long have you been in the Parks Department?

HAMILTON: About three weeks.

JUDGE: Did you have any law enforcement experience in the past?

HAMILTON: No.

JUDGE: So you didn't have any park ranger training or experience before your assignment to Tall Trees?

HAMILTON: No, but I was in the Boy Scouts.

JUDGE: Were you an Eagle Scout

HAMILTON: No.

JUDGE: I didn't think so. So you don't have any law enforcement authority to make an arrest?

HAMILTON: Well, I was the acting superintendent when I caught the Indian boy.

JUDGE: That's not what I asked you?

HAMILTON: I didn't think I needed any law enforcement experience. I was wearing a park ranger badge.

JUDGE: Hamilton, exactly what did you observe Komovi doing?

HAMILTON: Well, at the time, I was acting superintendent and was driving around the park to get a feel for the area and park operations. As I drove down the north boundary road, I saw someone moving around with a large bag. As I came closer, I observed a young boy within the park boundary putting pieces of wood into the bag. I also saw a sequoia tree [later identified as a cottonwood tree] that had been cut down [later determined to have been blown down]. I got out of the official superintendent's vehicle and asked the boy why he had cut down a tree in the park. I got no response whatsoever. So I told him to get into the car and drove him to the sheriff's office.

JUDGE: Didn't you tell the deputy sheriff, who by the way has been fired, that Komovi had cut down a sequoia?

HAMILTON: I didn't know the boy's name.

JUDGE: Well, you do now. Did you, yes or no?

HAMILTON: I thought it was a sequoia.

JUDGE: Yes or no, Mr. Hamilton.

HAMILTON: Yes.

JUDGE: Thank you. Now did you actually see Komovi cut down the cottonwood tree?

HAMILTON: No, but it seemed logical at the time.

JUDGE: So you didn't see him cut down the tree. Yes or no, damn it.

HAMILTON: No, Your Honor.

JUDGE: Well, thank you. We finally established the fact that you did not actually see Komovi cut down the tree. Now did you know that the Ropi tribe has a Special Use Permit that allows them to collect the roots of a cottonwood tree in the Tall Trees National Monument?

HAMILTON: No, I didn't. But why would they have the right to remove government property from a national monument?

JUDGE: Do you know anything about the Ropi culture?

HAMILTON: I know that they are Indians and live on the nearby reservation. So what's to know?

JUDGE: Hamilton, your lack of knowledge is only superseded by your insensitivity. Have you ever heard of spirituality?

HAMILTON: Yeah, but I don't believe in that kind of stuff.

JUDGE: Thousands of books have been written on spirituality and you call it 'that kind of stuff.' Have you ever heard of kachinas and kachina dolls?

HAMILTON: I'll have to ask my daughter. She has lots of dolls...ha ha.

JUDGE: I give up. Did you notify Komovi's parents that you had arrested him and that he was in jail?"

HAMILTON: No, I thought the deputy sheriff would do that.

JUDGE: You thought? What you did was a kidnapping. Do you realize the harm you have down to Komovi and his family?

HAMILTON: I was just doing my job.

JUDGE: If you didn't know what you were doing, why didn't you ask the chief park ranger?

HAMILTON: I've never asked him anything because he doesn't like me.

JUDGE: Do you realize that you violated Komovi's civil rights and his freedom of religion?

HAMILTON: Well, it appeared that he was stealing government property, and I arrested him.

JUDGE: Hamilton, where the in the hell did the Parks Department find someone like you?

HAMILTON: A friend of my dad who belonged to the same college fraternity and now works in the White House got me this job.

JUDGE: Stop, please, stop. I've heard enough. We will recess until tomorrow morning at 9:00 a.m. I'll give you my decision at that time.

The next morning when Tad Hamilton appeared before the judge and heard her decision, he fainted. When he was resuscitated by the EMTs, he was handcuffed and taken away by the US marshals. The liberal lady judge sentenced Tad to six months in jail and, upon release, two years of collecting cottonwood roots for the Ropi tribe. His father paid the $100,000 fine, which was given to Komovi.

Kitty Domenjovi hugged the young Komovi, and he said, "Good job, Grandma Kitty."

CHAPTER TEN

THE BIG BUBBLE CASINO

It takes a genius to get rich off the poorest of the poor. To make him and his riches, a national historic site takes a cabal of Spoilers and a few influential politicians. But it became a reality at the expense of the First Americans. How do you tell the story of a failed business enterprise and maintain that it has national significance like the Statue of Liberty? The entrepreneurial storekeeper executed the old-age business plan by exploiting cheap labor. He brought silversmiths from across the border (cheap Mexican labor) to teach the First American men how to make silver and turquoise jewelry (even cheaper labor).

The Ravajo women have been weaving for centuries, ever since the Spanish dumped horses and sheep on their Mother Earth and taught them the fine art. If the Indian trader could only get these stubborn women to weave the rug patterns that Easterners liked. The big department stores in New York and Chicago would stock them and the middleman, a.k.a. the Indian trader, would be on his way to even greater wealth. The poor, hungry Indian women finally came around, and a new Southwestern industry was born.

The women had some sheep and from the sheep some wool. They also grew corn and gathered pinyon nuts. The men had a few horses, an occasional welfare check, and together, the men and women lived in unbelievable poverty in the twentieth century in the United States of America. In exchange for the beautiful jewelry and the rugs they created, the storekeeper introduced them into a world of material civilization. He sold them (actually it was a barter system) soda pop, cigarettes, tobacco, coffee, sugar, potato chips, and Wrigley's chewing gum. Boots, pants, shirts, skirts, hats, and gasoline came later.

Inside the trading post was a new dimension in marketing, displaying, and selling. When a Ravajo silversmith or weaver entered the bulletin board door, they stepped into an open rectangle surrounded by high wooden counters. The counters were about four feet high and four feet wide and served as a barrier between the buyer and seller. This took care of an earlier problem of grab and go. The flooring behind the counter was about six inches higher than in the front. This did not go unnoticed by the Ravajo, who laughed that only tall Indians can work in the trading store. The shelves were filled with the goods that the Ravajo had recently acquired a need for. But only one of a kind or one brand was offered so as not to confuse the buyer. At the far end of the open rectangle, which was surrounded by the massive counters, was a potbellied, wood-burning stove. This open area between the door and the stove was called the Bull Pen.

The Ravajo Reservation Indians had no word in their spoken language for capitalism, revenue, earnings, wholesale, retail, or profit margin. They didn't ask about the price of goods but only how much credit they had left on the trader's books. They never received a copy of their credit report and simply took the word of the trader. The markup on goods and the profit margin gained by the Indian trader would have made even Old Scrooge drool. The trading post was isolated, and competition was nonexistent. The difference between what the trader paid wholesale for the goods and the price he charged the unaware Ravajo was at least triple. The profit he made off the silversmiths and rug weavers was fourfold. Tons of gorgeous rugs and exquisite silver, silver and turquoise bracelets, finger rings, necklaces, buttons, hat bands, bridles passed through the hands of the middleman—the Indian trader.

The Ravajo had little choice except to accept the white man's economic system. But they did enjoy socializing around the hot potbelly stove with other clan members, especially in the winter. They did figure out that the trader bought their wool by the pound, so putting heavy stones into the wool bags was one of their secrets and equalizer. And when the trader switched from canned Pet milk to Carnation because he got a better price, they refused to buy it. As one Ravajo clerk tried to explain to the boss man, "Milk come from cow, not flower." It was one of the few times that the Indian trader suffered a loss.

The Reservation Indian trading post was essentially a credit business. For example, the government welfare checks weren't delivered to the scattered Ravajo homes (hogans as they were called), but to the Indian trader. This strange and outrageous banking system worked as follows: The recipient of the welfare check would humbly appear before the trader, looking up at the man behind a giant, ornate desk and ask if "it" had come in. The trader would produce the paper as the Ravajo knew it, and he or she would endorse (thumbprint the back of *their check*) it. If the check was for, let's say, $35 and the debt on the trader's books was $19, the trader would inform them that they had $16 credit. No receipt, no cash offered of the difference. The trader might give the Ravajo a "seco," a coin good only at the trading post. The Ravajo never did know whether the trader was cooking the books, and the federal government didn't seem to care. The trader maintained that to try to explain the credit/debit accounting would only confuse them. Yeah, the trader surely didn't want to "confuse" them. Even the Ravajo clerks who worked in the trading post did not understand the trader's bookkeeping system, since they were never allowed to see the books—they were only Ravajo-speaking clerks.

When the credit on the trader's books reached zero, the credit would be extended, if the Ravajo had something to pawn. The trader's pawn closet was as they say a "cash cow." Indian jewelry, pistols, rugs, knives, axes, hoes, hatchets, saddles, even shoes found their way into the closely guarded trader's vault.

Sometimes these personal belongings were hocked to get food, sometimes to get the "seco," which could be sold at a discount to another Ravajo for cash. With the cash, the Ravajo could buy alcohol. They drank a lot of alcohol when they had the money—mostly cheap wine. And why did they drink to get drunk? There are many theories, even more scientific studies, but one reason might just be to escape the strange and powerful world of the white man. Anyway, if the pawn was not redeemed within thirty days, the Ravajo belongings became "dead pawn" and was sold at an enormous profit.

The Indian trader lived in a comfortable home with five bedrooms, a huge dining room, a splendid living room, fireplace, inside plumbing, bathrooms, and kitchen. On the walls of the trader's "castle" were numerous original paintings, artifacts, rugs, and fine furniture from back east. It was a pretentious Southwestern display of wealth, power, authority, and prestige. The Ravajo who produced the wealth lived in a one-room shack, about fifteen by fifteen, with a dirt floor, no running water, no electricity, no furniture, with bugs crawling all around.

So what happened to the Indian trader and his empire, some owning a dozen or more? Why had it failed? Why had it vanished? Was the trader outsmarted by seven-eleven? Some of the Ravajo say it was because of the spirituality and closeness of the Ravajo families. Brotherly love, unselfishness, caring, or maybe the inability to say no to another Ravajo. The Ravajo store clerks just could not abide the hungry women and children. It wasn't something planned, something dishonest, but something that came naturally to a people filled with spirituality. Actually it was quite simple—the Ravajo marketing and sales system. Buy one, get one free. Ask for one and you might get three. Buy one pair of shoes and take home shoes for the whole family. It was the Indian store clerk who saved his people from starving in the cold winters and who bankrupted the Indian trading business. It was something they did from the heart with a clear conscience. If the Ravajo people looked upon the trading post as a giant Christmas tree, it was the Indian store clerk who played Santa Claus.

The Spoilers and the politicians resuscitated the dying and decadent trading post and forced it upon the federal Parks Department as a national historic site. The state, the county, and mostly the Ravajo tribal parks wanted nothing to do with Bubble Trading Post. The Parks people didn't want it either, and serious questions were asked by some members of Congress. The old buildings were crudely built and not architecturally significant; the influence of the Indian trader was not of national significance. One historian said that "he was an agent of acculturation," whatever that means. He should have written that "he was an agent of exploitation." The paintings and artifacts were at best only of local or regional interest, but hardly worthy of national attention and taxpayers' money. Nevertheless, Bubble Trading Post became a national historic site, a boondoggle resulting from nothing more than pork barreling.

So what is the story? It is how the trader took advantage of the First Americans and exploited them for greed. Unlike the public school system, the churches, the government, they did little to uplift the Ravajo people educationally, spiritually, or improve their standard of living. The trader looked upon the Ravajo as children and treated them as children. So the story that is told about the Indian trader is one of a rich, benevolent father who showed the people the workings of capitalism.

There was one Ravajo who abandoned the spirituality of his people and became a very successful capitalist. He is Able Joe, who built the First American Reservation Gambling Casino. The Spoilers could do little to stop him, although they tried to thwart his attempts. Able Joe named his Las Vegas venture the Big Bubble Casino. And what did the Big Bubble have to offer? Cigarettes, cigars, liquor, beer, gasoline, hotel rooms, great food—all high quality at half the price. And national entertainment—professional boxing, wrestling, showgirls, dancing, dancing elephants, comedians, and most of all, *gambling*. It filled the need to get something for nothing, that insatiable appetite that the white man has for gambling. The closer the casino, the more they will come. Big Bubble was the first, and now there are Indian casinos everywhere, less than an hour away. The gamblers and the fun seekers keep on coming, especially the seniors who arrive by the busloads. They come to escape their self-imposed boredom and fill the coffers of their First American hosts. They play and pay at blackjack, roulette, poker, Texas hold 'em, bet on college and professional sports, and most of all, challenge the slots, those with one arms and otherwise. Twenty-four hours a day, every day. Their motto is "We're always there for you" and "You too can become a Millionaire."

There is fun for the family, even something for the little ones. Video games, high-tech interactive stuff, water slides, pony rides, a roller coaster, a petting zoo, twenty amusement park rides, babysitting for $50 an hour, including the baby food, and from 10:00 p.m. to 3:00 a.m. Ballroom dancing for the seniors and three discos for the younger and wilder big spenders.

Able Joe and all the other Indian reservation casinos give all their guests a brochure, which includes the following statement:

> We thank all of you, the young and the not so young, who find fun and friends at your wigwam away from home. We consider you a valued customer and appreciate your business. Because of you, we are able to provide every Indian family $5,000 a month from our business enterprises. Your generosity has solved our unemployment problems. Our young people are going to college and becoming teachers, dentists, doctors, lawyers, and we have our own First American anthropologist. We are now represented in the state legislature, and last year one First American became governor of a state and another became a US senator. Maybe one day we will live in the presidential palace. Everyone says you have to have lots of money to run for president. We have lots of money. Thanks to your support, benevolence, and participation in our casinos, we have found the American dream. Please read the back of this pamphlet for there is a poem that was written especially for you. It is our sincere thanks to the Indian trader of bygone days who was our teacher, our inspiration, and our role model. We sincerely hope you like it because it was written from our hearts,

The Indian storekeeper lived in a castle where he was king
When we traded with him, we lost everything
He taught us about the business and how to create earnings

Just Open a store and satisfy their yearnings
So we opened a place—an Indian reservation casino
Like Las Vegas and a town called Reno
You gambled and gambled until your money was gone
The old Indian trader hadn't been wrong
We loved having you here and want all of you to know
Our casino is your home if you have money to blow

The latter day Spoilers and eager politicians were fascinated by Able Joe and his Big Bubble Casino. He had become a rock star in the eyes of his people and was named First American Entrepreneur of the Year. Every political candidate he had supported and financially backed had won. He was becoming a power to be reckoned with.

It was one of Gotcha's few original thoughts. If the nation could have a national monument to a bunch of losers—Alcatraz Penitentiary came to mind—why not a national monument to winners. But was Big Bubble Casino of national significance? Well, it had revolutionized gambling. It legalized it, made it the thing to do. It created one of the biggest industries in the country and created a cultural phenomenon.

From the revenues it received, the federal government was now able to balance the budget. It was more American than apple pie. It was a living, authentic, glamorous slice of Americana. And it would not cost the taxpayers a dime. The proposal had the backing of the Conservative Party, and although the churches opposed it, Big Bubble Casino became a national monument. Actually, it was the president of the United States who authorized it, not the US Congress who had reservations about it. And Able Joe became the first superintendent of Big Bubble Casino National Monument. All those who knew and loved Able Joe just couldn't stop saying it. Ain't America Just Great.

CHAPTER ELEVEN

ART SOMEWHERE ELSE

Long before there were national parks, there were artists, painters, photographers, and sculptors who gave us images of what they would look like. The images meant different things to those who saw them. The pure scientist saw a research laboratory, the big oil companies saw a place to drill, miners dreamed of the gold that might be there, the entrepreneur salivated over potential profits, the future Disneys—a playground.

The artists see what they see and share that perception with those who have never been there. So when the Parks Department was approached about an Art in the Parks Program, it was really nothing new. The artists in residence were also welcomed by the park visitors as they were willing to share their creations and to teach others to create. The artists captured the beauty, the magnificence, the splendor, and most importantly, the soul of a national park.

But what is art? Who can define it? Who can understand it? Who can say? What is the role of the government? Can it judge, say yes to this and no to that? What are the standards? Who sets the standards? As the Art in the Parks Program grew, it became something that no one had ever anticipated. It got strange, bizarre, weird, even crazy.

A heavily bearded and tattooed hippie-looking man was arrested by the Capital City horse-mounted park police for chopping down a fifty-foot-high maple tree. The tree was estimated to be almost a hundred years old. The tree cutter was Christopher Bernardino who was thirty-two. Bernardino complained that his detention by the horse-riding policeman was an affront to his profession. To the police Bernardino didn't appear to be impaired or on drugs, but he couldn't understand the big deal about cutting down some old tree. He kept asking, "Why the hell am I in jail and get me a lawyer."

His personal possessions were inventoried and included a Mickey Mouse wristwatch, a wallet with $7, no credit cards, sixty-three cents in change, a can of snuff, a half roll of mints, a pocket knife, and two packages of Sweet and Low. In the worn suitcase he was carrying, there were one ax, one hatchet, two drawknives, many mallets, punches, burrs, brushes, fine chisels, a dovetail saw, a hand plane, a small box of micro-tools, a can of glue, three carving knives, a box of Brillo pads, numerous wood carving and wood sculpting magazines, and a book on the human anatomy.

The park police captain who was on duty got a call from Gotcha with orders to release him immediately. Bernardino's attorney arrived before he was released and threatened a lawsuit unless his client received an official apology from the arresting officer and that he be allowed to sculpt the downed maple tree. The apology was made, and the tree was set upright in front of a barn across from an old mill. Bernardino said that other commitments prevented him from sculpting during the day and that he needed floodlights on the maple tree so he could sculpt at night. So the park maintenance crew hooked up two floodlights for Bernardino. He then complained that someone had attempted to vandalize his artwork and demanded security. Six park policemen provided twenty-four-hour protection.

His increasing demands and the Parks Department ever acquiescing were an embarrassment to the parks rank and file. Little did they know. He proposed "A Day in the Life of a Sculptor." Capital City youngsters would learn the Bernardino way from the master's knee. He would visit two parks daily in the Capital City area at a cost of $500 a day. Bernardino also demanded that his sculpture be housed in the barn for all to see and enjoy. The old stone barn had been restored by the Parks Department, but funding was not available to furnish it with period historic farm tools, equipment, wagons, animals, and hay. The Society for the Ever Living Arts, mostly a group of rich, old, and bored aristocratic ladies supported Bernardino's idea and expanded it to include a permanent Art Barn. The shows would change every month and display the works of local artists.

Three park officials were invited to the home of the society's president, Ida Broomingburg near Stone Creek Park to discuss the proposal. At the end of the lunch, one of the Parks people drank heavily from the finger bowl and Ida Broominburg had it refilled for him. She thought the idea would be a slam dunk considering her hospitality, but it was turned down. The chief historian in the Parks Department considered it would be a prostitution of history. But one phone call from Broominburg and the Art Barn became a go. It cost $500,000 to renovate the old barn. Interior improvements included special lighting, heating, air-conditioning, meeting room, office, bathrooms, a sprinkler system, and an elaborate staircase. The exterior additions were landscaping and parking facilities for only an additional $150,000. The estimate for the historic refurnishing the barn was $30,000.

The master plan for the Art Barn would provide an opportunity for both professional and amateur artists. The contributions of children and senior citizens would be encouraged. The Art Barn would be open to the public seven days a week. The fine arts project would include paintings (oil, pastels, watercolors), pencil and ink sketches, photography, sculpture, and multimedia. Each individual artist would be responsible for delivery, setup, and removal of their works. The Parks Department would provide security, maintenance, and on-site personnel.

The interpretation programs at the art gallery would be provided by volunteers from the Ever Living Arts Society. All art-related projects, activities, displays, and advertising would be under the control of the society. The society would determine what was and was not appropriate for public viewing. The Art Barn shows would always be free, and there would be no solicitation or sales of the artworks. The Parks Department would assist in the printing and distribution of the brochures, flyers, posters, and catalogues. In other words, the government would pay for them but have no input into the content, graphics, or writing—no government censorship.

The grand opening of the Capital City Art Barn was on Halloween night, and it was cool with light snow. The time on the invitations that were mailed to a select group of patrons was 8:00 p.m. The treasurer of the "National Ascendancy of the Arts," a competing arts organization, arrived at 6:00 p.m. and was informed by one of the Parks people that the opening was at 8:00 p.m. She left, returned later, and the buzz was that her support was overwhelming—the only guest to come twice. Most of the invitees arrived half past the hour—a US senator, the secretaries of Interior and Commerce, one billionaire, numerous millionaires, two college presidents, too many high-ranking Spoilers, some with their wives, members in good standing of the arts community, and a few party crashers. Each guest passed through a welcoming line and was warmly greeted by Ida Broominburg, who was at the head of the line of six. They were presented with a beautiful ornate medallion, a slick colorful catalogue of the eighty art pieces on display, and a crystal glass of chilled champagne.

The twenty artists who created the paintings were there to interpret, entertain, and quietly solicit bids for their creations. Most of the attendees sipped one glass, acted interested, praised the hostess for her brilliance, dedication, and contributions to the art world, and slipped away within an hour. The ample spread of hors d'oeuvres was left mostly untouched. The Ascendancy bunch, the artists, and those who crashed the affair began downing the champagne right out of the bottles. No one remembers how it all started, but it was believed that two of the artists who were having an affair playfully tossed strawberries back and forth. It was an innocent attempt at foreplay that misfired, and one of the berries hit the drunken Ida Broominburg in the left eye. It looked like fun, so she threw a handful back, and the fruit fight was on. More and more champagne from the bottles fueled the flying figs, cheese balls, meat balls, olives, grapes, and peppermints. The park police were called in to stop the carnage and the park's maintenance custodians to clean up the mess. The Art Barn was to open in the morning for the third-grade class at

Stone Creek Elementary School where Ida Broominburg was president of the school board.

The three teachers and students were unaware of the Strawberry Exchange, but they were disappointed that Ida Broominburg and artists didn't show up. The park people did their best to conduct the tours and answer questions, but they lacked the artist's knowledge and affectation. The general public continued to be moderately interested in the Art Barn exhibits, especially when the artists put on their know-it-all show. Nothing unusual or controversial happened during the first year, but that would change in the second year.

Without warning, the changing Art Barn Art turned into anatomical sculpture. The materials employed were cedar, fir, maple, teakwood, tin, silver, ceramics, gold, bronze, and silver. Small figurines depicting eighteenth-century ladies' faces and hairstyles were the first offerings. This showing was followed by the upper body of women accentuating the bosom, some upright. There was a little concern from the mothers of nursing babies, who became restive and excited. The nude figures of full-figured women drew increased criticism from the visiting families who were not properly prepared for this level of sophistication. This was followed by the nude bodies of males, which made most of the teenage girls giggle. Over three hundred letters complaining about the displays were received by the White House. They protested the real-life sculpture and maintained that it was in poor taste.

The members of the Society for the Everlasting Arts were dismayed at the lack of appreciation for the contemporary sculpture, and the artists themselves were furious. Something had to be done to educate the public, maybe an art appreciation program. The society held a meeting with the park officials and presidential palace Spoilers before the next showing at the Art Barn. The negotiations were about the male genitalia sculpture that was scheduled as the next showing. The Spoilers supported the ladies and took the position of "letting it all hang out." The park people were appalled at the proposal and exclaimed, "Have you no shame?" It was decided that the Art Barn would be closed to the general public for one week and only members of the larger Capital City art community would be allowed to view the private parts. It was estimated that the total membership, those who kept up with their dues, was about 1,200. They would be issued confidential invitations and would be screened and identified before being allowed to enter the building. The administrative control would be the responsibility of the society. Two park police would be stationed near the building to enforce the "laws of decency" and keep the nonmembers out.

For one week those who had paid their dues lined up for the Members Only Showing. Minimum age was twenty-one. No cameras or sound equipment would be allowed, and touching would be strictly prohibited. The vice president of the society, Priscilla Peterson, who became rich the old-fashioned way, introduced the idea of charging a five-dollar admission fee, but was informed by a park policeman that it would take an act of Congress to support her money-making scheme.

As the lines grew longer, honey buckets were brought in and placed in appropriate places. Vendors were issued special passes to provide coffee, hot chocolate, pretzels, hot dogs, donuts, and candy. Teenagers hawked newspapers. Some sold pot. By the third day, over forty thousand alleged members of the art community had passed through the sculpture. Viewers were hustled through the exhibits, and it was in and out in ten minutes.

On the last day the Wrappers Against Artistic Decadence, a.k.a. WADS, began wrapping the windows and doors of the Art Barn with surgical gauze. This kept the park policemen busy unwrapping. Three park policemen or three who looked like them secured the building, locked and barricaded the doors from the inside. The show was over. It was estimated that over one hundred thousand membership cards legitimate and otherwise had been approved by the society. This exceeded the total number who visited the Washington Monument, the Jefferson and Lincoln Memorials combined for the same time period.

The sculptors, including Christopher Bernardino, were ordered to pick up their fetishes the following morning. When they arrived, they found that all the sculpture had been smashed. A small sign was tacked to the inside of the front door that read "Courtesy of the Peyote Society." The Art Barn was closed and never reopened.

After the Bernardo and Broominburg misadventure, the poor Parks people thought it was all over. It wasn't. The Parks coordinator for Special Events exclaimed, "Oh come on, this is off the wall. After what happened last year at the Art Barn. No way. I am fed up with the parks being misused by a bunch of self-serving politicians. I don't want to hear any more about hairdressing." He received a phone call from Gotcha that the hairdressers would be in his office at 1:00 p.m. to discuss the arrangements. His first question to the Head Hairdresser was, "When did hairdressing become an art form?"

Myrtle Myerstein was there to represent the hairdressers in general and herself in particular.

MYRTLE: It always has been.

Myrtle Myerstein was about five feet tall and weighed over two hundred pounds. She had bright silver hair and sported a huge fresh red rose. She owned seventeen exclusive salons in the nation's capital, Virginia and Maryland.

She continued, "In the ancient times, the peasants had short-cropped hair, and the aristocrats dressed their hair in rolls and let it fall over their shoulders.

It was an obvious class distinction more than anything else. Hairdressers were highly prized, and it was a profession that stayed in the family and was handed down generation after generation. Some of the earliest works of art, particularly statuettes of ladies showing elaborate hairstyles. Cleopatra would be the most obvious example.

COORDINATOR: "How about fingernails and toenails." Ha-ha!
MYRTLE: Young man, I own the most exclusive salons in the country, and I can assure you that we do not do any kind of nails. We only service the clients we wish to accept, and I have rejected thousands who do not have the political, economic, and social status that we require.

Coordinator: Oh! Well, what famous people have you had in your
    Red Badge Salons?
Myrtle: First of all, it is Red Rose, not Red Badge. Second, it is not
    just a beauty salon—it is a haute couture. Third, I don't divulge
    the names of my clients, but I can tell you that there have been
    many, many celebrities. Hairdressing is an extraordinary art
    form. When you transform a person on the outside, you change
    them on the inside. It gives the ladies confidence, pride, and it
    expresses their individuality And fourth, although I will deny
    that I ever told you this—the First Lady and all of her friends.

Well, that ended the questioning. Myrtle was given a one-time
special use permit. The restrictions were no advertising or marketing,
no posters, no flyers, no business cards, no soliciting. No Red Rose
Salon signs of any kind. It would be difficult to control the event, but
the Spoilers were only concerned about the millions of women voters
who had their hair done every week.

The site they agreed upon for the Hairdressing Artistic Show
of Shows was Laughanet Square, right across from the First Lady's
home. The small park displayed a statue of the famous Revolutionary
War hero from France. It was also the home of an assortment of
drunks, drug addicts, Vietnam vets, and those not playing with a
full deck. The only support these lost persons had were the wooden
benches where they camped and snoozed. They had no idea what was
about to descend upon them.

To be able to have her hairdressing ladies demonstrate the state-
of-the-art and the latest in hairstyling fashions would give Myrtle
invaluable visibility. All the major television stations would beam
it throughout the world with the White House in the background.
Myrtle set up six hairstyling stations complete with overstuffed Red
Rose Salon chairs. There were electrical outlets in Laughanet Square
(often used by the forgotten ones) so that each station was equipped
with all the necessary tools and accoutrements. The six professional
hair specialists were all scantily dressed in Red Rose Salon bikinis
especially created for the show. The six subjects were all Myrtle's
employees.

To enhance the festivities, Myrtle presented her bearded, raggedy, folk-singing brother, Barney, who still dreamed of being discovered one day. Myrtle herself would be master of ceremonies, enthusiastically showcasing each individual style. It would be a challenge because brother Barney wanted to howl all the time. Barney knew that this was his big chance, so he sang about "how the big oil companies had polluted and stole and the man in the White House just took their gold." The audience of over three hundred government employees on lunch break and sporting a paper Red Rose in their hair joined Barney in a loud and continuous chant.

And then the unfortunates returned to their homes away from home after foraging for cans and bottles left behind by the uncaring tourists. They were astounded and insulted by the gross spectacle of a bunch of floozies and government jerks trespassing into their sanctuary. The booze and drugs had already been induced, and they were ready to do once again what they had been trained to do—attack, attack, attack. They turned over the big, cushy Red Rose chairs, groped the gals whose hair was in disarray, and began to sing and dance to Barney's tune:

Before the park police could restore order, it began to rain, and the electrical connections started shorting out and then blew like it was the Fourth of July. The cheap red paper ribbons faded in their hair, and the government employees returned to their desks all red faced. The Secret Service agents dragged Barney off the stage and smashed his guitar over General Laughanet's head. Myrtle gathered up her girls and ran for cover crying about how the government always ruins everything.

CHAPTER TWELVE

WHEREVER HOSER THE FIRE

In May 1950, two men caused fires that swept through the Lincoln National Forest near Captain, New Mexico. On May 9, a black bear cub was rescued from a blackened snag, and his front paws and hind legs had been badly burned. The little cub was alone, charred, and scared before being found by a local rancher. He was flown to Santa Fe where his wounds were treated and bandaged. He was given the nickname "Smokey Bear" and flown to the national zoo in Washington DC. During the next twenty-five years, Smokey was visited by over one hundred million adoring fans.

During World War II, it was feared that the enemy would start catastrophic wild fires that would destroy the needed timber. A Smokey Bear first appeared on a poster in 1944 pouring a bucket of water on a campfire. He was dressed in blue jeans and a ranger hat. This icon with the message "Only you can prevent forest fires" became a national symbol before the fire in New Mexico. There were Smokey Bear toys, comic strips, and thousands of kids became Junior Rangers. In 1950 the little badly burned bear became the "living figure" of the fire prevention campaign. He would remind all of us that we have a personal responsibility not to be careless with fires.

Smokey Bear, not Smokey the Bear, which was a cute and popular tune, was known all over the world as a symbol for fire prevention. He was the spokesman for eliminating careless, man-caused fires and no doubt helped save thousands of lives and millions of acres of forest. But he didn't say that "all fires were bad." And he never told us that we needed to extinguish all the fires. But he left the impression that all fires were a threat to human life, and the public bought into the myth. Smokey Bear became too popular, too believable—a national celebrity.

Smokey Bear's message to prevent mindless, careless, unnecessary fires is as relevant today as it has ever been. It is true that nine out of ten forest fires are caused by people. But forests have been borne out of fire, created by fire. For example, the lodgepole pine trees depend upon fire for reproduction. Their pine cones need to be exposed to extreme heat before the seeds can be released from the cone itself and germinate. Fire plays an essential role in nature along with rain and wind. Fire suppression became an obsession only after the big lumber companies like Wherever Hoser bought off the politicians. Fire has a natural role and is a necessary tool for restoring and maintaining healthy forests to use and enjoy.

A woods is not just wood, and a forest is not just trees. Sometimes you can't see the trees for the forest because of something called a future fuel supply. The ground beneath the tall trees, a.k.a. the forest floor, can be covered with all shapes and kinds of foliage. Diseased and dead fallen trees. branches, leaves, roots, grass, vines, weeds, decaying animal remains and lots of other stuff make up the forest floor. All of this mess can get quite deep and can grow higher, wider and even dryer. It waits for months, years, decades and generations for something or somebody to come along and change it into fire and smoke When a forest becomes overwhelmed with tons of debris it is simply a disaster waiting to happen.

Some forest management scientists believe that if the fuel supply is low, a surface fire can be a good thing because it is manageable and the forest can quickly restore itself. But if the fuel supply is allowed to get bigger and higher and it catches fire, disaster will happen. Money and manpower are then wasted in futile suppression efforts. A massive fuel supply on the forest floor and extending up the tree trunks is just one element of a future catastrophic wildfire. The other two elements that make up a fire are oxygen and heat. When a combustible fuel comes in contact with oxygen at high temperatures, a natural phenomenon occurs—fire. Remove any one of these three elements and the fire will die. The fuel and the oxygen in a forest need a lightning strike or a careless human act. Questions about wind are always asked because of its effect on forest fires. How strong is the wind? Which direction is it blowing? How quickly can it change direction? Every fire is different, and every fire is unpredictable.

The forest fire scientists divide the fires into three categories depending on intensity and severity.

Ground fires are the least damaging to private property and human life. They burn the humus—dead plant life mixed in the soil beneath the leaves. They are usually slow-moving and not significantly affected by the wind. These fires may not appear on the surface and may go unnoticed for a period of time. Surface fires burn grass, leaves, twigs, shrubs, and fallen bark. These fires travel faster than ground fires but are easier to control. This type of fire can prevent more catastrophic fires from occurring. They also release numerous nutrients and spur germination of conifers such as giant sequoias and lodgepole pine by releasing the seeds from the cones. Crown fires are of two types: dependent—when the fire creeps up the trees to the crown or top. It happens when the winds are low and the trees are spaced far apart. Running is the second kind and are fires that burn extremely hot, travel rapidly, and can change direction quickly as they leap from the tops of the trees. These are the most dangerous and destructive and produce firestorms and tornadoes. They also create spot fires in all directions at high speeds. The running crown fires are a firefighter's worst nightmare. They burn through everything including all the trees, the wildlife, and the forest firefighters who try to stop them.

Considering the scientific knowledge, the memorandum from Gotcha to Big Lodgepole National Park was surprising, unbelievable, contrary to established forest management and an affront to common sense. Henceforth, it read, "The forested land within Big Lodgepole would be thinned out." The title of the memorandum was "Twelve Steps to a Lusty Forest."

1. Prescribed burns are evil. They are against the will of God and His plan for managing nature and stuff. They are now outlawed forever.

2. Controlled fires are stupid. Any simpleminded person knows that you extinguish a fire—first, foremost, and always.

3. Suppression is always good. Never forget that Smokey the Bear tune—"Get me out of here."

4. Redheaded woodpecker. The overreaction to the plight of this weird bird is unfounded. They can just go and peck somewhere else.

5. Forest insects. Part of nature, always have been. We're not sure what it is that they do, but we know they don't like fires.

6. Fire cache. Must be inventoried twice a week to ensure that all necessary equipment and tools such as fire rakes, chainsaws, those Pulaski and McLeod tools, and whatever that other stuff is—is ready when needed. There should be two backpack firefighting pumps for each person in case of leaks—that is, the pumps can't do much about people who leak and ensure that copious amounts of both potable and portable water are on hand. You never know how much is enough sometimes.

7. Global warming nonsense. It's cold in the winter, and in the summer it can get hot as hell in some places. People seem to like it that way. It has nothing to do with fires. Deny this unscientific crap because it ain't good science.

8. Campfires are prohibited. If a campfire is discovered, those responsible will be banned forever from camping in, around, or near a national park.

9. Scientific science systems. In the future, this will always be referred to as SSS since it will be easier to remember. SSS is the intellectual basis for the program of thinning. Clearing could have been used, but thinning is in these days and clearing is not always clear.

10. The goose and the gander. The thinning of the national forests is to include the thinning of the national parks because in most people's mind they are one and the same. As we know, many national parks are within larger national forests, but the public is not always aware of this. Maybe one day they will be the same because the federal government takes care of both of them. And we want you to make sure that all of your visitors understand that saying the Forest People are a bunch of "cut and runners" is unfair. They are simply doing their job as prescribed by Congress.

11. Forest folks lead agency. Because the national forests are larger and have a history of cooperating with the United States of America Timber Industry, they will manage and supervise the thinning.

12. Wherever Hoser the Fire was selected as the best qualified, easy to work with, and most experienced timber company. They have the management style that can ensure success—exploitation. Their rape and ruin procedures are the envy of the world. They will be given the privilege of extracting the tall trees in the Big Lodgepole National Park because of their commitment to destroying the small trees in the process.

The memo was so ridiculous and outrageous that the park superintendent of Big Lodgepole tossed it in the trash without sharing its contents with the park staff. Two weeks later, lightning ignited a small five-acre fire. The park rangers monitored the fire but let it burn. When the Spoilers learned that the park had maintained a "control burn" operation, they descended on Big Lodgepole in a fury. The superintendent denied ever seeing a "Twelve Steps to a Lusty Forest" memorandum. He was demoted and transferred to the district office as assistant EEO officer. The head of the investigation team was Hank Handshaw, who had previously worked for Wherever Hoser before being appointed as coordinator for Protection of Natural Resources. Handshaw brought in the Forest Service faithful and ordered them to immediately extinguish the small ground fire.

The park staff, including the confused park rangers, were corralled into the park visitor center theater where the "lost memo" was explained to them. Before the brainwashing was halfway through, all the employees walked out. If Handshaw didn't have their support, "So what," he said to himself. He would teach them a lesson in loyalty. His Wherever Hoser buddies, along with the Forest Service loyalists, established positions on the boundaries of Big Lodgepole and were ready to do what they were famous for—cut and run.

Of course, that it was against the law to cut a tree in a national park didn't deter them, since they rationalized that the park was inside the forest and the boundaries were blurred. And as the Wherever Hoser Company president often said, "Wood is wood." He looked upon those crybaby, tree-hugging environmentalists as the enemy.

It was a quid pro quo agreement between the United States government and the political arm of the Wherever Hoser Company. The lumbering giants would clear out the younger, smaller trees and open up the forests in the forest and in the parks. They would get the big prize. They called it "thinning and winning." They would get the best and biggest of the tallest trees for their timber mills. The noise they made could be heard three miles away, and Hank Handshaw said it was 'the most beautiful sound he had ever heard. A parade of chainsaws—chopping, hacking, mangling, tearing, ripping away the unwanted ground growth buildup. But it was torturously hot, and the wind blew the sawdust, the leaves, the small chopped-off limbs and the slash off the forest floor into the open air pockets between the tall trees and then up the trees. It was the beginning of a roaring fire.

The Wherever Hoser choppers dropped their gas-filled noise makers and ran for their lives. The fuel supply on the forest floor was the deepest anyone remembered, and it extended six miles long and one mile wide. The winds whipped up to sixty mph with gusts as high as a hundred. The gigantic firestorm sent the red-hot flames two hundred feet high into the air. It burned and burned and burned out of control, impossible to stop. The Spoilers in their three-piece suits and pointy-toed Florsheim shoes danced around pointing their fingers, casting blame on anyone and everyone except themselves.

The Spoilers flew in Ropi rain dancers and prayed in and out of church for rain or an early snow. No rain, no snow, and the Rope rain dancers danced but not the rain dance because two of them were Peyote Society members. Under the personal direction of Hank Handshaw, the Wherever Hoser workers built fire breaks where the Ropi dancers danced. There was maximum crowning—treetop to treetop. It was too late. They should not have built the fire breaks where the Ropis indicated. The fire roared and raced through the Forest Service land, bypassed the park, and headed straight for the Wherever Hoser properties.

It destroyed the company's famed hotel and resort center. The massive sawmill, which held two million board feet of lumber, was burned to the ground. The fire scorched the golf course and consumed a total of thirty-eight company buildings and eighty pieces of heavy equipment. The company lost over five hundred million dollars. No big prize, no tall trees, no quid pro quo. The Wherever Hoser company cut off all political contributions to the incumbent administration.

CHAPTER THIRTEEN

FIFTY-STAR FLAG RAISING

Keith, representing the US senator from Hawaii, yelled, "It's our state that's being added to the Union, and the fiftieth star represents Hawaii, not the White House." "Well," exclaimed the White House Spoiler, "the flag represents the United States of America and all the states." It was the same old hassle between the executive branch versus the legislative branch. The question was, "Who would pull on the nylon rope to raise the first fifty-star flag?" The president said that the honor should go to him, and he would be represented by the secretary of Interior. Actually, it would be one of the Parks people, a Peyote, who would ultimately decide the question.

The secretary was a loyal Spoiler and a former newspaper hack who had bounced around several federal agencies. The Spoilers wanted their man to pull the string on the flag since it was an election year.

The senator from Hawaii was a World War II wounded hero who had lost an arm in defense of his country and the recipient of the Medal of Honor. The issue escalated and would have gone before the US Supreme Court, but the senator, being a true patriot, was willing to acquiesce to the president. To the people of Hawaii, it was an insult, but their man simply said, "Let the jerk, jerk."

The forty-nine-star flag, which had honored Alaska as the forty-ninth state, had only flown for one year. It first flew at Fort McFriendly National Monument and Historic Shrine. On July 4,

1960, the forty-nine-star flag would come down, and the fifty-star flag would be raised in its place. In commemoration of the event, a special replica of the fifteen-star flag, which flew on September 13–14, 1814, would also be flown during the ceremonies.

The singing of "The Star-Spangled Banner" in schools, colleges, and at sporting and military events would forever remind one of Francis Scott Key and the bombardment of the fort. The British who had folded its tent in the American Revolutionary War thought they might have another go at it—it was called the War of 1812.

The young nation, the United States of America, refused to be pushed around by the biggest navy in the world. It would not ignore the British attacks on our ships and interfering with our shipping, commerce, and seizing our sailors. As the naval war ensued, the British moved up the Patusent River and landed troops at Benedict, Maryland. They moved toward the Capital City, which had fewer than ten thousand people living there. Less than one hundred soldiers defended the presidential palace. As the English soldiers moved toward the Executive Mansion, the president's wife, cheerful Molly, grabbed a painting of the first president and fled across the river into Virginia. The British General Bobby Boss and his savages threw rags soaked with oil through the broken windows of Molly's home and set fire to the building. They also torched the Treasury Building, the Capitol, Library of Congress, and the Naval Yard.

The Mother Country's torches headed back to their boats and sailed to a big, much bigger target—Baltimore, a major center of shipbuilding and trade. The city was defended by Fort Mcfriendly under the command of Major George Annistood. The big guns at the fort held the British ships at bay, two miles down the Parapcso River. On that day, September 13, 1814, a special flag of defiance was flying one hundred feet high above the ramparts of the fort. The flag was huge, thirty feet by forty-two feet with fifteen stripes and fifteen stars (Kentucky and Vermont had been added to the Union) and made of eighty pounds of dry wool bunting by Mary Pickersquill and her daughters.

It was too big to be sewed together in the Pickersquill home, but there was ample room in the nearby beer brewery. Each white star was over a foot long. She was paid $405.90 for the flag materials and the sewing. It was this flag that inspired Francis Scott Key, although he may not have seen it at dawn's early light. Key was aboard a British ship pleading the release of Dr. Billy Means. The ship was two and a half miles down the river from the fort, and it had rained heavily throughout the British bombardment. The flag was soaking wet and hanging limply from the flagpole.

After the retreat of the British, Key completed his poem in the First American Hotel in Baltimore, writing and rewriting. The poem was first entitled "The Defense of Fort Mcfriendly" and ironically put to the tune of an English drinking song "To Anacreon in Heaven." The title was changed to "The Star-Spangled Banner" and surprisingly did not become the national anthem until March 3, 1931. Americans with normal vocal cords have been embarrassed ever since. The British were gone, but they had given America a song.

The heated arguments at the planning sessions for the fifty-star flag ceremony now centered on the fireworks. This was heralded to be the biggest and most extravagant fireworks spectacle in the United States. Thousands would ooh and aah in person, and millions would see the brilliant lights and hear the popping sounds on television. The history of fireworks used by the Greeks and Romans was recorded some six hundred years before the Savior came to save the world. The Chinese were credited with the discovery of gunpowder, and some say that fireworks have the power to fend off evil spirits. Since the American Revolution, July 4 was the date that America would blow up the sky with fireworks shows that would always dazzle the kids. The local park staff wanted a fireworks display that was the safest and of the highest quality. A first-class theatrical that would include red, white, and blue images of historical American flags, pinwheels, comets, rockets, roman candles, fire balls, repeaters, spinners—all the bells and whistles and then some. The Spoilers were at the planning session to ensure that their man got the lucrative contract.

Another thorny issue was, Who would present the principal address? The Spoilers maintained that it had to be the secretary of Interior because he was representing the president. And why didn't the president himself attend? He was too busy on the political trail campaigning for the party pols. The secretary did agree to recognize the senator from Hawaii, who was of course from the opposition party. The fifty-star flag event would be used by the secretary to highlight his questionable achievements. The parking of cars would be proudly provided by the Eighty-Second Airborne in dress uniform. The honor guard would be represented by all four branches of the armed services as was the custom. The seating arrangements would be handled by the Boy Scouts of America. The Eagle Scouts would seat the other dignitaries—those who were not on the red, white, and blue grandstand. Refreshments were offered by an anonymous local merchant, much to the chagrin of one of the Spoilers who wanted his uncle to get the gig. The United States First Marine Band was selected to play patriotic music. The all-Negro Southern Baptist Church Choir of Baltimore would sing the expected oldies and one special soul rendition.

It was now the evening of July 3, 1960, and the attendees would forever remember "O say can you see, by the dawn's early light." The massive fifteen-star, fifteen-stripe woolen flag "whose broad stripes and bright stars were so gallantly streaming" was lifted by a gust of wind, and it rose up and up higher, and everyone who saw it applauded. And the choir sang, "And the land of the free and the home of the brave." Then the flag of defiance was lowered, folded, and secured for posterity It was 11:55 p.m. July 3, and at exactly midnight, the sparkling brand-new fifty-star United States of America flag would be raised for the first time anywhere by a stand-in for the president. The park rangers attached the fifty-star to the ready-made clasps on the halyard. The wind was back, and Old Glory was flapping in their hands as all waited for that historic moment. It was becoming difficult to hold, and one of the rangers, Cool-Head Fred, said "Where are they—let's get this flag up."

The Marine Band was playing, and the Baptist Choir was finishing "Home of the Brave." And finally Secretary Jerk began jerking to uplift the flag in coordination with the music. Timing was most important, but no rehearsal or dry run had been made because no one anticipated a problem. As the red, white, and blue reached half mast, the rope slipped off the top roller, and the flag was stuck as the

Marine Band and the choir were on "The land of the free." The jerk jerked and jerked, but nothing happened. Cool-Head Fred jumped into the fray, pushed the secretary out of the way, made a lasso loop movement, which flipped the cord back onto the roller. He then pulled the senator from Hawaii to the top of the heap, and with one arm, the Hawaiian war hero propelled the Fifty Stars to the top of the flagpole. As the flashbulbs burst from the worldwide news organizations, the senator was once again an American hero. In the days that followed, his beaming face was on television, newspapers, and magazines everywhere.

It was destiny, it was right, it was beautiful. The fiftieth state and its senator were honored as it should be.

There were no pictures of the secretary since his face was hidden by a large park ranger hat with shiny silver acorns on the dark leather hat band. The image of the gallant senator from Hawaii had been sealed forever in the minds of people for eternity. The Spoilers who had planned, controlled, and directed the ceremonies were burning with rage.

An investigation was initiated, and all the park people who were present during the event were interrogated. The entire scene of the rope jumping off (how did he do that?) and then jumping back on was studied in detail. The Spoilers brought in a cherry picker so they could examine the roller on top of the flagpole for manufacturing defects, inept installation and possible tampering. They found nothing.

Because it all happened so quickly and the cameras were aimed at capturing the historic movement, there were no pictures taken of the incident. The investigation was dropped. All the park people who were there as the fifty-star flag was hoisted received a Special Achievement Award and a check for $5,000 from the United States Congress.

The president was looking for an excuse to dump Secretary Jerk who was now a major political liability. The story of the inquisition was leaked to the press, and the jerk resigned. The White House Spoilers would never forget the humiliation that they suffered at the fifty-star flag raising. However, none of the Spoilers ever remembered that Cool-Head Fred had been there. It was a costly mistake.

CHAPTER FOURTEEN

WE'RE FROM THE GOVERNMENT, AND WE'RE HERE TO HELP YOU

L. F. Wing was born the year of the stock market crash, and he grew up during the Great Depression, a time of severe unemployment, and even worse, segregation. His father was a Baptist preacher in the Deep South, and his grandfather had been a sharecropper on a small farm. His family always called him LF, and he developed a love of reading, finishing high school at the age of fifteen. He completed college, earned a doctorate in theology, and became the pastor of a church in a small town in Alabama.

Both his words and his "follow me" actions resulted in a bus boycott that lasted for over a year in Montgomery, Alabama. He later returned to Atlanta, Georgia, his birthplace, and became pastor of the same church his father had served. But it was the civil rights movement where he focused his time, talent, and energy. Dr. Wing was arrested over twenty-five times for "civil disobedience." His leadership in demonstrating for the poor and uneducated African Americans led to the right to vote for millions of men and women. He was the most charismatic public speaker of his time, and he became famous for his "Freedom Is My Dream" speech in the nation's capital. He was recognized around the world for his achievements, receiving the Nobel Peace Prize, the highlight of his short life.

It was during his efforts to help the garbage workers receive a fair pay for their work that he was murdered by a hired gun. The death of this forceful civil rights crusader at the age of thirty-nine incited race riots throughout the United States and mourning all over the world. He was a prophet in the truest sense of the word, and he was honored for his contributions to justice and equality by a saddened but grateful nation.

After his untimely death, his wife, Rebecca, established the L. F. Wing Center for Freedom and Peace, a living memorial to his legacy. The center is devoted to continuing his ideas and philosophy in always confronting the cruelty of man's inhumanity. Through Mrs. Wing's leadership and guidance, the movement blossomed to include the civil rights of women, the right of equal pay for equal work, the rights of gays to get married and receive government benefits, and the rights of children to receive proper parental care. The forum for an all-inclusive society began in Rebecca Wing's home, but it grew and developed into a beautiful architectural structure next to Dr. Wing's crypt.

The Wing Center would function as the centerpiece for service and teachings of L. F. Wing's life and commitment to his fellow man. Dr. Wing was successful in gaining equal rights for millions without physical force, military might, or war. The center would coordinate its efforts and programs with other organizations both public and private to carry out its mission. The Wing Center housed a visitor center with exhibits, an auditorium for viewing the historical footage of Dr. Wing's endeavors, a library, museum storage, archives, a gift shop, and administrative offices. The Wing Center was the central point of a larger historical complex that included Dr. Wing's birth home, the church where he was pastor, and the crypt, which was nestled in a Reflecting Pool. Visitation to the to the historical area grew rapidly, and it became the most visited place in the city. The center developed outreach programs to educate schoolchildren everywhere. The educational efforts would help prepare children for leadership in the struggle against poverty, racism, violence, and war in the spirit and tradition of Dr. Wing's life.

As public interest in the Wing historical complex grew to the point where the family could not handle the overwhelming crowds, they asked for help from the federal government. It was not only in the interest of the US government, but also it had a moral responsibility to support one of the most important chapters in American history. The Parks Department was the logical agency since it had the expertise in historical preservation and in providing interpretive services to the public. The parks detailed the Black Band-Aid Brigade from the Capital City to come to the rescue of its brothers and sisters in Atlanta, Georgia. These were African American career Parks Department employees who had been mesmerized by Dr. Wing and were enthusiastic followers of his civil rights movement. Along with the personal services support, the area was given a new designation—national historic site.

The cooperative agreement with the Wing Center stated that the Parks Department would always be in a supportive role, and its involvement would be limited to technical support and minimal financial aid. The Wing family and the board of directors would continue to be the major institution for providing information directing the research program, interpreting and controlling the legacy of Dr. L. F. Wing. The parks would lease the birthplace from the center and provide tours of the home. The parks would provide assistance at the Sweetgum Baptist church with an exhibit, but the church volunteers would provide the tours and information services for those who visited the church.

The Parks Department would have no land acquisition authority, and they would never be allowed to develop a visitor center that would compete with the Wing Center. The Parks would only cooperate with the other property owners and city officials to promote historic structures preservation and public use.

During periods of heavy visitation, they would station personnel in the gravesite area to answer questions and provide orientation. The Spoilers in the Capital City now had their foot in the back door, and in time they would attempt to usurp the control and total management of the L. F. Wing National Historic Site. That it was confusing to the park visitor as to who knew what, who did what, and who was responsible for what is best illustrated by a conversation between a park visitor and a park employee.

Birth Home of L. F. Wing Park Visitor: This is a pretty big house.

Park Person: It's a two-story wood frame house and has fourteen rooms.

PV: How old is it?

PP: It was built in 1895, and L. F. Wing's grandfather purchased it in 1919.

PV: And it was in this house where Dr. Wing was born?

PP: Yes, he was born here in 1929 and had an older brother and sister.

PV: What room was he born in?

PP: The one over there.

PV: How long did he live in this house?

PP: His grandfather, grandmother, his mother, father, sister, and brother all lived in the home. They sold it in 1941 and moved a few blocks away.

PV: Did Dr. Wing have any children?

PP: Two boys and two girls.

PV: Who owns the house now?

PP: The Wing Center bought the house to ensure that it would be preserved as the historic site of Dr. Wing's birthplace.

PV: So the Parks Department just helps out with the tours?

PP: Well, not really. As I understand it, the Parks Department has a cooperative agreement with the Wing family who actually owns, controls, and manages the national historic site. We lease the home from the Wing Foundation and are responsible for the interpretation and preservation of the home and grounds. We also completed a furnishing plan to document the interior of the home to the historic period. The original furniture, rugs, pictures, family memorabilia all belong to the Wing family. Also, we provide the security, protection, and public safety.

PV: Is the home open to the public throughout the year?

PP: Except for major holidays like Thanksgiving and Christmas.

PV: How many people visit the home every year?

PP: Over one million visit the national historic site, and about fifty thousand take a tour of the home, which usually takes about twenty minutes.

PV: So the Parks Department will always preserve the home and provide the tour services?

PP: Yes, ma'am.

PV: Will the Parks Department buy the home someday?

PP: Oh no, the home will always belong to the Wing family. As we told Mrs. Rebecca Wing when we first arrived, "We're from the government, and we're here to help you."

And at the gravesite of Dr. L. F. Wing

PV: How long has the gravesite been at this location?

PP: In 1968, the body of L. F. Wing was carried upon a farm wagon drawn by mules to Southern Cemetery. In 1970, Dr. Wing's remains were taken from that cemetery and moved to its present site of entombment. The crypt is constructed of Georgia marble, which acknowledges his Southern roots. As you can see, in the center of the Reflecting Pool on a raised platform is the L. F. Wing crypt.

PV: What is the inscription on the Wing crypt?

PP: The engraving on the crypt reads "Pastor, L. F. Wing, 1929–1968, Free at Last, Free at Last, Thank God Almighty I'm Free at Last."

PV: Will other members of the family be buried here?

PP: Yes, that is my understanding.

PV: Who is responsible for the preservation and protection of the gravesite?

PP: The Wing Center owns the complex, which includes the gravesite. I suppose if we were asked, the Parks Department would help out, but only if it was requested. It's kind of a sensitive issue.

PV: I noticed a flame or something over there. What is that?

PP: That's the Eternal Flame, and it symbolizes Dr. Wing's lasting memory.

PV: Will the Parks Department ever take control of the gravesite and Wing Center since it was designated a national historic site.

PP: Oh no, never. It belongs to the Wing family forever. As we told Mrs. Wing when we first got here, "We're from the government, and we're here to help you."

PV: Well, I am confused. I see the park people at the Wing home, and I see them here at the Wing Center, but you keep telling me you're just here to help.

PP: Yeah, we're just here to help them along.

And at the Sweetgum Baptist Church

PV: How old is the church?

PP: It was completed in 1922, and a school was added in 1956. As you can see, it's a Gothic revival style of architecture.

PV: Did Dr. Wing preach here?

PP: Yes, he did, and his father and grandfather before him.

PV: Is it open to the public, I mean besides the regular church services?

PP: The members of the church has a group of volunteers who regularly offer tours of the church.

PV: Is there a charge or fee?

PP: No, but that has been a problem. If you take the tour, you can make a donation if you wish. The Parks Department felt that donations should not be accepted, but you've got that separation of church and state thing.

PV: Who owns the church?

PP: Sweetgum Baptist Church.

PV: I heard a lady on the tour bus say something about a murder at the church?

PP: It's something we don't usually talk about, but Dr. Wing's mother was murdered by some deranged man while she was playing the organ. That's all I know about it.

PV: I'm sorry. Was Dr. Wing's funeral held in this church?

PP: Yes, it was.

PV: Will the church become part of the national historic site?

PP: Oh no. We told the church members that we're from the govern-ment and we're just here to help you.

As long as Dr. Wing's remarkable wife, Rebecca, was at the helm of the Wing Center and the Wing Historic District, the legacy of her husband would remain safely in the family's hands. She successfully lobbied the United States Congress to honor her husband with a national holiday. Her efforts became a reality and ensured her posi-tion as an energetic force in the fight for justice and equality for all. Mrs. Wing became a national icon because of her tireless support of disadvantaged citizens, and she gained international stature in the eyes of the world. Rebecca Wing was almost equal to her legendary husband.

As Mrs. Wing became older and in failing health, she eventually relinquished the leadership of the Wing Center to her family, the board members, and ultimately to her son, Baxter. She exclaimed that we need a new vision and fresh ideas to continue the work and philosophy of L. F. Wing. Her son had professional experience in mass communications and in producing and directing modern tech-nological documentary films and music. He incorporated the Wing estate and copyright protection of his father's work and lifetime accomplishments. He began making plans for an interactive theme park to serve as both an educational tool and experimental study in promoting the meaning of Dr. Wing's life. He would employ the latest in communications to show how peaceful demonstrators suf-fered at the hands of segregationists and brutal law enforcement tech-niques. He wanted to create an edu-tainment approach, which was beyond what the Parks Department had ever envisioned.

Visitors to the national historic site would experience some of the same misery that civil rights workers, both black and white, endured. Through real-life theatre and historical plays, the public would experience firsthand how Dr. Wing and his followers were subject to racial taunts, harassment, and bullied by fearful segrega-tionists. And how out-of-control law enforcement officers attacked them with powerful streams of high-pressured water from fire hoses, billy clubs, gas bombs, and police dogs. The civil rights brothers and sisters were peaceful, offered no resistance, were passive demonstrators, and exerted a force that became known as the people's power. The play would also depict the methods of passive resistance, such as sit-ins and sit-downs, that were successfully employed. In addition, the program would include interactive and participatory exhibits with original tools, weapons, and techniques used by the police and the segregationists.

The Spoilers back in the Capital City also had a dream to enlarge the park system and the Wing National Historic Site would be a significant inclusion. They persuaded the Congress that the national historic site should be administered by professionals and not allowed to deteriorate. And what better agency to manage the site than the Parks Department. What was needed, the Spoilers said, was a new visitor center to provide better services to the visitors. They hustled the local politicians for support promising to clean up the neighborhood—meaning buying local buildings at inflated prices. After all they would have to have room for parking, administrative space, and housing for the park employees. The Big Double Cross was now in motion.

In the beginning the government had pledged that they would never acquire any land or buildings or build a competing visitor center. Now the Parks Department would tell the story of the civil rights movement without the constraints and interference of the Wing family. The earlier sleazy smile, the cold handshake, the "you're the architect and we're the carpenters" would soon vanish.

One member of the Black Band-Aid Brigade, who once served in the Southwest and unknowingly had friends in the Peyote Society, was devastated to see what the Spoilers were planning. Before the community building was acquired by the Parks Department for a visitor center and on receiving a tip from a friend from the past, he alerted Mrs. Wing that she was about to be sandbagged by the government. He would be her eyes and ears and keep her aware of the nefarious plans of the Spoilers. Although he was not in the Parks Department inner circle, he would pass on the information from those who were. He would not stand by and let the government disparage the Wing family.

A strange little uncivil war was developing. When the Wing family learned of the government's skullduggery, they exploded in uncontrollable rage. Mrs. Wing held a press conference and screamed that "it was never a possibility that a Parks Department that I trusted would usurp our role as guardian of the Wing historic district. At first they congratulated us on becoming a member of the National Register of Historic Places. Then they made the Wing Historic District a national historic site. It is not the loving people who gave the tours of my husband's birthplace but the evildoers in the capital. It was they who slew the dreamers, but they will not slay the dream."

Mrs. Wing wrote a letter to the president demanding that the government honor its original cooperative agreement that explicitly stated that the government would not develop a visitor center that would compete with the Wing Center. She wrote, "You are stealing what we created" and "You came at my invitation as park guides, now you're trying to direct the play." The response came not from the presidential palace but from the Parks Department's sinister Spoilers. It began by stating that it was all a misunderstanding and a "matter of semantics." The park's exhibits would not conflict with "your role" in presenting the story of the civil rights movement. We will do the history thing, and you can continue to do the "vision thing."

And it went on with words like "partnership," "joint venture," "mutual understanding," and "common interest" that replaced previous obsequiousness as supportive, aid, assist, backing, help. Mrs. Wing well remembered "we're from the government, and we're here to help you." The relationship with the parks went from warm and fuzzy to alarm, to shock, to incredulity, to outright hostility. If the Parks established a competing visitor center across the street from the Wing Center, they would have overwhelming resources—taxpayers' money. They would significantly reduce the role of Dr. L. F Wing, his philosophy and legacy.

Their master plan deleted his opposition to the Vietnam War, his support of organized labor, his defense of women's rights, and his deep concern for all poor and disadvantaged people regardless of race or ethnicity. The battles that Dr. Wing and supporters had fought against, inequality and injustice, were too important to be told by a government that bugged his telephones, kept him under surveillance, and did everything it could to destroy his name and his movement.

Mrs. Wing and the Wing Board of Directors banned the Parks Department from her husband's birthplace and the gravesite. She forbade any Parks Department officials from setting foot in the Wing Center. All the Wing family memorabilia, civil right artifacts, speeches, letters, documents, personal items, pictures, photographs, paintings, awards, gifts, films, were secured away from the government, protected and stored in private hands. The government could build their visitor center, but they would only display empty cases and boxes. Mrs. Wing now understood why Mount Vernon and Monticello and Williamsburg were all in private ownership. With the help of big cola money, the Wing Center and its historic properties remained in the Wing family forever.

CHAPTER FIFTEEN

GETTYSFIELD

The venerable Confederate Army of Virginia was again victorious, December 1862 at Fredericks and on the first day of May 1863 a brilliant victory at Chancelsburg. After these two battles, the general knew that his army was weakened and that needed provisions were in short supply. He also knew that he could no longer continue to fight defensive engagements and that is was time to take the fight to the Yankees in Yankee territory.

It would be the challenge of his life since "his right arm," General Thomas Jonathan Jackmon, had been shot off his horse accidentally by Confederate troops from North Carolina. Jackmon had suffered three bullet wounds and it was hoped that if his arm was amputated he would live. At the first major battle of the Civil War, he had gained the nickname of Stonewall. The name stuck, and his soldiers never called him General but simply Stonewall. He had always been aggressive, unpredictable, a spirited risk taker who helped win victory after victory. When he died a few days after being wounded, the general exclaimed, "It is terrible a loss, and I am grateful to Almighty God for having given us such a man." He addressed all the Confederate troops saying, "The daring, skill, and energy of this great and good soldier are now lost to us. But while we mourn his death, we feel that his spirit still lives and will inspire the whole army with his indomitable courage and unshaken confidence in God as our hope and strength."

"Let his name be a watchword to his corps who have followed him to victory on so many fields." The general assured the president of the Confederacy that if he did not take the offensive the Union Army would surely regroup and invade once again. The Northern newspapers proclaimed that the Northern people were losing confidence in their military and political leaders. The lack of support could have an effect on the army's will to fight. A decisive victory up north could bring recognition and possible intervention from England and France. And the Confederate soldiers needed food, shoes, horses, guns and ammunition, which could be gained from an invasion into Northern territory. Without the leadership and military genius of General Stonewall, it was a gamble, a serious risk, but doing nothing was an even greater risk.

The Confederate commander reorganized the Army of Virginia into three corps—a total of 75,000 battle-proven veterans. His army pulled out of eastern Virginia headed west toward the Shenandoah Valley and then crossed the Potomac River. The army then moved north into Pennsylvania. The famed Confederate Cavalry leader Jeb Pruitt pushed his cavalrymen on a long swing east of the Union Army. It was a costly mistake that would affect the inevitable battle. The Union Army under General Pleade was on the Confederate Army's flanks, and the general was considered competent and cautious. Neither side anticipated that the greatest battle of the Civil War would take place in the little market town of Gettysfield. Some say that the fight happened there because the Yankees stumbled on a few Johnny Rebs trying on some new boots.

The First Day—Wednesday, July 1, 1863

The Union Army endeavored to position its forces between the Confederate Army and the nation's capital to protect the president. The night before the battle began, a Union officer said that "the Confederates will attack us in the morning and we must hold on." Both sides were desperately waiting for their scattered reinforcements to catch up and form an organized, disciplined, ready-to-fight Army.

The soldiers in the gray uniforms did attack in the early morning, but it was mostly reconnoitering, probing, feeling each other out. But they did engage, as one reporter wrote, "the most desperate fighting ever waged between the Artillery and the Infantry at close range without of cover on either side—bullets hissing, humming, and whistling." A Confederate general who had lost a leg in an earlier battle was hit again in the same place. He exclaimed that "he heard the thud, but it don't hurt at all to be shot in a wooden leg." The Johnny Rebs pushed the Billy Yanks over to Chopwood Hill as night came upon the battlefield. The first day was won by the Confederate Army, so say the historians.

The Second Day, Thursday, July 2, 1863

The Confederates were late moving into action on July 2. In the afternoon, the Confederate artillery blasted away at the Union left flank. A Rebel force of infantry then advanced through the apple orchard and the cornfield and took command of the Devil's Dig below Little Flat Top. The Johnny Rebs began climbing up the slopes of the hill unaware that the Union defense had just received reinforcements. The two armies battled each other until nightfall, and when the ammunition was all spent, they fixed bayonets and fought toe-to-toe. The Blue left flank held, and the Rebels were repelled. The Confederate attack on the right flank at Coventry and Gulp's hills was face-to-face, eyeball to eyeball. They clubbed each other with rifle butts, cannon rammers, and even bashed each other with stones. It was personal, mean, and savage.

The Union counterattack drove the Confederates back to their original positions. It was darkness, and the second day was over. The second day clearly went to General Pleade and his Union Army. That evening the Confederate commandeer believed that the Union flanks were strong but the center was weak. The Union commander concluded the same and reinforced the middle. The defenses were formidable protected by stone walls, stacked fence rails, and they had the high ground.

The Third Day, Friday, July 3, 1863

It was hot, and it would get hotter. The Army of Virginia's artillery, some 150 cannon, was only a mile from Cemetery Ridge. Morale was still high, and the general believed his army could accomplish the mission. The Rebel artillery pounded the entrenched Union forces, but their aim was too high and did little damage. The next tactic was audacious, but poorly planned and executed. Six battle-hardened brigades plus General Wickett's fresh division, 15,000 strong, advanced, the Johnny Rebs yelling, yelling, through a half mile of open field without any protection. It was not Wickett but General Armistood who led the charge. "Follow me" he yelled, cheering the Rebels forward with his cap on his upraised sword. "Give 'em the cold steel." The fight became hand to hand, and a Billy Yank remembered "an overwhelming resistless tide of an ocean of armed men sweeping upon us. On the move, as with one soul, in perfect order, over ridge and slope and through orchard and meadow and cornfield, magnificent, grim, irresistible."

The Union artillery and infantry fire from above on Cemetery Ridge was relentless and merciless. It was not irresistible but a gamble that failed miserably. The Southern soldiers were slaughtered, and Armistood was killed. An observer later wrote that the battle noise was "strange and terrible, a sound that came from thousands of human throats...like a vast mournful roar." The Johnny Rebs limped back down the slope defeated, almost completely destroyed. The Confederate general rode out to receive the remnants of the once-glorious Army of Virginia and said, "All this has been my fault."

The battle of Gettysfield was now history. The total losses for both the Union and the Confederacy (killed, wounded, and missing) was 51,112. Remarkably, the only civilian killed was Jennie Wade, who was hit with a bullet that went through the door of her home before hitting her. On July 4, there was no celebration in the Army of Virginia, as the devastated Rebels limped back across the river into Virginia.

The Union Army's failure to pursue, attack, and destroy the Confederate Army was a major blunder. The president was furious when General Pleade reported that he had repulsed the Confederates at Gettysfield. He wanted the Confederate Army destroyed and the war to end. Nevertheless, the Confederate general had been defeated and never invaded the North again.

As Johnny Reb and Billy Yank abandoned the battlefield, they left behind some 21,000 wounded and dying for the people of Gettysfield to clean up. To these caregivers, the aftermath was worse than the battle itself. The stench from the dead soldiers and animal carcasses was overwhelming. Over six thousand brave soldiers from both the Union and the Confederate armies had been killed in the battle, and their bodies had been left behind on the battlefield.

The governor of Pennsylvania led a movement to purchase seventeen acres of land for a proper burial of the fallen soldiers. All the Union states contributed funds and participated in the planning and the establishment of a cemetery. The Cemetery commissioners, to honor the men who had died at Gettysfield, held a dedication ceremony on November 19, 1863. To consecrate the burial grounds, they chose the most renowned orator of the day, Edward Windpiper. Windpiper, president of Harvard College, gave the performance of his life—it lasted for two hours. The 12,000 attendees were there to pay their respects and see where their loved ones were buried. The cemetery was not to become a federal cemetery until 1872, so inviting the president was almost an afterthought. The president spoke for only a few moments, but his words will forever be remembered: "We cannot dedicate, we cannot consecrate, we cannot hallow this ground. The brave men, living and dead, who struggled here, have consecrated it far above our poor power to add or detract. The world will little note, nor long remember what we say here, but it can never forget what they did here. It is for us the living, rather, to be dedicated here to the unfinished work which they who fought here have thus so far nobly advanced. It is rather for us to be here dedicated to the great task remaining before us—that from these honored dead we take increased devotion to that cause for which they gave the last full measure of devotion; that we here highly resolved that these dead shall not have died in vain; that this nation, under God, shall have a new birth of freedom; and that government of the people, by the people, for the people, shall not perish from the earth."

The first veterans' reunion, the twenty-fifth anniversary in July 1888, was attended by thousands of Union and Confederate veterans. This was the singular most important event for the preservation of the battlefield. Under the leadership of General Dan Fickles, Gettysfield veteran and now a US congressman. The battlefield was established by an act of Congress as Gettysfield Military Park in 1895. This was the same Dan Fickles who shot and killed Philip Barton Key, the son of the author of "The Star-Spangled Banner" for having an affair with his wife. He pleaded temporary insanity and was found not guilty—the first in an American courtroom.

The fiftieth reunion in 1913, attended by some forty thousand veterans, was highlighted by a reenactment of Wickett's charge to be met by outstretched open hands of friendship from the Union survivors. The seventy-fifth anniversary in 1938 was a memorable occasion with the lighting of the Eternal Flame and the dedication of the National Peace Memorial by the president who said, "All of them we honor, not asking under which flag they fought—thankful that they stand together under one flag now." There were 1,845 Civil War veterans present at this dedication, sixty-five of whom had actually fought in the battle of Gettysfield. The average age, ninety-four.

When the Parks Department assumed responsibility for Gettysfield National Military Park in 1933, the mission for the department was well established. It was "to provide for the enjoyment," "leave them unimpaired." To the public historians, "enjoyment" meant "education." What could be more educational than park historian—storyteller on one end of a log and a student on the other end. It was something like this at one time because not many Americans visited Gettysfield during the Depression and World War II. At that time, the individual visitors were greeted with "Where you folks from?" It was personal, and their questions were answered with a talk using a relief map of the battlefield, an excellent teaching tool, and onsite guided tours. The visitor center was small, dingy, and dusty and displayed a few original muskets and uniforms.

After the war and into the 1950s through the end of the twenti-eth century, more families had automobiles some two or three. They were on the move, and with so many places to go and see and so little time, the old educational approach was replaced with the "New Interpretation." The visitors were accustomed to exciting and dra-matic fast-paced movies and then television. So the parks changed to meet the demand.

Media professionals and communication specialists could tell the whole story in less than one hour. New interactive exhibits, dioramas, audiovisual programs, and reenactments. Then there was the private Electric Map, and a Cyclorama, and the Tower. All daz-zled the folk who seemed to enjoy it. The story was the same, but the telling had changed—it had been enhanced, embellished, even more glitzy.

Fifty years ago the Electric Map was the in thing. It was a half-hour show that explained both the Union and the Confederate troop movements during the battle. It was a must-see, advertised in travel books. For $5. It was once free, then 25 cents, then 50 cents, $1, $2, etc. The family experienced a quick, sanitized overview of the battle. The marvel of electronics—no smoke, no blood, no maimed or dead bodies.

The Parks Department bought the Electric Map in 1971, and the twinkling continued to entertain. When the parks acquired the Cyclorama("cycl" circle, "orama" to view) of Wickett's Waltz into hell, a special architectural dream, as it was called, was constructed to display the 359-foot-long, 27-feet-high artwork. It was a 360-degree panoramic painting to give one the illusion of being in the middle of the battle. After viewing the awesome visual of smoking cannons, battle flags, galloping horses, broken wagons, dead horses, leg and arm amputations, faceless and headless soldiers, bloody corpses, one visitor murmured that after the viewing the Parks Department should ask "all those who enjoyed being in the middle of a killing field, please raise your hand." Oh yeah, "to provide for the enjoyment?"

Another enhancement was the Tower. It's ugly. An abomination on sacred soil, an eye sore, should never had been built. These were some of the comments of career Parks people, especially the historians and architects. Even the director of the Parks Department said, "Of all the projects planned and carried out, this tower is the most monstrous." But it was built to the surprise of the Gettysfield park staff, the townsfolk, the director, and even the governor, who promised that the tower would never rise. But it did rise, all 307 feet high, 14,000 steel bolts, and 508 steps. It was touted as "the classroom in the sky," "breathtaking," a unique panorama of the battlefield minus the fighting and dying American soldiers. The tower boasted high-powered telescopes, a narration even in foreign tongues, an oversized gift shop, a snack bar, all for the visitors' enjoyment.

So why was it built? The Parks people say it was a mystery. A mystery? Well, somebody sold out. A victory for the Spoilers. And it happened in the same year that a disgraced president quit the White House. Nevertheless, over one million sightseers experienced the power of the tower, and it stood for twenty-six years. And for twenty-six years the owners collected the revenues and met increased criticism. So finally, they said to the government, "You want it, it's yours for six million."

During the summer holidays, a single mother took her two young children to see the famed Electric Map. After the twinkling died out, her ten-year-old son was seriously disappointed. "Mom!" he said, "I thought there was going to be a battle—that was no battle. It was just boring. Can I go to the car and get my Nintendo? This place sucks." In the modern world of video games, computer graphics, interactive games, in the home, in the school, and the real fun in the arcades, the Electric Map has lost its twinkle. The story is the same but the reverent. Educational telling has been supplanted by the Walt Disney entertainment and amusement approach.

The unique and handsome edifice designed only for displaying the Cyclorama art was dysfunctional as a visitor center and public use building. The plans are now to rehabilitate or destroy the Cyclorama building and build a visitor center that meets the needs of the present-day visitor and the needs of the park staff.

Years of neglect will cost the Parks Department about ten million to replace the structure. And the mighty Tower finally hit the dust—blown up in just eight seconds. This visual intrusion on the barren battlefield cost the taxpayers six million.

There is, on the horizon, yet an another extravaganza to "provide for the enjoyment." It will not be built on the historic battlefield and will not be another intrusion. It is a joint effort of big business and weak government. No old-time and antiquated history lessons. This will be the virtual reality experience—the show of shows. The one-billion-dollar development will forever be known as the "Gettysfield Grand Kitsch." It will be bigger and glitzier than anything in Las Vegas. Three gigantic floors each with historic names: the First Day, the Second Day, and the Third Day—each floor three hundred thousand square feet.

Underground parking for ten thousand cars, fifty floors of spacious and expensive rooms. Ten five-star restaurants—the Wicketts, Fickles, General Pleade, Confederate Commander, Armmistood, Little Bald Top, Seminary Stand, Devil's Digs, Big Bald Top, and Gulps Hill. The Gambling Casino on the First Day Floor an array of two thousand one-arm bandits, poker, blackjack, and three new games—with a minimum bet of $50,000—the Right Flank, the Left Flank, and the Center Charge.

For the daring and the adventurous, an authentic 1863-style wedding chapel and a modern-day divorce chapel, the largest gift/toy shop in the world with replica Confederate Colt six-shooter, Enfield muzzle-loading muskets, a double-edged Bowie knife, twelve-pounder Napoleon cannon, bayonets, swords, minié balls, cannon balls, caps, belts, belt buckles, regimental insignias, and too much to name plastic junk.

On the Second Floor a Sharpshooters Gallery—a shooting range where one can pick his favorite targets. General Bluster and General Fickles were the two favorites. Shooters are equipped with an authentic Springfield muzzle loader and six minié balls—help is available in loading and aiming at an extra fee. A photo studio with both union and Confederate uniforms; eleven bars serving Southern comfort; a cannon firing demonstration; a practice bayonet exercise; A Day (actually only thirty minutes) in the Life of Billy Yank and a Day in the Life of Johnny Reb. Each evening at eight and ten a special real-life play of Wickett's Charge into Hades, with battlefield sounds, smoke, blood (not real), and the Rebel yell.

The Southern and Northern soldiers who fought, died, and were buried at Gettysfield were just plain tired of it all. Their collective voices cried out, "Please stop it, please." They were tired of being written about, talked about, second-guessed, the untruths, the half-truths, the one-upmanship, the war games played by both adults and children. The twinkling Electric Map, the inaccurate painting of the carnage, the movies, the museum exhibits, the know-it-all historians, and most of all the damn politicians. And from their graves, they asked, "Why did we have to die here?" "Why didn't our leaders resolve the problems peacefully?" "Don't you know the battle here was brutal, savage, horrible, so unnecessary?" "Why can't the living let us rest in peace?" "We just fought and died here not understanding why?" "Now all the monuments, memorials, granite generals, old artillery cannon, unthinking hordes trampling all over this sacred ground. Do they think this was some kind of nineteenth-century game?" "Did not the president say 'The brave men who died here have consecrated it far above our poor power to add or detract?'"

The Peyotes were listening and heard their cry. They had seen the Spoilers seal greedy deal after deal. They had seen the encroaching commercial developers, parasites, sucking the blood from the fallen for profit. Gettsyfield was becoming a profitable crazed carnival, a place for family vacationers to waste their time and money on foolish schlockish souvenirs. All of it so dishonored those who lost their lives here.

The Peyotes would take action to right the wrongs. They would restore the battlefield back to nature, to the tranquil farmland, as it had been before the slaughter. On a dark snowy night, the Peyotes moved onto the battlefield with bulldozers, front-end loaders, and dump trucks—all provided by the Friends of Gettysfield, the National Coalition for Decency, and Greenplease. They knocked down, pulled down, ran over, bulldozed, flattened, crushed, and squashed hundreds of man-made granite and marble statues, monuments, markers, and tablets. It took just three hours. They hauled it away and dumped all of it in the Gettysfield Grand Kitsch monstrous swimming pool. The land was then restored to the silent countryside as before. And the peach orchard would overflow with ripe fruit, and the wheatfield harvest would be abundant, and the grass would grow back, and the mocking birds would sing, and there would at last be peace at Gettysfield. Someone said they heard thousands of cheering voices from over near the cemetery.

CHAPTER SIXTEEN

HOW OLE IS THE HOLE

PRESIDENT: This is the most impressive resume that I have reviewed in my seventeen years as president of Nit Wit University. It says here that you were once employee of the month, that you were once a drunk, and you hold the gullible Book of Records for patching up river rafts.

TALL TALE: Yes, sir, it's true, bless the Lord.

PRESIDENT: You actually met Jesus, and He told you that the Great Gulch was made by Him 4,500 years ago on Thursday, February 18, at 9:12 a.m. by Boah's fertile flood. Must have been a helluva lot of water.

TALL TALE: Well, I don't curse anymore, praise the Lord, but it's all there, all of it, in my book *How Ole Is the Hole*.

PRESIDENT: And you sold over three hundred copies of *How Old Is the Hole*.

TALL TALE: Well, maybe a few more. I gonna make those park people rich, yes, sir—selling my book in that government store.

PRESIDENT: And in all those years of rubbering on the Big River you never lost a soul?

TALL TALE: Not even one. And thousands of souls were baptized right there in that holy water, praise the Lord.

PRESIDENT: And you and you alone were responsible?

TALL TALE: Oh no, the Lord was with me on that river. I was never alone.

PRESIDENT: And you have a reference from that distinguished author and lecturer, the father of faith-based Research, Dr. Jerry Rightthink?

TALL TALE: Me and him is buddies. I could never have wrote *How Ole Is the Hole* without him. Bless the Lord.

PRESIDENT: Exactly. We are most grateful to have someone of your caliber, creative intelligence, intelligent creativity, God-inspired achievements. You have that vision thing deep down inside you, boy. So I would like to offer you the position of dean of the Pseudoscience Department. It includes God's teachings on geology, biology, chemistry, paleontology, geophysics, tectonics and geomorphology, and stuff like that. I may have left out a few of theologies, but I'm not sure what the hell they do anyway. Do you think you can handle all that?

TALL TALE: Piece of cake.

PRESIDENT: Great, I knew you would say that. Everybody likes a piece of cake. Now I have a problem with a few knuckleheads— those pipe-smoking, wine-tasting, cardigan-wearing nerds who have lost their faith in our Lord and think science is their god. We got to do something about these troublemakers before they ruin everything.

TALL TALE: Well, I would begin with one of them management reorganizations like Jack Belch said.

PRESIDENT: Brilliant. Just how would you do it?

TALL TALE: Simple. I would give all of them a faith-based test, and those who failed would be sent to a rehabilitation center for lost souls.

PRESIDENT: Why didn't I think of that myself. Tall Tale, you are truly a genius. Who would replace them?

TALL TALE: I would establish a new science college exclusively on faith-based research. Young, easily persuaded Earth creationists would head the faith-based departments. The new studies would include the Bible Tells All, Religion Trumps Science, Biblical Time Scale Methodology, the Genius of Genesis, Faith of Our Fathers Documentation, the Lord Is My Shepherd syllabus, Evangelical Evolution, and a Jesus Loves Me Know study group.

PRESIDENT: Awesome, just awesome. Would your book *How Ole Is the Hole* be required reading?

TALL TALE: Absolutely. God's glorious gorge is so deep, so vast that it cannot be understood unless you read my book. The book demands that you go down into it and bathe in the holy waters. Here you will find the overwhelming evidence of the power of Mother Nature, who works with God. Amen.

The First Americans say they first discovered the Great Gulch and then showed it to the Spanish conquistadors under Toronado in 1540. The first study that in detail revealed the canyon to the world was the Major John Wesley Howell Expedition shortly after the American Civil War. This was the beginning, and hundreds of scientific studies would follow. The Great Gulch is filled with cliffs, slopes, buttes, spires, and temples colored in gold, red, pink, orange, and many shades of green. It is the rays of the sun that gives it its spectacular colors. Scientists maintain that the earth was formed four and half billion years ago give or take a few million. Some of them say that the canyon is ten million years in age. *Big* is the word for this canyon—277 miles long, about nine miles wide, and one mile deep. It is a devastating example of water and wind erosion. It has been called "the world's most wonderful spectacle, ever changing, alive with a million moods." Sunrise bathes the canyon in a hot-red hue; at midnight it is a mystery, dark and brooding.

There are many Indian legends, many more than the nearby Indian tribes. The one story still believed by most of today's First Americans is told by storytellers in many different ways. But they all say, "My grandfather knew that the river was from nowhere and went everywhere. River fast, much power, move big and higher—roaring always roaring. It was moving for a long time as old as the sun and the moon. River take much rock and leave some. River still taking it away today but not like before. River good to us—give water for corn and squash—no flood, no Boah boat, no faith, but hand of the spirit. River do it all—great-grandfather know from great-grandfather before."

It was first a national monument and then became a national park in 1919. The president, who was known as the great conservationist, exclaimed, "To mar the wonderful grandeur, the sublimity, the great loneliness and beauty of the canyon—leave it as it is. You cannot improve on. The ages have been at work on it, and now man can only mar it. What you can do is to keep it for your children, your children's children, and for all who come after you." One can hike down a rim trail to the bottom or by mule down the more popular Devil's Trail. But gawking and gazing is what most people do from the top of the south rim—about five million do so each year.

So does it really matter how old the canyon is or how it was created? We know that it was created a long time ago and that water, ice, wind, and snow all played a part in its creation. To the harried sightseer, the causal tourist, and the lonely visitor who don't fathom the difference between a thousand, a million, or a billion years, isn't it enough to enjoy the beauty and mystery? Perhaps that is too simplistic, unintelligent for the scientific mind and the true believers of the scriptures in the Bible. They continue to fight over when and how the canyon was formed. It could have been a flood or river or maybe both that carved the Great Gulch. It could have been five thousand years ago or 10 million or even more. Those in the scientific community and those in the faith-based camp will never reach an agreement simply because they don't want to. Each side knows they are right and cannot grasp the arguments of the other. They cling to their positions as if all the knowledge of the world is at stake, and maybe it is. They will never come together, they will never agree, they will never compromise—because their mind-set will not allow them to. It is impossible.

Tall Tale's book, *How Ole Is the Hole*, for sale at the national park bookstore, claims that it was at the time of Boah and the great flood that the canyon was formed. The book states that it was only 4,500 years ago and it was a flood that carved the gorge. The author says that it's right there in the book of Genesis, the first book of the Bible, a book that God dictated to Moses on Mount Sinai. The creationists maintain that the evidence of God's existence is seen in the things he made. The flood theory is known as the classic flood geology and is so obvious that the evolutionary geologists just don't get it, explains Tall Tale. And the canyon is a solemn witness to the mighty power of God. It took a lot of water, much more than the river could deliver, to dig and create a canyon. The book is illustrated by beautiful and awesome pictures by a photographer who doesn't agree with the creationist's story. When asked for truth about the creationist's belief, they offer something like, "If God didn't mean that He created everything in six days, why did He do it and why is it in the Bible?" The basis for the formation of the canyon is found, they say, in the book of Genesis.

Genesis 1:1–31 and 2:1–3.

> In the beginning God created the heaven and the earth and God said, Let there be light and there was light and God called the light Day and the darkness he called Night. And the evening and the morning were the first day. And God made the firmament and divided the waters which were under the firmament from the waters which were above the firmament: and it was so. And God called the firmament Heaven. And the evening and the morning were the second day. And God called the dry land Earth and the gathering together of the waters called the seas and the earth brought forth grass and tree yielding fruit And the evening and the morning were the third day. And God said Let there be lights in the firmament of the heaven to divide the day from the night and let them be for signs, and for seasons and for days and years. And God made two great lights, the greater light to rule the day and the lesser light to rule the night, he made the stars also. And the evening and the morning were the fourth day... And God created great whales, and every living

creature that moveth and every winged foul and
God blessed them, saying be fruitful and multiply, and fill the waters in the seas and let the foul
multiply in the earth. And the evening and in
the morning were the fifth day. And God said,
Let us make man in our image, after our likeness:
and let them have dominion over the fish of the
sea So God created man in his own image, in the
image of God created by Him; male and female
created He them. And God saw everything that
He had made, and, behold it was very good. And
the evening and the morning were the sixth day.
And He rested on the seventh day.

There is a second creation story: Genesis 2:4–25. Mostly about
Adam and Eve, but it adds nothing to the basis for the age of the
earth. So there you have it—all of it. When asked for further evidence that supports their claim of six thousand years and that the
Great Flood happened in 2348 BC, the creationists refer to something called the Bible timetable. Shortly after the Dark Ages, an Irish
cleric determined that the creation took place in 4004 BC. It was
based on the age of various kings and a long list of begats. The secular
scientists say the methodology is unscientific and totally unworthy of
any intelligent consideration.

When asked for documentation that the canyon was formed by
Boah's Great Flood, the early earth creationists offer Genesis 7:17–24
and Genesis 8:1–16.

And the flood was forty days upon the earth; and
the waters increased, and bare up the ark, and it
was lift up above the earth. And the ark went upon
the face of the waters. And the waters prevailed
exceedingly upon the earth; and all the high hills,
that were under the whole heaven, were covered.
And every living substance was destroyed which
was upon the face of the ground. And the waters

prevailed the earth an hundred and fifty days. And God made a wind to pass over the earth, and the waters assuaged. And after the end of one hundred and fifty days the waters were abated. And the ark rested on the seventh month on the seventeenth day of the month, upon the mountains of Ararat. And it came to past in the six hundredth and first year, in the first month, the waters were dried up from off the earth and Boah removed the covering of the ark and looked, and behold, the face was dry. And God spake unto Boah, saying, Go forth of the ark, thou wife, and thy sons and thy sons' wives with thee.

So the flood came and went, and Boah and his family and the animals were saved and returned to the dry land. The creationists say this was the beginning of the gutting of the gorge. It was not a river but the great flood they affirm. When the scientific world asked for specifics based on geology, the author of *How Ole Is the Hole* replied that he had talked with the Lord and that the Lord said that it was the flood that did it. He added that the scientists are all wrong, that God created everything, and they should not question the authority of the scriptures. "The Bible is the Word of the Lord and they better believe it," Tall Tale said.

Scientists, always seeking absolute proof, assert that the leading biblical scholars conclude that no one knows for certain who wrote the book of Genesis or when it was written. And to them, the Genesis story doesn't provide any evidence as to how old the earth is. The scientists are exasperated because the creationists don't read the scientific experiments and resulting studies. Geologists and other scholars offer an impressive array of tests and dating methods such as stratigraphy and cross dating, radiocarbon—CJ4, correlation by fossils, biostratigraphy, paleomagnetic and archeomagnetic dating, radiometric timescale, thermion mass spectrometry, and cosmic ray exposure dating. The conclusions of these methods and tests were that the earth is over four billion years old.

Scientific studies for the past one hundred and fifty years have provided increasing conclusive evidence on the gorgeous canyon. The most recent studies show that the canyon was carved by a continuing flash flood on the Red River, millions of gallons of water taking with it sand, silt, rocks, and boulders the size of a house.

The erosion was gradually made by the surging water as land around it was uplifted. Hundreds of studies of the canyon have been made as geologists test and retest new methods to date the rocks. They say the rocks don't lie. To date, they conclude that the canyon is at least five million years old, if not older. The scientists say the creationists have nothing to offer and it's the same old "we're right and you're wrong." They have no evidence, no proof, no nothing.

The book entitled *How Ole Is the Hole* attracted little notice until Dr. Willie Pelt, a highly respected university geologist, picked it up during a visit to the canyon. He was flabbergasted by the book's assertions and subsequently published a scathing review of the book. He maintained that the hypothesis and resulting conclusions were illogical, unfounded, unscientific sophistry, and wooly headed thinking. It is a blatant example of phony baloney, he wrote, a crude attempt to proselytize by biblical literalists using a beautifully illustrated multi-authored book about a spectacular and world-famous geological feature. Pelt claims that allowing the sale of the book within a federal government nature preserve is unconstitutional.

He writes that the government is approving the creationists' poppycock and their fundamental beliefs. In his review, *Creationism Is Ignorance*, he writes that the silly book tries to undermine the scientific research of scholars from all over the world. Saying it's a work of God does not make it so. It's an embarrassment to the park ranger naturalists who are trying to explain the natural history and formation of the canyon.

You can preach about Genesis in churches. But don't display religion along with scholarly books.

Another scholar from the Paleontological Society writes that the canyon was formed millions of years ago. He states that it is the responsibility of the Parks Department to present the best scientific information to the public, and the book is nothing but pseudoscience. And another concern from a public employees organization states that the park should present only science and not provide a forum for debate.

Seven presidents from the most prestigious scientific organizations: the American Geophysical Union, Society for Vertebrate Paleontology, American Geological Institute, National Association of Geosciences Teachers, Association of American State Geologists, the Paleontological Society, and the Geological Society of America sent a letter to the park superintendent, which was supported by the one hundred thousand professional membership. The letter urged the superintendent to remove *How Ole Is the Hole* because it is not science but a religious tract. They maintained that the federal government endorsement of the book attacks the scientific scholars of the world who support the scientific findings of the formation of the canyon.

The book is contradicted by the park naturalists and all the interpretive media they use to tell the story of the formation of the canyon—the museum exhibits, films, audiovisual programs, nature walks and talks, the popular campfire programs, and the scientific literature written by the park staff and the scholars from academia. One park naturalist exclaimed, "We give the park visitor scientifically correct information based on the best available research. The canyon will always be a natural outdoor laboratory for thousands of geology students who study here each year. This book has no scientific basis." As result of the professional criticisms from both within the Parks Department and the scientific community and the legal advice of a Parks Department lawyer, the superintendent pulled the book off the government bookshelf.

Almost immediately, in defense of God's truths, an ultra-conservative, right-wing fundamentalist law firm threatened a lawsuit if the book was not restored to its rightful place on the bookshelf. In a letter to the Parks Department in the Capital City, they argued that abolishing the sale of *How Ole Is the Hole* was a patent violation of the US Constitution. The book they asserted was an alternative scientific point of view. They accused park naturalist Bettye Bates as the instigator in having the book removed. Finally, the law firm God's

Given Law preached that the secular evolutionists have their theory and the earth creationists have the Bible. To preclude Tall Tale's book from the bookstore is contrary to the first amendment.

In response to their letter, Gotcha overruled the superintendent. He said the legal advice that the superintendent received was from a land acquisition park attorney who was deficient in constitutional law. The book *How Ole Is the Hole* would be restored but placed in the mythological, inspirational section of the bookstore. This decision satisfied no one as the ACLU responded with a lawsuit stating that the book, although beautifully illustrated, was a false scientific interpretation and pseudoscience. The National Union of Federal Employees joined in claiming that the right-wing zealots in the presidential palace and the Parks Department were consistently overruling the local park superintendents.

The dilemma was what to do with the book now and the nagging constitutional question. When the issue first surfaced, the Spoilers stayed on the sidelines and passed the buck to the park superintendent. He had the authority to decide what was sold in the bookstore. But when the self-interest groups threatened lawsuits, the Spoilers were caught between Scylla and Charybdis. No decision was forthcoming. They would vacillate, say a decision was forthcoming, then stonewall. The one thing that all parties agreed upon was the photography. The visuals in *How Old Is the Hole* were beautiful, elegant, spectacular, majestic, outstanding, and awe-inspiring. The photographer Bruce Ansel Hillson, who created the artistic pictures, was devastated that Tall Tales had stolen his pictures. He filed a law suit and retained his photography from the book which was removed from the store. Bruce produced a beautiful coffee table edition of his pictures that became a best seller.

CHAPTER SEVENTEEN

WHAT WOULD OLE ABE SAY TODAY

The question being asked by both the right-wing Christian fundamentalists and the left-wing secular liberals is what would ole Abe say about a short, eight-minute documentary being shown at his marble memorial. The video features a divergent group of American citizens crying out at rallies and marches beneath his feet for equality and justice. Since the burning issue of his time was slavery and the preservation of the Union, who knows how he would view some of the troubling issues of today. Civil rights, feminism, gay rights, homosexuality, women's right to choose, abortion, and separation of church and state. The federal government show includes all these concerns highlighting the "I Have a Dream" rally in 1963. Those who knew him say he was humble, sensitive, compassionate and had a vision for all people to be free. He was born on February 12, 1809, near Hodgenville, Kentucky, and grew up in the backwoods of a small farm. Although he had less than one full year of formal education, his inquiring mind led him to read and write at an early age. He was six feet four inches tall, awkward looking with huge hands. He farmed, cut wood, clerked in a store, became a lawyer, a legislator, and was elected to the US Congress in 1846. He was respected for his honesty, integrity, and straightforwardness.

As one studies his life, his humanity would support the view that he was deeply concerned about fair play and "love thy neighbor as thyself." He definitely believed in God but was not a regular churchgoer. He personally hated slavery, but his single-minded vision and unshakeable imperative was the preservation of the Union. He was elected president in 1861, again in 1865, and when the Civil War ended, he was asked about retribution from the defeated Confederacy. He replied, "I'd let 'em up easy, let 'em up easy."

He was assassinated on April 14, just five days after the surrender at Appomattox. If anything he wrote or said might have indicated what he would say about the eight-minute show, it would be his Second Inaugural Address on March 3, 1865: "With malice toward none, with charity for all, with firmness in the right, as God gives us to see the right, let us strive on to finish the work we are in, to bind up the nation's wounds, to care for him who shall have borne the battle, and for his widow, and his orphan—to do all which may achieve and cherish a just, and lasting peace, among ourselves, and with all nations."

The marble monument to ole Abe looks like a Greek temple. The thirty-six Doric columns arranged in a colonnade around the exterior represents the number of states in the Union at the time of his death. The statue of the sixteenth president stands nineteen feet tall and made of Georgia marble. It was dedicated in 1922, and today over four million visitors seek inspiration from his benevolent countenance. The monument is a special place for all Americans, especially those who march to and rally at the memorial. About slavery he once declared, "It is difficult for us, now and here, to conceive how strong slavery of the mind was and how long it did, of necessity, take to break its shackles, and to get a habit of freedom of thought established." The memorial is a symbol of American democracy throughout the world. It is a sacred place where any American can stand, speak, and solicit attention for causes and issues that continue to divide the country. On August 28, 1963, about 250,000 people heard a southern preacher proclaim "I have a Dream." Since then millions have appeared before his benevolent countenance seeking understanding and acceptance of their passionate pleas.

Visitors to the monument ask just as many questions about the marches and rallies that have taken place there as they do about the memorial. The most frequent inquiry is where is the spot where L. F. Wing stood when he gave his "I have a Dream" speech. Other questions are about gay rights and women's rights rallies. As a result of the interest in the causes and rallies at the memorial, a group of high school students in 1994, with assistance of the Parks Department, produced the eight-minute film. The cost of the production was funded through donations from thousands of students, mostly in the Washington DC area.

The events depicted in the short film included real-life marches and rallies against the Vietnam War, in favor of gun control, abortion rights, civil rights, gay rights. Some of the scenes show signs, which read, "I am pro-choice," "Stop the killing," "Keep abortion legal," "National Organization for Women," "Christians support homosexuals," and "The Lord is my shepherd and knows that I am gay." The video is narrated by a voice that purports to be ole Abe, and he takes the story through historical times from the Civil War to civil rights and beyond. The program has been seen by at least ten million of the forty million visitors during the past ten years. Then in 2003 a right-wing Christian fundamentalist preacher complained.

The barrage began with the preacher man shouting that the video was an outrage—nothing but left-wing putrid propaganda designed to allow homosexuals and abortionists to piggyback on the civil rights demonstrations, which of course he also opposed. He exclaimed that it was a perversion of American history, shamelessly slanted to promote ultra-liberal causes. The video would make one believe that President Abraham would have supported the cruel abortionists and the sick homosexuals. He screamed, "Stop the travesty, stop the lies, or you will feel the wrath of God." Preacher man was able to solicit the aid of a Midwestern conservative politician who proclaimed that "as long as our man is in the White House, we can put an end to this garbage." They both railed against homosexuals whom God had punished by inflicting them with AIDS. And the women having abortions were murderers, defying the sixth commandment. (They both supported the Vietnam War that took the lives of 58,000 American men and women.) They complained to the Parks Department that the eight-minute film ignored the "Promise Keepers" march (a group of conservative Christian husbands); The "Stop Abortion" rallies and the "Gays Are Sinners" sit-down. (None of these events ever came within a mile of the Memorial.)

The students who created the video were surprised and alarmed at the Christian fundamentalists attack. The students maintained that they had both liberal and conservative input when the film was being developed. One student said that he was delighted that the ignorant cleric was outraged—that he should be outraged but at the injustices that still exist in our country. Another wrote that "the Christian zealots are just plain mean-spirited, and they condemn homosexuals and abortionists without any knowledge about them." The father of one of the students, a seventeen-year-old girl and an honor student, relished the opportunity to confront the preacher man.

Debate between Loving Father and Preacher Man:

LOVING FATHER: I have two daughters and two sons. One of my sons is gay. I love him the same regardless of his homosexuality. Am I wrong?

PREACHER MAN: Yes, you are wrong. You should give him parental guidance and not let him live in sin.

LOVING FATHER: He doesn't believe he's living in sin. He says that as a young boy he was always attracted sexually to other boys. He is deeply in love with his male partner and feels that it is natural for him to feel this way. They are both dentists and responsible citizens.

PREACHER MAN: So what. He is living in sin, and it is wrong.

LOVING FATHER: How do you know this?

PREACHER MAN: It's right there in the Bible.

LOVING FATHER: You accept everything in the Bible as absolutely true.

PREACHER MAN: Everything in the Bible is absolutely true. It is the Word of the Lord.

LOVING FATHER: Who wrote the Bible?

PREACHER MAN: It was dictated by God to Moses and other apostles.

LOVING FATHER: Wasn't the Old Testament first written in Hebrew, then translated into Greek, then Latin, and finally into English? Isn't it possible that the meaning of some of the words was lost or changed in the translations?

PREACHER MAN: That is not possible. The Bible is the revealed Word of the Lord.

LOVING FATHER: Many biblical scholars from divergent religions and denominations interpret the meaning of the scriptures and have come to different conclusions.

PREACHER MAN: Let me tell you again. The Bible is the inerrant Word of God.

LOVING FATHER: I'm sure that you are aware of the story of Sodom and Gomorrah. When the mob came to Lot's door demanding to have sex with his male guests, Lot replies in Genesis 19:8, 'Behold now, I have two daughters which have not known man, let me, I pray you bring out unto you, and do ye unto them as is good in your eyes. Only unto these men do nothing.' I ask you what kind of father would do something like that? And why would God let Lot sacrifice his daughters?

PREACHER MAN: You're missing the point. God destroyed Sodom and Gomorrah because of the sins of the people.

LOVING FATHER: Yes, I understand that. But if you accept the Bible as God's inerrant word, what's the meaning of Lot giving up his two virgin daughters for mob sex?

PREACHER MAN: If God said that is what Lot did, then that is what Lot did.

LOVING FATHER: You didn't answer my question.

PREACHER MAN: God destroyed Sodom and Gomorrah, and that's the meaning of the story. That's the end of it. You're trying to make it say something different.

LOVING FATHER: So you don't know. Why do Christian fundamentalists condemn gays? They are born homosexual. Can you imagine a young boy saying to his third-grade teacher, when I grow up, I want to be a homosexual?

PREACHER MAN: One can choose evil, or one can choose righteousness.

LOVING FATHER: It's not a matter of choice, Preacher Man, don't you understand that. Are you homophobic because you fear something you can't comprehend?

PREACHER MAN: The Lord is my shepherd, I fear no evil.

LOVING FATHER: Is King David one of your heroes?

PREACHER MAN: It was David who slew Goliath, and Jesus was a descendant of the House of David.

LOVING FATHER: Do you know about the relationship between David and Saul's son, Jonathan?

PREACHER MAN: What about it?

LOVING FATHER: How do you interpret the inerrant Word of the Lord in 2 Samuel 1:26? "I am distressed for thee my brother Jonathan; greatly beloved were you to me: Your love to me was wonderful, passing the love of women.

PREACHER MAN: They were just good friends.

LOVING FATHER: Just good friends, no physical attraction or contact?

PREACHER MAN: They may have hugged, but nothing more.

LOVING FATHER: And that's your interpretation? They may have hugged. Many scholars would disagree with you. Whatever. Okay, what did Jesus say about homosexuals?

PREACHER MAN: Jesus is Lord. Whatever God said, Jesus said.

LOVING FATHER: I thought Jesus was the Son of God?

PREACHER MAN: He is God the Father, God the Son, God the Holy Ghost.

LOVING FATHER: Well, I can't find anything in the New Testament about Jesus saying anything about homosexuality.

PREACHER MAN: That's because it's in the Old Testament.

LOVING FATHER: If crucifying homosexuals is paramount in Christian fundamentalism, you'd think that Jesus would have least commented on it.

PREACHER MAN: What God said, Jesus said. That's good enough for me.

LOVING FATHER: Did you know that some Christian denominations accept gays? There are even some gay priests and gay bishops. They must interpret the Word of the Lord differently than you.

PREACHER MAN: They are not Christians. They will receive the wrath of God and are doomed to go to hell.

LOVING FATHER: How do you know that, Preacher Man?

PREACHER MAN: Because they have sinned against our Lord.

LOVING FATHER: So once again you don't know.

PREACHER MAN: You must first believe, then you will know.

LOVING FATHER: Believe? Know? Aren't they two different things? Oh well. Now what is your knowledge of Paul's letters in the New Testament?

PREACHER MAN: You mean St. Paul?

LOVING FATHER: Okay, St. Paul.

PREACHER MAN: Well, he was a saint.

LOVING FATHER: In St. Paul's letter to the Romans 7:14–18, he writes, "I am carnal, sold under sun. I do not understand my own actions. Nothing good dwells in me that is my flesh. For I do not what I want, but do the very thing I hate." So what does that mean to you?

PREACHER MAN: It means what it means.

LOVING FATHER: How about the part 'nothing good dwells in me in my flesh?

PREACHER MAN: Well, just like all of us, sometimes he didn't feel too good. But although he persecuted the early Christians, he was forgiven because he saw the Lord.

LOVING FATHER: Once again you dodged my question. Some scholars maintained that Paul may have been a homosexual.

PREACHER MAN: That is blasphemy. He was a saint like I told you already.

LOVING FATHER: In the scientific world, the research of many prominent psychiatrists reveals that homosexuality is innate. Some people are born with that sexual orientation. So how can you condemn them for being themselves?

PREACHER MAN: They weren't born that way, they chose to sin.

LOVING FATHER: And just how do you know that?

PREACHER MAN: Because one of our leaders in the Fundamentalist Christian World, James Smallhead, said that the Lord told him that all homosexuals are sinners.

LOVING FATHER: So you reject what modern science concludes about homosexuality?

PREACHER MAN: Absolutely. And not only will the homosexual sinners suffer eternal damnation but also those heathen scientists and all those who preach against the Word of the Lord will burn in hell.

LOVING FATHER: Some people say that you are a bigot and are prejudiced against gays.

PREACHER MAN: They can say what they want. I am a man of God, and I know what is right.

LOVING FATHER: The Christian church once condoned slavery, were anti-Semitic, believed that lepers and epileptics were sinners. Do you still believe that?

PREACHER MAN: I'm talking about homos here.

LOVING FATHER: So today you hate the gays and abortionists—your scapegoats.

PREACHER MAN: They are both sinners and will be punished by God.

LOVING MAN: And how do you know that?

PREACHER MAN: Because the Bible tells me so.

LOVING FATHER: Well, I couldn't find the word *abortion* or anything about abortion anywhere in the Bible.

PREACHER MAN: It's right there in the Bible, you don't know where to look.

LOVING FATHER: Okay, where, what book, chapter, and verse?

PREACHER MAN: I'm not going to tell you, you'll have to find it for yourself.

LOVING FATHER: So once again you don't know. Don't you believe that a woman should have a choice?

PREACHER MAN: If she chooses abortion, she is committing a sin.

LOVING FATHER: And if your wife's life was threatened during her pregnancy or if your daughter was raped?

PREACHER MAN: It don't make no difference. In the eyes of the Lord, abortion is abortion.

LOVING FATHER: Do you think that you and your Bible are misogynistic?

PREACHER MAN: What does that mean?

LOVING FATHER: That you hate women. In Deuteronomy 25:11, it states that 'a woman who grabs a man by his private parts shall have her hand cut off.' Isn't that a little severe?

PREACHER MAN: It's the Word of the Lord, brother.

LOVING FATHER: I understand that your wife is a Sunday school teacher and also sings in the choir.

PREACHER MAN: Yes, sir, she is a good Christian woman.

LOVING FATHER: Does she know about Paul's letter to the Corinthians?

PREACHER MAN. She knows her Bible better than me.

LOVING FATHER: Well, you better refresh her memory about 1 Corinthians 14:34–35: "Let your women keep silent in the churches; for it is not permitted unto them to speak. If they will learn anything let them ask their husbands at home."

PREACHER MAN: You insult my wife, my daughter, and the fine Christian people who live their lives according to the Bible. What is that you are trying to do?

LOVING FATHER: I'm just trying to find the truth.

The presidential palace Spoilers would take charge on this one, for they didn't want Gotcha Butcher to screw it up. It was politically explosive, and if not handled properly, it could cost the Conservative Party millions of votes. They proclaimed to the media that they had a responsibility to present a balanced approach with the eight-minute film. The government filmmakers working for the Spoilers requested footage of right-wing religious events from the major news organizations, such as "Anti-abortion zealots," "Gays should be ashamed," "Women should stand by their man," "Ban criminals, not guns." When questioned about the request for the right-wing film clips, they stonewalled and said that government agencies routinely receive news from the media.

The local park people who face the visiting public every day strongly supported the eight-minute program as is, since it answered myriad questions about public events at the Memorial. Two pro-abortion groups filed a lawsuit requesting documents about the film footage the Spoilers received and an explanation on how they would revise the eight-minute show. The government complied with the Freedom of Information Act and released 1,500 documents that were heavily redacted and paragraphs blackened out. The Spoilers lived up to their reputation as masters of manipulation, obfuscation, vagueness, and obscuration. When the Chief Flack was pressured to respond to mounting inquiries, he answered that it was "untimely and inappropriate to make any concrete statements one way or the other because he wasn't sure of the context in which the question was asked." He added that "it is preposterous for us to provide any credible information on the status of a project that may not have been undertaken by top management because decisions were not always forthcoming."

An additional request from the media for expenditures was turned down by the Spoilers. Someone leaked (a local park employee, and a member of the Peyote Society believed it was Cool-Head Fred) that to date $126,630 had been spent in an effort to revise the Memorial video, and an additional $70,000 was still available for further revisions. This opened up a flood of inside information from park people who hated the Spoilers. They were, of course, anonymous, but all of them were given full coverage by the media. One said, "After removing the eight-minute video three months before the election, the White House claiming it was lost, it was reinstalled after the election." Another leak stated that "the Parks Department, after extreme intimidation from the White House, are exercising truth and replacing it with right-wing propaganda."

And "they are trying to erase feminism, war protesting, and gay rights rallies from American history." And a bombshell, "The administration is turning the Parks Department into a right-wing political agency. The Spoilers have now spent all the $200,000 and are asking for more funds to complete the eight-minute film." The Spoilers were being undercut on all fronts.

Two years had elapsed, and no solution to the controversial video had been forthcoming. When threatened with another lawsuit, the Chief Flack was back with "I'm reluctant, quite frankly, to provide any public information because I have no idea when and if a new revision will be released anytime soon. As of the present, the original video will be available for viewing by the park visitors if that is what they choose to do with their time. However, it will continue to be optional and not an integral part of their visit." So after a waste of taxpayers' money, the Spoilers were clearly defeated. The crisis was over for the time being, but there would be another and another. And another.

The question remains, What would ole Abe say today about a video that played fifty times a day in front of his ever-present countenance. Considering his life, what his biographers have written, and what those who knew him said, it is clear that he was not a Christian fundamentalist. In fact, he may not have been a Christian at all. His Gettysburg Address and Second Inaugural speech reveal his strong belief in humanity. He did not believe in a Bible that supported slavery.

Paul wrote in Ephesians 6:5, "Slaves be obedient to those who are your Masters." And Jesus said in Matthew 10:24, "The disciple is not above his master, nor the servant above his lord." About the political attempt to revise the eight-minute video, Abe would have said, "You can fool some of the people all the time, and all the people some of the time, but you can't fool all the people all the time." About the humanitarian causes of the feminists, the gays, the abortionists, the African Americans, and the Native Americans, it seems certain that ole Abe would have proclaimed, "Free at last, free at last, thank God Almighty, they're all free at last."

CHAPTER EIGHTEEN

A CONFLICT OF CULTURES

The Russian delegation was to arrive in the Capital City tomorrow. Careful planning had been put into play to ensure their safety, and hopefully they would leave with a favorable impression of the United States. This was the first visit for the president, Georgie Breztakov, and his delegation of twenty-party faithful. A grand tour of the nation's capital and its historical heritage was the responsibility of the Parks people. Cool-Head Fred was chosen to plan, coordinate, and direct the activities, which included advice from the presidential palace, the State Department, and of course, the Central Intelligence Agency. The bus tour included stops at the presidential monuments and memorials, the Smithfield Institution, Arlington Cemetery, and lunch at the Cannery Center.

It was a challenge to befriend the Russian representatives because the cold war was still in effect and the Berlin Wall was still standing and was a symbol of our differences. All the members of the delegation were knowledgeable about the United States, especially the military. The spokesman for the Russian group was Viktor Stolvorin, and he made it clear that they were not interested in the usual tourist sites but wanted to visit the Pentagon, Andrews Air Force Base, CIA, the Naval Fleet at Virginia Beach, the War College, the Naval Academy, and any nearby missile sites. They weren't even interested in visiting the Russian Embassy since they knew it was bugged. Cool-Head Fred tried to explain that some of those places were even off-limits to our own citizens. Viktor replied that they thought the United States was a democracy.

The first stop was at the Jefferson Memorial, and they didn't even bother to get off the bus until lured by a Häagen-Dazs ice cream bar. One of the members believed to be a KGB agent mumbled in Russian, "Who cares about your Declaration of Independence?" The next stop was at the Washington Monument, but since the elevator was broken, only one member ran up and down the 898 steps, and he did it backward. It was something this Olympian always wanted to do. Thank God the air-conditioning worked, for it was a hot August day. The bus just drove by the Lincoln Memorial, and Viktor narrated about old Abe and his ending slavery. Another Russian asked, "They have no Siberia?" So far not one Russian had bothered to take a picture. One of the Parks people who knew a little Russian tried to make a little small talk but was rebuffed as an American spy. He tried again hoping to provoke some response and asked if they had any dentists in their country. An unamused delegate responded bluntly, "No shortage of tooth pullers. Why you care?" "Well, please don't get me wrong," said the park employee, "but I noticed that none of you people ever smile." "No have bad teeth. Only fools like you Americans do smile. Nothing to smile about."

To the man, the Russian group, except for Viktor and Georgie, who appeared well fed, had a tired, hungry look about them. They were uptight about something, unsure, uneasy—perhaps they were afraid to be friendly; maybe their military mind prevented it. This posture was about to change as the tour entered the Arlington Cemetery. The Russians became alive, alert, interested, if not ecstatic. Here was something they understood and appreciated—discipline, country, the ultimate sacrifice. During World War II, millions of their people—their fathers, uncles, brothers, sisters, and friends—had died fighting the nasty Nazis. They were proud, and it was this pride in their country that led to their mantra: "We are not afraid to die."

The bus stopped at the Tomb of the Unknown Soldier, and there was a pushing, shoving, a stampede as the Russians peeled off the bus. Out came the cameras, snapping over and over again. This is what they wanted to take back home. Although there were a dozen or more non-Americans buried at Arlington Cemetery, there were no Russians. Nevertheless, the first picture they took was of a plaque that read "Arlington Cemetery – Tomb of the Unknowns – Changing of the Guards." What was it that so attracted them to what was also known as the Tomb of the Unknown Soldier. The most photographed sign was "Here Rests in Honored Glory an American Soldier known But To God."

The tomb is guarded twenty-four hours a day, 365 days a year by volunteers attached to the Old Guard, the Third United States Infantry. Remains of unknown American soldiers have been buried at Arlington since World War I. The changing of the guard takes place every half hour, and it was this scene, this respect, this honor that mesmerized the entire Russian delegation. An impeccably dressed relief commander appears on the plaza to announce the changing of the guard. The new sentinel unlocks the bolt of an M-14 rifle to signal to the relief commander to initiate the honorable tradition. The commander marches out to the tomb and salutes, then faces the spectators (the Russian delegation) and asks them to stand and stay silent, which they obediently do. The commander then conducts a detailed white glove inspection of the weapon; then he and the relieving sentinel recognize the retiring sentinel in front of the tomb. All three soldiers salute the Unknowns. The commander commands to the retiring sentinel, "Pass on your orders." The new sentinel responds, "Orders acknowledged." He then sharply marches at a cadence of ninety precision steps per minute. He smartly turns and marches twenty-one steps and once again turns.

After each turn, the sentinel executes a precise shoulder-arms movement to place the rifle on his shoulder. It was an experience that the Russians would cherish, and it would be the highlight of their visit. They stayed for two hours and finally ran out of film. As they got back on the tour bus, each Russian shook hands with Cool-Head Fred and sincerely thanked him for taking them to the Tomb of the Unknown Soldier.

At the Rullis Airport waiting for their departure back to Moscow, they were greeted by a Spoiler from the presidential palace who extended his hand to the tour leader and said, "The president looks forward to doing business with you Russians." Viktor exploded, "I no shake hands with capitalist sons of bitch."

The other culture that descended upon America that summer was the Chinese communists, sophisticated, gracious, ingratiating, most of them educated in the United States. The director of the Chinese delegation was Dr. Lin Dong Wong, a graduate of both Stanford and Princeton. He would serve as the group's interpreter although they hardly needed one. These Chinese were the crème de la crème.

Always friendly, ever smiling, but hidden beneath their six-button jackets were undetectable recording devices. Unlike the rough and rude Russians, these communists were appreciative of every little courtesy. They relished the historical tour of the nation's capital, especially the Smithfield Museum. They paid their respects at the monuments and memorials but were not enthusiastic about Arlington Cemetery and the Tomb of the Unknowns.

The luncheon for the Chinese representatives was held at the Cannery Center, the cultural heart of Washington DC. It was so easy to engage them in social conversation, and one subject that really got them animated was ping pong, which all of them had played since childhood. The Chinese were the world champions, and it was the number one sport in their country. When asked, they explained that the reason that most of their players held the ping-pong paddle like holding a pencil was that it gave them a more powerful and stronger forehead smash. Their winning strategy with their big, big forehand had always been to attack, attack, attack.

At the cocktail party, which preceded the sit-down luncheon, Paul Puffington, who was a multimillionaire, patriot of the presidential palace, and chairman of the Cannery Center got smashed.

He hated all communists, especially Chinese communists and everybody at the Cannery Center. He only served as chairman because his wife forced him to or she would expose his propensity for booze and illegal government contracts. He resented all the hoopla over the Chinese and was furious that the Parks Department had given them a grand tour of the city. He told Cool-Head Fred that it was a waste of taxpayers' money and they would be hearing from ole Puffington.

Though they didn't say anything, the Chinese guests were suspicious of the chop suey and rice and had it tested before picking up their chopsticks. Puffington, who had just downed another double scotch, was outraged that the Chinese didn't use the table forks since they were in America. He was seated next to Dr. Wong and began to pepper him with obnoxious questions. Did your mommy and daddy work in a laundry? Why are your men oversexed? When are you people going to whack off those bug-infested pigtails? When are you going to take down that wall, Wong? He remembered President Reagan saying "Take down that wall." Dr. Wong responded that the Great Wall of China will never come down. And Puffington continued, "Did you know that all our Christmas toys were not made in China? And why did you people forsake a Bethlehem Jew for a Jewish economist?" And finally, to be solicitous, "You likey your soupey."

Dr. Lin Dong Wong was the keynote speaker at the Cannery Center, and he was a dynamic, articulate, charismatic defender of communist China and their way of life. He praised what communism had done for the poor peasants. He damned the capitalistic United States for its treatment of Native Americans, Chinese Americans, Jews, women, Negros, and homosexuals. He blasted Paul Puffington and described him as an ignorant drunk, a boorish pig, and an example of the American government. As Dr. Wong returned to his seat and began sipping a cup of hot tea, he said to Puffington, "You likey my talkey?"

CHAPTER NINETEEN

BLUSTER BATTLEFIELD GONE FOREVER

The United States government failed in its attempt to buy the Black Hills for $6 million. The Sioux Indian chiefs may have known that piles of gold lay beneath, but they refused to sell because the Black Hills were sacred and of strong spiritual value to them. The government's next ploy was the Treaty of 1868, signed at Fort Laramie, Wyoming. On the surface it appeared to give the Sioux and Cheyenne what they hoped for: the Bozeman Trail would be abandoned, Forts Kearny and Smith would be abolished, and they would be settled on the Great Sioux Reservation, which included the Black Hills. It also included the Powder River Country, which contained abundant game and fish. The treaty, which was made by the Committee of Indian Affairs, hopefully would integrate the Indians into the United states with eventual citizenship. The United States Army was furious because it gave back established military forts and territory, which had cost them much blood. The generals considered the Indian treaties a waste of good ink. They ignored the Fort Laramie Treaty and quietly let the gold miners establish the mining town Deadwood.

From their base in Deadwood, the gold hunters illegally ventured onto the exclusive Indian territory to grab the gold. The general attitude of the Army and their perception of the Plains Indians was best expressed by one whom the Sioux called "Long Hair" or

Yellow Hair." Colonel Bluster had said, "Stripped of the beautiful romance with which we have been so long willing to envelop him, the Indian forfeits his claim to the appellation of the noble red man. We see him as he is, a savage in every sense of the word." The Indians settled on the reservation planning to live in peace with the United States, but the continuing encroachment of the gold miners and settlers and their need to hunt buffalo off the reservation made that impossible. The US Army was ordered to keep the Indians on the reservation and, if need be, punish them for "trespassing." The Indian chiefs—Sitting Bull, Crazy Horse, and Gall—blamed the Army, and the Army blamed the chiefs. The official policy from President Grant and his White House advisers was that if they didn't remain on the reservation, "they shall be deemed hostiles and treated accordingly by the military force." Since the government had violated the treaty, the Sioux defended themselves against what they considered treaty breakers and white intruders.

There were many Indian fights after the violations of the ineffective government treaties, but the most famous was the Battle of Little Bighorn in Montana, June 25–26, 1876. The US Army strategy agreed upon by all present on the supply steamer *Far West* on the Yellowstone River was to surround the Indian village and then attack with full force. The commander of the Seventh Cavalry was Lieutenant Colonel George Armstrong Bluster. For whatever reason—glory, ego, stupidity—the boy general divided his forces into three battalions, headed by Meno, Canteen, and himself. Each would attack the encampment from different directions, and with surprise on their side, they would overwhelm the Indian village.

But the Sioux-Cheyenne encampment west of the Little Bighorn River extended for almost three miles. Major Meno was the first to attack and had his men dismount, deploy in a skirmish line, and fight on foot. The superior Indian force swarmed all over this cavalry battalion and sent it into full retreat. Meno's engagement, defeat, and retreat lasted less than one hour, and he lost forty-seven men killed and fifty-three wounded. The Indian warriors for whatever reason did not pursue their advantage.

Some three miles north, Bluster and his battalion of about two hundred and twenty-five men descended down a deep ravine near Medicine Tail Coulee. He had wanted to attack the Sioux/Cheyenne from the rear, but he grossly underestimated the strength of the Indian village. Bluster's troops, some of them untrained, were exhausted from a forty-mile forced march. After he realized that he had made a drastic mistake in fragmenting his command and now being outnumbered at least ten to one, he dismounted his troops along the ridge and assumed a prone position against the coming onslaught.

The lay of the land gave the Indians a tactical advantage, and they encircled the pinned-down Seventh Cavalry. The warriors attacked with both arrows and bullets, and some of them were armed with repeater Spencer and Winchester rifles. Bluster's troops were equipped with only single-shot Springfield rifles. Perhaps realizing the hopelessness of his position, Bluster dispatched his orderly/trumpeter Sergeant John Martini with an urgent message for Captain Canteen.: "Come on—big village, be quick, bring packs" [ammunition].

Canteen was hunkered down giving support to Major Meno's troops, especially caring for the dead and wounded. A lame attempt was made to aid Colonel Long Hair, but Canteen turned back before reaching Bluster's Last Stand. Yellow Hair's men were hemmed in and taking devastating blows from Chief Gall from the south and Crazy Horse from the north. The attacking Indian force stampeded the cavalry horses and with them the badly needed ammunition. The Last Stand troops shot their remaining horses to provide cover against the never-ending arrows and bullets. The young, spirited Indian braves were everywhere on the battlefield and killed all 225, every last man on that hot Sunday. The close and intense fighting was brutal, savage, and an Indian chief said they never considered taking prisoners. Many of the dead had been scalped and mutilated. Contrary to some rumors, Bluster was not scalped, but his naked body had received mortal wounds to his left temple and left chest. Along with his two brothers and a nephew, Bluster and over two hundred Seventh Cavalry were buried on June 28 on the battlefield. The estimated number of Indians killed was sixty. The Indian dead were removed from the field and buried elsewhere. The only surviving participant on the US Army side was a horse who was badly wounded. His name was Comanche. This living memory of the Seventh Cavalry was nursed back to health and officially retired with military honors. The famous horse was never ridden again, and he made hundreds of military appearances, saddled, bridled, and paraded at special patriotic ceremonies. He died at age thirty at Fort Riley, Kansas, home of the Seventh Cavalry.

The boy general, a brevet brigadier general at age twenty-five during the American Civil War, was well known as a fierce and brave leader of the Union cavalry. His reputation for boldly defying established military tactics and taking unbelievable risks with great success did not play out that day, forever known as Bluster's Last Stand. And he must be held responsible for one of the most disastrous defeats and total annihilation on American soil.

Bluster had often said that "there are not enough Indians in the world to defeat the Seventh Cavalry." He may have truly believed that, and so did a nation that was celebrating the one hundredth anniversary of the Declaration of Independence and the birth of the United States of America. It was not until July 5 that the nation learned about the Bluster Massacre at the Little Bighorn River. The telegraph key punched out "Bismark, D. T. July 5, 1876. General Bluster attacked the Indians June 25 and he with every officer and man in five companies were killed." The day before the proud and happy Americans had celebrated with parades, patriotic speeches, picnics, music, festivities, and lots of drinking and merrymaking all over the country.

On the following morning, the merrymakers needed something to assuage their collective hangovers, not the shocking and humiliating news of disaster on the Little Bighorn.

To the stunned nation, it was unbelievable how a bunch of wild savages could destroy the pride of the US Army, the Seventh Cavalry. When General Grant became president, he supported a sympathetic and tolerant policy toward the First Americans. It seemed to him that past military intimidation had been a failure. That was about to change immediately. The newspapers, politicians, and those westward expansionists, all portrayed Bluster as a hero and his soldiers as victims. They mobilized public opinion to settle the First American problem once and for all. Now the emphasis would be on opening up the northern plains for white settlers. Manifest Destiny was alive and well.

The country wanted revenge for the brutal defeat and death of the flamboyant General Bluster. For the US Army, the Bluster Massacre was a major turning point. They now had the full support of the president, the Congress, and most importantly, the American people. They all wanted unconditional surrender, and unconditional surrender is what they got. The War Department dispatched three additional regiments to the Dakota Territory and built two new forts. In less than two years, the Plains Indians would be forced onto reservations that would control and isolate them from the outside world. Chief Crazy Horse and Sitting Bull did not realize at the time that Bluster's Last Stand would be the end of their nomadic life.

The US Army declared all-out war on the Sioux and Cheyenne. Those who resisted confinement on the reservation were hunted down and ruthlessly slaughtered. Along with the completion of the Continental Railroad in 1869, the fun killing of the buffalo by the train passengers, and finally an unnatural confinement to a small piece of land with boundaries, spelled the end to the free-spirited way of life for the First Americans.

The public wanted to know what happened at the Battle of Little Bighorn. An inquiry was held in Chicago, but the results were not released for seventy-five years. Popular writers and even some historians exclaimed, "We will never know," "We cannot be certain," "The truth is lost forever," "We don't know the facts," "It will never be known," and "The only survivor was a horse."

Well, what about the memories, recollections, oral accounts of the victors? They were discounted because who would believe a bunch of "illiterate savages." And "under the circumstances you can't believe what they might say," "They would say anything to save their own skins," "What was being written about the battle was written by subjective Indian haters, and most of it was conjecture, guess-work, white man's history," say the descendants of the Indians who

133

fought there. There were numerous Sioux and Cheyenne eyewitness accounts that were recorded shortly after the battle, and at least two of them are plausible.

Chief Crow King was interviewed and said, "When they saw that they were surround they dismounted. They tried to hold on to their horses, but as we pressed them closer, they let go their horses. We crowded them toward our main camp and killed them all."

Is there anything inaccurate, implausible, outrageous, or inflammatory about this statement? It seems reasonable, probable, doesn't provide any gruesome details or suggest any heroics. And Chief Low Dog remembered, "As we rushed upon them, the white warriors dismounted to fire, but they did very poor shooting. They held their horses reins on one arm while they were shooting, but their horses were so frightened that they pulled the men all around, and a great many of the shots went up into the air and did us no harm."

Does it sound believable? Doesn't it confirm Chief Crow King's account? What is it that the white man doesn't get?

Two days after Bluster's Last Stand, Captain Canteen surveyed the battlefield, and his troops identified the dead bodies of the Seventh Cavalry. The following day, they were buried in shallow graves, and wood stakes marked the place of the burials. George Bluster's remains were exhumed in 1877 and reburied at West Point, New York. The first memorialization of the white soldiers was in 1879 with a temporary monument made of cord wood and filled in the middle with bones of the killed horses. The site was established as Bluster Battlefield National Cemetery by the secretary of War on January 29, 1879, to protect the graves of the white Seventh Cavalry soldiers. An enduring granite monument replaced the cord of wood and rotting horse bones and was erected on Last Stand Hill in July 1881. In 1890, over two hundred permanent marble markers replaced the first wooden stakes that marked the burial sites. In 1926, the Meno-Canteen Battlefield was added, and in 1940 the battlefield was transferred to the Parks Department. On March 22, 1946, it was redesignated as Bluster Battlefield National Monument.

The Parks people told the story of Bluster's Last Stand from the white man's government perspective.

The free official government brochure was "white and blue" and referred to the Indian warriors as "hostiles" and" savages." The Bluster myth was propagandized far and wide in literature, plays, paintings, and later in the movies. It was one-sided government history. It was once said that the victors write the history, but not in the case of the Battle of Little Bighorn. The United States government treated the battlefield as a holy ground like Gettysburg, Appomattox, and Arlington Cemetery.

A generation had passed, and on June 25, 1901, there was a gathering of family and friends to honor those Union soldiers who died on that date twenty-five years earlier. It was a solemn, worshipful observance, the first of a ritualistic homage that would further perpetuate the heroic image. The tragic defeat was still in the minds and memories of the worshippers. Many wept uncontrollably, asking themselves how in the hell could this possibly have happened. There was no gathering, no respect, no consecration for the Sioux Cheyenne and Arapahoe Indians. Their descendants were not invited nor wanted. At the fiftieth anniversary, the federal government on June 25, 1926, refused to allow any word or sound, anything that would even acknowledge that real, live Indian people fought, died, and defeated the United States Army. A heartfelt letter was sent to the Department of the Army from Mrs. Thomas Beaverheart asking for a marker for her father, Lame White Man, who was killed and buried along Battle Ridge. She never received a reply to her request, and her repeated efforts to gain recognition for her father were ignored.

Another generation and another remembrance of the government's story of the battle took place on June 25, 1951. A young Parks Department buff remembered fifty years later that it was a grand and glorious military celebration. Three-star generals and colonels and flags and drums and bugles, and they all dedicated a museum for ole Bluster. They drank good scotch whiskey from the general's bottle and honored the Seventh Cavalry and their fearless leader. It had been seventy-five years since the Little Bighorn Massacre resulted in the permanent reservation life of the First Americans, yet they were still not invited to participate in the event—one that they had created.

They were not welcomed, did not attend, and did not taste the general's scotch. The whiskey was for the losers, not the winners. The Blusterites drank and drank and cried in their good scotch, "How did this tragedy happen?" Did they really want to know? If they had invited the descendants of the victorious First Americans, they would have been delighted to enlighten them.

And yet another generation had come and gone, and now it's June 25, 1976, the centennial of the Bluster bravado. The planning for the one hundredth anniversary would formally include those who had been denied participation for a century. In the tradition of the spectacular reenactments of the Civil War battles at Manassas and Gettysburg, some of the First Americans wanted another battle at Little Bighorn; the local whites wanted nothing short of revenge, and the government could provide the referees. After some tense arm wrestling, it was agreed (this was not a peace treaty) that a quiet, dignified commemoration would be the compromise.

The Parks Department volunteered one of its own as the principal speaker (they still didn't get it) and as usual the government would call all the shots. At the commemorative ceremonies, the government historian's Bluster Blather was disrupted by a (communist radical as they called him) Russell Cleans, and two hundred and fifty noble red men sporting red berets marched toward the government's grandstand dragging an upside down American flag. The dreaded AIM, American Indian Movement, was there to protest, and all hell broke loose. The uninvited guests crashed the official party, and Chief Russell Cleans, the most notable First American of his time, pushed aside the government spokesman and harangued the shocked audience. He cried out that the federal government would not allow a monument to the victors, Sitting Bun and Crazy Horse. He promised that one day the Indian warriors would have their memorial on Last Stand Hill.

Twelve years later, on June 25, Chief Russell Cleans returned dressed in a buckskin coat (some believed it once belonged to George Bluster) for the Indian warriors carried away hundreds of souvenirs that once belonged to the Seventh Cavalry. He wore US Cavalry boots and spurs and was mounted on a great brown stallion named Comanche. Chief Russell Cleans rode up to Bluster Hill and cemented an iron plaque over the mass graves of the union soldiers. This was the first, if not permanent, monument to brave Braves who died defending their freedom and their land. Finally, at last on Last Stand Hill, there was an Indian monument. It read, "In honor of our Indian patriots who fought and defeated the US Cavalry to save our women and children from mass murder."

This defiant, courageous act did more to attract public attention to the unjust, arrogant, and official government treatment of the present-day Indian tribes and to their forefathers. Cool-Head Fred was successful in planting the first native American – Russell Cleans as superintendent of the national monument. Russell Cleans opened the door to the First Americans and encouraged their efforts to tell the Indian side of the story. A Cheyenne US senator, Ben Bigfoot, persuaded his fellow senators to support his bill to have the name changed from Bluster Battlefield to the Battle of Little Bighorn. The Bluster love feast was finally busted, and the Bluster Temple worshipers were furious. There right-wingers railed at the revisionist history, even if it was true, and most of all about Rusell Cleans. They cried that he was a no-good troublemaker and appointing him to be the superintendent was pure sacrilege. To them, it was the world turned upside down.

When they learned that not only was the name changed but also that an Indian Memorial would be placed adjacent to the 1881 Bluster Stone, they proclaimed that it was comparable to building a monument at the Alamo to the victorious Mexicans. Led by a local politician and businessman who threatened to further impoverish the reservation Indian families, he blasted the Cheyenne senator for eradicating Bluster's good name. And to build an Indian Memorial was to dishonor the brave white Seventh Cavalry soldiers who lost all at the Battle of Little Bighorn, the local right-wingers lamented. They wailed that Bluster Battlefield should be a mecca for whites only.

On June 25, 2003, one hundred and twenty-seven years after Bluster was killed, the First Americans claimed another coup. A Sioux spiritual leader said, "It's time to bury the hatchet forever, and a memorial should serve its total purpose. It must not only be a tribute to the dead but also a message for the living. Power through unity." And that is the message today.

CHAPTER TWENTY

THE ONE-DOLLAR TIP

His name was Bobby Joe. Everybody called him Bobby Joe even though he had been a teacher, a football coach, a high school principal, and a preacher with a PhD. He had been interviewed many times and was always asked why they called him Bobby Joe. He always replied, "Well, that's what my mammy named me, what my grandma called me, and it kinda stuck. You got a problem with it?" He cherished the summer months where for the past thirty-six years he had served as a park historian at the Barber's Ferry National Historical Park. He had mastered the life of Jahns Braun and respected, even revered, Braun more than any other man black or white. Bobby Joe maintained that while other men talked, Braun acted on his beliefs. It was Braun who set the stage for the American Civil War resulting in the freedom of the American slaves, one of whom was Bobby Joe's grandfather. Bobby Joe had been giving talks, tours, and answering questions about what Jahns had done at Barber's Ferry and what it meant to all people, longer than any person alive. And no one did it with more passion. He was dedicated to setting the record straight, to banish the lies that had been written in high school textbooks, biographies, and the Civil War literature. To Bobby Joe, Jahns Braun was the greatest man in American history, even greater than Washington or Jefferson who both owned slaves. How could these two giants, presidents both, he often wondered, what was in their hearts?

It was Braun with eighteen men including his sons who on October 16, 1859, raided the federal arsenal at Barber's Ferry to take the Yankee guns and arm the slaves. Bobby Joe decried the way Braun had been portrayed as some loony bent on some impossible task. The writers even said his mother and grandmother were demon possessed. They gave him little credit for being the most important catalyst for freeing the slaves.

Bobby Joe had published a scholarly article in the *American Historical Review* based on original research that concluded that Jahns Braun was a true American hero. He wrote that Braun had proclaimed that though his attack of the federal arsenal had failed, it would make a stunning impact on the conscience of men everywhere. That Braun was a man filled with love of his fellow man, and those who knew him believed that he was of sound mind and righteous heart. Billy Joe also believed that Braun had received his inspiration from God Almighty and that God was acting through him.

When Braun was brought to trial and convicted by the southern government for treason, criminal conspiracy, and murder, he exclaimed to the world that "had I so interfered in behalf of the rich and powerful, it would have been right. Now your court finds me guilty for doing what was only justice and now you want to take my life—well, so be it—for to try and free the slaves whose rights were taken away by wicked, cruel, and greedy slaveholders and their false government is what has to be done. If you choose to kill me for what God knows to be true, I say, then, let it be done." Braun was hanged on December 2, 1959, in Charlesburger, Virginia.

Bobby Joe wrote "that church bells in the North rang loudly and freedom lovers everywhere praised Braun's life and deeds and mourned his death." In less than eighteen months, the country would be in a long and bloody civil war. Northern soldiers would march into battle in his defense singing "Jahns Braun Body, and as he died to make men holy, let us die to make men free." Freedom for all people was the essence of Bobby Joe's philosophy. When he told his tale of Braun at Barber's Ferry, it could break your heart. Often his eyes could not hold back the tears, and he always ended it with, "Thank God for Jahns Braun, thank God Almighty." He could have performed a one-man show on Broadway and packed the house every night.

After each talk or tour about Jahns Braun at Barber's Ferry National Historical Park, visitors would shake his hand, and they always applauded. Some would hug him, and a few tried to tip him. Yes, give him money, but he would just smile and say, "Please don't forget old Jahns Braun."

One day, Bobby Joe went up to the park superintendent's office and told Russ that a lady had given him a $1 tip. Russ would have just normally put it in the canteen coffee jar, but this time Seymour, the loyal Spoiler flack, was in his office. He was in the park to investigate complaints from the director of the veterans retirement home, who, while on tour in the park, had been stung by a batch of stinging bees.

Seymour said, "What are you going to do with that dollar bill?" Russ replied, "Well, we usually put it in the coffee fund." Seymour yelled, "You can't do that. This is an official donation by a United States citizen, and there must be an accountability. I'll take it back to the Capital City and get a ruling from the solicitor's office. Can you image what might happen if the media got ahold of something like this. 'Park historian accepts bribe.' I can't let that happen, not with an election this year. Now about the purpose of my being here today, the bee stings."

The veterans who had been stung by the bees had been in the Veterans' Hospital since World War I where they had been treated for battle fatigue and shell shock, which today is diagnosed as post-traumatic syndrome. When the bees attacked them, they assumed the battle-ready position and maintained an attack mode. The source of the Bee Bombardment was Russ's hobby of making a wine known as Mead. His honeybees did most of the work in the attic of one of the historic buildings. After the stinging complaints, Russ moved the operation to an isolated structure away from the tourists. Seymour was unable to find any bees, but he did have the $1 bill. He had known two party-loyal congressmen who had gone to jail for taking contractor's money, so he was going to get an opinion on the $1 tip. He remembered that his mother had given the postman Charlie a plate of homemade cookies, but this was different—this was cash. Seymour took the issue to the Federal Bribes Investigation Agency— the under $100 section.

The FBI investigated the Barber's Ferry Bribe and concluded that because of Bobby Joe's passion for interpreting the life of Jahns Braun he must be a communist. They were unable to discover who made the bribe. Gotcha Butcher got involved since if the Parks Department accepted handouts, then Congress would start cutting their budget and nobody wanted that. The director of the FBI told the supervisor of the under $100 section to put the dollar bill in his pocket and forget about the investigation.

Russ, back at Barber's Ferry, was informed that the case was closed, and he passed it on to Bobby Joe. "They can't do that. I want my $1 tip back," exclaimed Bobby Joe. He could have cared less about the $1, but it was the actions of an indifferent and arrogant government that he would not let pass. Then he had heard that the FBI said he was a communist, and that did it. His lawyers from the National Association of Abused Minority Employees sued the FBI to avenge this gross injustice. The $1 tip was returned to Bobby Joe with an apology. He had it framed and gave it to Russ. Somehow the $1 tip ended up in the underground museum of the Peyote Society and is one of their most cherished mementos.

CHAPTER TWENTY-ONE

A STANDARD FOR FREEDOM

Just what does the Stand for Liberation stand for? Who does it represent and speak for? Is every ethnic, religious group and race included? What peoples are excluded or have been ignored? When it was dedicated on October 28, 1886, the president of the United States said, "We will not forget that Liberty has made her home nor shall her chosen altar be neglected." What was the intent of the French people when they presented America with the Freedom Statue? What was the meaning of the New Colossus when it was first written? Why did it take another thirty-four years before women were allowed to vote? Why did it take more than seventy-five years after the statue was dedicated before First Americans and African Americans could proclaim "Free At Last?" How does the federal government present the story today?

The Stand for Freedom, originally called "Liberty" or "Lightning the World," was a gift from the people of France to the United States to commemorate the friendship first established during the American Revolution. The idea for the meaningful gift allegedly was formed at a dinner at the home of Ted Latourque in the summer of 1865, near Versailles. Latourque was a jurist, historian, and outspoken abolitionist who believed that the end of slavery was a fulfillment of the ideals of the Declaration of Independence. He promoted the mutual love of democracy and freedom between the two nations and called France and America "The Two Sisters." He fervently pursued his dream that the French people present the United States with a statue that would be a lasting memorial to the idea of human liberty.

After the assassination of the Civil War president, the French— and it was from the hearts of all the people—presented the fallen president's wife with a gold coin. The beautiful piece was inscribed with the words "Dedicated by the French democracy to Lincoln, twice-elected president of the United States. Honest Lincoln who abolished slavery, reestablished the Union, and saved the Republic."

Latourque persuaded the celebrated sculptor Frederic Bouholdo to go to America and propose a joint effort between the two countries to establish the monument. Bouholdo favored the New York City Harbor as the site after meeting with the president, senators, and distinguished artists and literary figures. It was agreed that France would build the statue and that America would construct the pedestal. Raising the needed money from the American citizens would be a challenge.

Emma Lazard was a Jew through and through. She was born into a wealthy uptown New York City family and received a classical education in the arts and languages from the ever-present private tutors. Ralph Waldo Henderson, Harriet Beecher Roe, James Russell Powell all encouraged and admired her early literary efforts. The singular event that transformed her life and her poetry was the heartbreaking scene of poor, sick, and uneducated Jewish refugees from the anti-Semitism of Eastern Europe getting off the steamers in New York City. She became enraged at the rich Jewish Americans who did nothing to help them and considered the refugees an embarrassment.

She personally met the new immigrants at the docks as they departed the boats and gave them food, money, and clothes. Helping these people who held the same beliefs as she did only strengthened her faith, and the Jewish refugees became her cause célèbre. She helped them get jobs, obtain an education, and become successful Americans. She wrote about them in her essays and poems: "Until we are all free, we are none of us free." In an effort to raise money for the pedestal, there was a contest and auction held in her city. She responded by writing the poem "The New Colossus," which contrasted the statue with the Greek Colossus of Rhodes, an awesome warrior. In the "New Colossus," her hero was a nurturing woman, the mother of exiles, who welcomed all to the land of the free. Her poem was auctioned off at a fund raising in a benefit sale for $21,500, a large sum for any person at that time. Her immortal words became the credo of all immigrants coming to America and became the universal symbol and were inseparable from the statue:

> Give me your tired, your poor, your huddled masses yearning to breathe free, the wretched refuse of your teeming shore. Send these, the homeless, tempest—tost to me, I lift my lamp beside the golden door.

Freddie Bouholdo was a distinguished French sculptor who began his artistic career as a painter and architect, but it was as a sculptor that he was to express his patriotic spirit and gain world fame. At the age of eighteen, he had received a commission to create a statue of a famous French general. As a sculptor, he favored huge, oversized patriotic monuments. During the Franco-Prussian War, he had served as a major in the French army and was inspired by the defense of Belfort, a French city. He carved the "Lion of Belfort" out of the red sandstone hill that towered over the city. It was no surprise that he was selected to produce a statue that would be an international symbol of freedom. He began the actual work on "Liberty Enlightening the World" in 1875.

Bouholdo began with the same model he had shown all over New York and Washington DC. The French folks had responded early and generously with sufficient funding for the statue. The major challenges were an acceptable design, the size, scope, and the material to be used in the statue. Bouholdo then made a larger, more workable model—four feet in height and finally an expanded one that was thirty-six feet tall.

Copper was chosen as the primary metal because of its light weight, its durability, and it was readily malleable. It would be reinforced with steel, which would not affect the appearance of the copper.

Carpenters made wooden molds and frames to which copper sheets would be pressed and hammered forming each section. To reinforce the copper forms of the statue and provide stability, four huge iron posts were installed from the top to the bottom with supporting beams extending throughout all the sections. Over three hundred thousand French paid to watch the work in progress—twenty men working ten hours a day and seven days a week. The raised arm and torch were completed first and were on display in Philadelphia for the 1876 Centennial Celebration. When completed, the statue was 111 feet tall from foot to head. The hand sixteen feet long, and the index finger eight feet, the head seventeen and the nose four feet. From bottom of the pedestal to the top of the torch 305 feet.

An often overlooked shackle, which the sculptor displays broken, lies in front of her right foot—escaping from the tyranny of slavery. The completed statue represents a woman fleeing from the cruel system of bondage. Her right hand holds aloft the flaming torch of liberty. In her left hand a book of law, which is inscribed with the "Declaration of Independence: "All men are created equal." She is wearing flowing classical robes and a spiked crown.

The American-built pedestal overcame difficulty with both fund raising and in the construction process. It was a harbinger of more contentious times when the government missed the original meaning of the gift from France and the immortal words associated with it. Did not the man who first had the idea for the monument intend for it to be a symbol of the end of slavery in the United States? Did not the author of "The New Colossus" intend that the statue represent liberty and freedom for all people? It would seem that the people who would tell the story of immigration through a museum to be housed in the bowels of the pedestal would have understood this. Is it not obvious that the idea for a memorial to freedom came from a well-known abolitionist? Was it not the end of slavery in the United States the reason for the statue?

Is there any doubt that the tragedy of the oppressed Jew inspired the poem for the statue? Is this too difficult to grasp, or is it more convenient to hide these salient events in a larger melting pot? The man and woman behind the idea and the words welcomed all enslaved and oppressed people. So why is the heart and soul of the story of liberty given short thrift by an all-white male jury?

It was 1972, an election year, so why not have the president use the Lady of Liberation as a backdrop for the president's political campaign? He could say just the right words, something for everyone, and how many votes that would bring in. As one of the Spoilers in the presidential palace exclaimed, "It was a time of conflicting ideologies when the competition for the loyalties of groups and individuals was keen."

The Immigration Museum would become the voice of nationalism at the expense of history. The museum exhibits planning team consisted of four white males: Jim White, Joe Mann, George Males, and Sam Smith—all-white, Anglo, Male, Protestant, known as the Wamps. The pressure was on to get it completed before the 1972 election. Would it not have been more timely to dedicate the museum in 1976—the bicentennial of America or in 1986, the centennial of the birth of Lady Liberty?

The Wamps exhibit team took the approach that everyone wanted to come to America and that they were willing to give up their old ways and assimilate into some mythological melting pot. Since the Wamps were all descendants of European immigrants, why not glorify their ancestors? They all agreed that they should glorify the good old boys and make them the centerpiece of the immigration story. They would offer seventy-five exhibits, enough to cover the whole European continent. They ignored the common wisdom that most visitors were not students but tourists who might spend ten minutes in the museum between visits to the restrooms and the hot dog stand. The result of the exhibiting planning was that the exhibits were too pedantic, too complex, too European—a plan that excluded or ignored the First Americans, African Americans, Mexican Americans, Chinese, Japanese, Russian, and South Americans who did not embark from Europe.

The rush to complete the plan to meet the political deadline and to glorify the heritage of the European Americans incurred the wrath of those who were slighted. When the minorities complained about how they were being unfairly treated, they were told that it

147

was too late to make any changes and even minor revisions would be impossible. The African American critics were furious that the exhibit on their ancestors was built around a slave ship, leaving out their contributions to American history. They wanted the entire planning team fired because of its racist attitude. The criticisms continued and included professional, religious, and academic organizations, which pressured the Parks Department to scrap the entire exhibit plan and start over again. A new plan could be developed and produced easily in time for the 1976 bicentennial. Since the money for the museum had dried up, the exhibit planners would have to get money from the taxpayers. It was unfortunate for the Wamps because both cultural and political America was changing. They would have to appear before the congressional subcommittee on parks and museums. The members of the committee would demand radical changes in the exhibit planning that reflected the contributions of their forefathers.

There were five members who would interview the Wamps. Actually it was more of an inquisition and an experience that the Wamps would never forget. The chairman was an African American and a former college president, a First American who was an attorney and tribal chairman, one lady lawyer whose sister was Gloria Fienhamm, a Jewish rabbi, and a Chinese millionaire businessman.

The first question was asked by the chairman:

AA: You refer to the African Americans as 'involuntary immigrants.'
Is that a euphemism for slaves?
WAMPS: We deleted that title.
AA: That's not what I asked you.
WAMPS: Yes, that's correct.
AA: What is at the bottom of the statue's feet?
WAMPS: A shackle.
AA: A broken shackle?
WAMPS: Yes, that's right, a broken shackle.
AA: What does a broken shackle mean to you?
WAMPS: Freedom.
AA: Freedom from what?
WAMPS: Freedom from slavery.

AA: Did you ever interview Malcolm X?

WAMPS: Who?

AA: Malcolm X.

WAMPS: No, we didn't.

AA: Why not?

WAMPS: It never occurred to us. What would he be able to offer?

AA: The tragic plight of the black people in American history.

WAMPS: Okay, we'll interview him.

AA: So why doesn't your exhibit plan highlight the progress of the black people rather than some childish story of a day in the life of a slave on a slave ship?"

WAMPS: We will. We will. The slave ship exhibit will be eliminated, and the full story of the African Americans will replace it.

AA: Your exhibit also portrays the dietary habits of the slaves. Do you think they preferred to eat chitlins, hominy grits, and collard greens? Maybe they would have liked a pork chop or a steak if they were allowed to. Why doesn't your plan include the African American success in the fields of medicine, education, music, fine arts, government, armed forces, literature, and science?

WAMPS: That's exactly what we plan to do, sir. Already our historical researchers are at work to accomplish it.

AA: I want you to understand that I'll be looking forward to reviewing the completed exhibit plan.

The next member to question the planners was the rabbi.

RABBI: When you think of the Jewish people, what comes to mind?

WAMPS: Very smart, successful, rich.

RABBI: All of them?

WAMPS: Well, that's the popular image.

RABBI: Well, some of us drive taxis, work in factories, some are policemen.

WAMPS: Yeah, that's right. I once get a ticket for speeding, and I found out later the cop was Jewish.

Rabbi Do you believe the Jewish people have given of themselves to our country?

WAMPS: Absolutely.

RABBI: Then why do you emphasize their religious beliefs and customs? Your exhibit on the Jewish immigrants explains Yum Kippur, Rosh Hashanah, Bar Mitzvah. Is this appropriate in a government museum? You are aware of a basic tenant of our constitution—the separation of church and state?

WAMPS: Well, we believed that it was important for the viewer to understand what a Jew is. So we feel the exhibit identifies a Jew.

Rabbi, *laughing*: In addition to being a United States congressman, I'm also a Rabbi, and I don't even know what a Jew is.

WAMPS: It seems to us that more than most ethnic groups, the Jews cherish their religion and customs and in many ways remain separate from mainstream America."

RABBI: Let me correct you. We are not an ethnic group. And except for our religion, we are very much mainstream America. Are you still including the melting pot theory in your exhibits?

WAMPS: We no longer use the term 'melting pot,' but in the revision we prefer to use "cultural pluralism."

RABBI: Would it be too much to ask that you broaden your coverage of the Jewish community?

WAMPS: We will be happy to do that, sir.

It would get a little tougher for the Wamps as the First American began his inquiry.

FA: Do you think that Custer deserved what he got at the Battle of Little Bighorn?

WAMPS: It was definitely a one-sided fight. Custer is not looked upon favorably by most historians. There are a few Custer buffs who consider him a hero.

FA: What people think he's a hero?

WAMPS: Well, you know, the military and the right-wing folk.

FA: Why did you ignore the First American in your previous museum planning?

WAMPS: They were not immigrants. They were already here. And they didn't come from some European country and pass through Ellis Island.

FA: Do you consider them a part of your melting pot?

WAMPS: We don't have a melting pot anymore. But they don't seem anxious to assimilate since they live on reservations.

FA: Don't you know that the word 'assimilate' is terrifying to my people?

WAMPS: No, we didn't know that.

FA: Why do you think they live on reservations?

WAMPS: I suppose because they want to.

FA: Have you ever interviewed Russell Beans to get his point of view?

WAMPS: Who?

FA: Forget it. Do you believe that the First Americans received justice from the United States government?

WAMPS: Well, that was in the past. Let bygones be bygones. If they let go of the past and left the reservation, they could become more American.

FA: More American?

WAMPS: They could get educated, get better jobs, and wouldn't have to live on welfare.

FA: Are you a racist or just ignorant of the history of the First Americans? You don't know why they live on reservations, you've never heard of Russell Beans, the most prominent Indian living today, you don't know what 'assimilate' means to the Native Americans. Now I demand that you contract with a Native American exhibit planner for the First Americans exhibits. If you can't find one, I'll find one for you. Do you now understand?

WAMPS: Yes, sir.

The Wamps were unprepared for the next drilling from the Congresswoman.

CW: Do you consider yourself a misogynist?

WAMPS: I don't know what that word means?

CW: It means you hate women.

WAMPS: Oh no. I'm a married man and have two daughters.

CW: Well, good for you. When you view the Statue of Freedom, what do you see?

WAMPS: A symbol of freedom.

CW: The Statue of Freedom is a woman, and the words that she cries out are from a woman. Do you not see a free woman?

WAMPS: Well, I guess so.

CW: You guess so. Why is it that your previous exhibits almost totally ignored women and children?

WAMPS: We didn't realize that we had slighted women and children. We concentrated on men because they were considered the head of the family at that time and the women and children just followed.

CW: Why is your exhibit planning team all white males?

WAMPS: I don't know, really. It just evolved that way.

CW: I cannot understand how you can tell the story of American women if you don't involve a woman.

WAMPS: Yes, ma'am.

CW: Don't "yes ma'am" me. Did you interview Gloria Fienhamm?

WAMPS: No, ma'am, we didn't.

CW: I didn't think so. What do you think a woman's role is in American? One of your previous exhibits shows her standing over a stove holding a baby. Is that it—she just makes babies and cooks dinner?

WAMPS: We didn't think it would be viewed that way.

CW: How else could one view such insensitivity? I'm going to change that right now. I will not fund any additional funds for your exhibit planning that does not include at least two women as members of the team. You all-white male group are oblivious to the economic, social, and political contributions that women have made. You are blind to the facts of history, and I will not let that happen again. Do I make myself clear?

WAMPS: Yes, ma'am.

The last congressman to question the Wamps was the Chinese entrepreneur. He would show no mercy.

CHINESE: Something wrong here. You show Chinese as clothes washerman while eating soup with chopsticks. Only stupid white man would do that. What you know about Chinese people?

WAMPS: We visited the Chinese community in Chinatown.

CHINESE: Community? We are Americans—Chinese Americans. You talk with Michael Chang? He could have told you about Chinese. No talk to him?

WAMPS: We are aware of what the Chinese community has contributed to American society.

CHINESE: No more community talk. You think all Chinese people do is play ping pong? Did you know that I own electronics company, hotels, restaurants, and Chinese college?

WAMPS: We knew you were a role model to your people.

CHINESE: No role model, but very rich. You know who built railroad that go to California and New York and connect country together?

WAMPS: I believe it was the Irish workers.

CHINESE: No Irish. Chinese build railroad. Irish goof off. Irish always drunk. Don't know how to build railroad. Watch Chinese do all work.

WAMPS: We didn't know that.

CHINESE: You know how many Chinese doctors and dentists in America? Chinese go to Stanford, MIT, Harvard. And best ping-pong players in the world. You know why? Start young, work hard, good coach, practice, practice, practice. Never give up. Chinese people proud. You make Chinese look like pigtail coolie. If you want Chinese congressman to give taxpayer money for museum, you tell truth.

WAMPS: We make Chinese look good.

CHINESE: Don't try talk like Chinese American.

WAMPS: I'm sorry.

CHINESE: You sorry. Okay. Chinese exhibit all wrong. Now you make new Chinese exhibit and make right.

WAMPS: Yes, sir. Make right. Okay.

The subcommittee provided the necessary funding for the Statue of Freedom Museum. It was revolutionary, inclusive, fair, honest, intelligent, and the visiting public praised it. One of the members of the subcommittee was a friend of the Peyote Society. Guess who.

CHAPTER TWENTY-TWO

WHERE HAVE ALL THE GLACIERS GONE?

A glacier is a river of ice that moves. It is created by enormous amounts of fallen snow over a long period of time. About 10 percent of the earth is covered by glaciers mostly in the Antarctica and Greenland. In the United States, most are located in the northwest and Alaska. Simply stated, no snow no glacier. Some glaciers are as small as a football field, and one known glacier is over four hundred miles long. A glacier is formed by the accumulation of snow and extremely cold weather. The weight of more snow compacts what snow that has already fallen, and it becomes a huge mass of ice.

Glaciers change size. The more snow, the larger it becomes—less snow with melting and it becomes smaller. If the glacier becomes bigger, the weight of the ice mass and the melting at the bottom make it slippery, and it will begin to move. That's what makes glaciers unique—the ability to move. When it begins to move, it is like a flow of hard mud. It behaves like a twister—ripping, gouging, moving anything in its path—rocks, boulders, trees, soil, shrubs, even animals. The flowing ice can break away and form small and large crevasses.

Glaciers provide drinking water and irrigate crops. They are often named by the shape and size of its ice mass. Because they absorb all colors of light, they give off a bluish hue. When a glacier completely melts and vanishes, it leaves a gouged-out area called a glaciated valley.

Global warming is the number one enemy of all glaciers. It is the rise in the temperature of the earth that ultimately destroys them. And the enemy is getting hotter and hotter. There is an increase in the number of extremely hot days and a decrease in the number of cold days. The hottest ten days on record have occurred since 1990. In 1995, the hottest year on record, global temperatures went up about a half of one degree. The increase in temperature cause more wildfires, dust storms, massive flooding and make hurricanes stronger and more dangerous. The increases in gases—carbon dioxide, methane, water vapor, nitrous oxide—form what is called the greenhouse effect because like a glass-enclosed greenhouse the gases cannot escape.

The global warming is the direct result of selfish, greedy, and foolish actions of people. The industrial plume, chimney smoke, forest fires, road dust, vehicle emissions, and other pollutants trapping the sun's heat and causing the planet to heat up. Coal-burning power plants are the largest producers of carbon dioxide in the United States and cause most of the global warming. The US is only 4 percent of the world's population but produces 25 percent of the carbon dioxide pollution. In 2002, about 40 percent of the carbon dioxide in the US stemmed from coal burning to produce electricity and 20 percent from vehicles. And where are the blue skies?

It was the US Congress that preserved that once spectacular land now known as Moraine National Park. In the park there are over one million acres of mountains, valleys, two hundred lakes, and extensive forests. If you look, you can find flowers—Indian paintbrush, purple aster, heather, hollyhocks, and glacier lilies. Birds—hawks, owls, ravens, woodpeckers, harlequin ducks, bluebirds, swifts, and mockingbirds. Trees—spruce, Douglas fir, cottonwood, hemlocks, lodgepole pine, and red cedars. Animals—white-tailed deer, bighorn sheep, red fox, grizzly bear, mountain lion, wolf, elk, and moose. Lakes—St. Marie, Two Pills, McKenzie, Truebom, Trinnel, and Towcurrent. There are Roads going to the Moon and Bogan Pass, but the park is a hiker's paradise with over seven hundred miles of trails.

The Great Northern Railroad reached the park on the eve of the twentieth century. Hotels were built, and thousands came to see the scenery, especially the glaciers. Today, over two million people visit the park to see it all, including the twenty-four small glaciers that exist from over one hundred and fifty a century ago. Scientists predict that all the glaciers will evaporate, vanish, within thirty years. A Moraine is what's left when the glaciers melt away. To see how fast the earth's glaciers are disappearing, look no further than Moraine National Park where ice formations thousands of years old are no more. The fact that glaciers are melting rapidly are evidence that global warming is a reality. In the last ten years, Trinnel Glacier has lost 20 percent of its size. The problem is the park isn't getting enough snow. The quickening de-glaciation of the park's glaciers now threatens to upset the mountain ecosystem. The animals, fowl, lakes, streams are all out of balance. Yes, they will still be there—only the glaciers will be gone.

There are solutions. The biggest culprit is carbon dioxide. The Kyoto Protocol of 1997, signed in Japan, has been subsequently ratified by 162 nations, but not the United States. It mandates a reduction in greenhouse gases by 2010. Rather than continue to use more fossil fuels, we must further develop and use other sources of energy such as wind, solar, and nuclear. We have been preaching conservation for the past fifty years but not taking any serious actions. Stronger incentives are needed for conserving our natural resources and penalties for wasting energy. The United States Congress should enact such legislation and do it now.

Gotcha Butcher was appearing before the Senate Committee on Conservation and Parks to defend the administration policies as they affected the Parks Department. He was questioned by Senator Carson, a native of Montana and former professor of geology.

CARSON: The EPA submitted a report to the United Nations that explicitly states that human activities have a profound negative effect on global warming. It predicted environmental doom unless people change their habits and lifestyles. It is obvious that the president and his White House advisers do not agree with these findings. Can you explain this, Mr. Butcher?

GOTCHA: Well, Senator Carson, I don't speak for the EPA.

CARSON: Yes, I know that, but career park employees, your best scientists, openly support the report and have been punished for doing so.

GOTCHA: Well, you're either with us or against us. The employees you referred to are old-school environmentalists They have been reassigned to jobs that they can handle.

CARSON: Don't you understand that when you ruin the careers of devoted park employees who don't submit to your agenda you will alienate the environmentalists, like me?

GOTCHA: Like I said, you're either with us or against us. Our creationist scientists have advised us that the global warming theory has not been proven. They say it could easily turn around and we could have a cooling period. The president has political capital, and he intends to spend it. American citizens voted for a president who will protect their jobs and not buckle under to the extreme environmentalists. You sound like a member of Greenpeace, Senator Carson.

CARSON: No, I'm not a member of Greenpeace [but he was a member of the Peyote Society]. I'm a United States senator from Montana who is deeply concerned about global warming. The landmark agreement negotiated in Kyoto was an important beginning because it sends a political message that the leaders of the world support a major reduction in fossil fuel emissions. But your administration refused to sign it."

GOTCHA: And rightfully so. The Kyoto Protocol was totally inadequate. It gave China and India a free pass and put all the blame for global warming on people. It disregarded the actions of the sun, which is a major source for global warming.

CARSON: You and your administration have no scientific data to support your position. The leading scientists in the world strongly disagree with your indifferent policies. Your administration has skewed the scientific data and initiated a massive political campaign to mislead the public. You have zero credibility in the scientific community. Your Bible-belching creationists are an embarrassment to our country.

GOTCHA: And your scientists present no evidence, only theories. We can't afford the luxury of you being wrong.

CARSON: We are not wrong. The country's addiction to oil and gasoline that emit carbon dioxide contributes enormously to global warming. Your solution is to drill, drill, drill and dig, dig, dig. The first rule of holes is that when you're in one, quit digging. Our solution is conservation and using other sources of energy. You people know the price of everything and the value of nothing.

GOTCHA: Do you want another Great Depression like in the 1930s? Do you realize how many jobs would be lost if we stopped burning gasoline and natural gas? Just think what would happen to employees at Enron, Halliburton, Exxon, and General Motors. Oil is the life blood of our country. We just need more of it, and we're going to get it.

CARSON: "You people don't give a damn about conservation and protecting our natural resources. You have sold out to the big oil companies, the automobile manufacturers, and energy-producing companies. Your administration is in the pockets of the lobbyists who circumvent the environmental laws and regulations. You have fought every congressional measure to protect public health and the environment. You have tried to gut the Endangered Species Act and drill for oil in the Artic Refuge in Alaska. Our political system is paralyzed in the face of what may be the single most important challenge of our time. And your administration is in deep denial about how drastic the problem really is.

GOTCHA: You want to tell the American people how bad it is, well, be my guest. Go ahead, scare the hell out of them. We are trying to protect our workers' jobs and keep the economy moving ahead. If we listen to you, we'll be paying $10 a gallon for gas at the pump. You want to bankrupt the economy?

CARSON: You are here today representing the Parks Department, and my immediate concern is the disappearance of the glaciers at Moraine National Park. Global warming is indeed a global problem, but we have to do something now in our own country to continue to preserve and to protect our national parks. They are our nation's crown jewels and represent what is best about our democratic society. We must leave them unimpaired for those who follow us. That is the law.

GOTCHA: The sky is falling. The sky is falling. Is that what you're saying?

CARSON: How can you be so blind? The disappearance of glaciers all over the world, especially in Moraine national Park, is real, visual evidence of global warming. The rise of three degrees in temperatures can have a devastating effect on the park's streams, lakes, forests, and wildlife. I can't save the world, but I can do something about preserving our national parks.

GOTCHA: Oh, you bleeding heart liberals. You're taking about a piece of ice. Parks are for people.

CARSON: Our national parks are not a playground just for the rich. When my great-grandchildren ask me to take them to see a glacier, I'm not just going to show them a picture.

GOTCHA: Senator Carson, you can't just lock a national park and throw away the key

CARSON: Gotcha, that's exactly what I'm going to do. You're dismissed.

The United States Congress alone has the authority to establish a national park—not the president, not the courts, only the congress. To Senator Carson they have a responsibility to do it right, and to look out on the glacier's alpine beauty is awe-inspiring. It is something that our children and our children's children should not be denied. Congress controls the funding, and the senator was successful in persuading his colleagues in both the Senate and the House to cut off the funding. Two weeks after dismissing Gotcha, Moraine National Park was closed.

The entrance sign reads,

MORAINE NATIONAL PARK
STAY OUT

NO ADMITTANCE
A free flyer available at the closed entrance station says,

THE UNITED STATES CONGRESS HAS THE AUTHOR-
ITY TO ESTABLISH A NATIONAL PARK AND THE
POWER TO DE-ESTABLISH. THIS PARK IS CLOSED
TO THE PUBLIC FOR RESTORATION AND REJUVENA-
TION. IT WILL REMAIN CLOSED SO THAT THE PARK
CAN RECOVER FROM THE CARBON DIOXIDE PRO-
DUCED BY YOUR AUTOMOBILES. WHEN THE PARK
IS FULLY RESTORED AND THE GLACIERS RETURN, IT
WILL BE REOPENED ONLY TO ELECTRIC CARS.

THE FORESTS, THE TREES, THE SHRUBS, THE
PLANTS, THE FLOWERS, THE LAKES, THE STREAMS,
THE GRIZZLY BEAR, THE FOX, THE DEER, THE
SQUIRRELS, AND THE REMAINING GLACIERS ALL
THANK YOU.

CHAPTER TWENTY-THREE

CELEBRATING THE INTERNATIONAL FOLKS

This was the first time the global folks festival would be held in the Capital City of the good ole US of A. The two organizations responsible for the planning, development, and execution of the gala event were the federal Parks Department and the world-famous Peoples' Museum Institution (Institution, not Institute). The festival grounds would spread from the memorial to the man who freed the slaves to the end of a reflecting pond, within spitting distance of the monument to the first president. The Parks people would provide the nuts and bolts for the really big show. They would set up the performing arts stages and enclosed facilities for ethnic Performing Arts and Fine Arts, little known Crafts and Fabulous Folk Food; the platforms, chairs, public address systems, special lighting; first-aid stations; lost and found booth (a separate nursery for lost babies); facilities for too-numerous concession stands; free water stations; public parking and public safety provided by the US Parks Horse Mounted Police; comfortable lounges for the press; even better lounges for the VIPs; trash and garbage removal, and omnipresent restrooms (actually 103 portables contracted for with Honey Buckets, Inc.)

The Peoples' Museum Institution flaunted their sophistication, knowledge, and experience in rounding up the folk life artists from the small villages and hamlets here and abroad except for the

Baretookies Backwoods folk singers, dancers, and craftsmen, which the Parks people proudly paraded. The Peoples' identified, located, promoted, and delivered on time the major stars of the International Folk Life Festival. The performers were routed out of the low and high hills of the Balkans, First American singers and dancers forgotten on the isolated plains reservations; the trade workers union from somewhere; and the local AfroAmerican jazz musicians and vocalists.

The Balkan musicians, singers, dancers, and storytellers were all nonprofessional—true artists who were still pure and original, untouched by any form of capitalism. They played, sang, strummed, danced, and shared their traditions for the love of it—yes, for the love of it, as their fathers and mothers had before them. Few folk life followers had ever heard the Balkan Tambura—the sounds of the pear-shaped, long-necked wooden string instrument—the way they played it. The Tambura produced a metallic, tingling sound. It was played by plucking the strings with one's thumb, but most pluckers preferred something called a plectrum—an artificial thumb.

The Blue Collar Tradesmen—men who build our homes and who are strong union members—demonstrated their skills, their worth, and their pride. There were carpenters, bricklayers, plasterers, plumbers, stone masons, electricians, and painters. They not only demonstrated how to do it but also let the venturesome have a go at it. There was always a waiting line of home owners looking for help and the latest in "fixing it up." The sign in front of their showcase was "The Trade Has Been Good To Me."

The First Americans whose great-grandfathers had performed for George Custer at the Little Bighorn almost a hundred years ago were back. They performed a reenactment on the sacred grounds of the Grand Mall. They brought their flutes, their drums, their costumes and voices and mesmerized the viewers.

The Afro Americans representing those who came over on slave ships brought the blues as only they could do. The Gospel singers were there too, with original renditions of "Amazing Grace," "Take Your Troubles to the Lord," and everybody's favorite, "We Shall Overcome."

And Bantookey brought their backwoods performers—fiddlers, banjo players, quilters, basket makers, singers, dancers, and their fantastic food. But they also brought their whiskey makers, tobacco growers, and horse breeders. The tobacco hustlers were a major concern for the Parks people who were overly sensitive to First Amendment Rights. The tobacco people planted their tobacco plot right in front of ole Abe, and the anti-smoking crowd soon appeared. The protesters were peaceful, polite, well-disciplined and just walked around with their signs: "Tobacco Kills" and "Don't Let Your Kids Smoke." They were simply making a statement as they had so many times in the past.

Although the Bantookeys put the blame on them, the Anti-Tobacco Bunch denied any involvement—it just wasn't their style to be destructive. The night before the opening someone, or maybe more than one, dressed up as Parks Department maintenance workers and pulled up about half the tobacco stalks in the Tobacco Growing Exhibit, an area about twenty by thirty feet. The Whiskey Making Exhibit area was also hit. All the Bantookey hooch was poured into the Tobacco Patch. There had always been a sisterhood between the tobacco and whiskey bashers.

The US Park Police were late in arriving at the scene because of the size and layout of the festival grounds. They reported that they saw some park maintenance workers running away from the tobacco field. The Bantookies blamed the Society for a Smoke-Free World and the ever-present homosexuals.

The Park Police were unable to make any arrests, and it was never determined how they got there and who spoiled the big smoke in. But more importantly, it was the bigmouth, big-belly politician from Bantookey who blamed the Parks Department. The senior senator Jack Daniels Marlboro accused the Parks people of deliberately sabotaging (I wonder how he knew) the sovereign state of Bantookey. He was already upset about a previous incident that happened two days before. During a dry run, a former Bantookey derby horse threw her jockey and then jumped into the reflecting pond. It was over one hundred degrees in the Capital City on that Sunday. The Parks Department festival director, Jim Lee, was summoned to

Senator Marlboro's office at 8:00 a.m. on opening day of the folk life festival. Marlboro was beyond rage, and he, his arm, his hand, and his Cuban cigar, all shook with terrifying furor.

MARLBORO: Boy, do you know who I am?
LEE: Yes, sir, Senator.
MARLBORO: Do you know that I'm chairman of the Parks Department Oversight Committee?
LEE: Yes, sir, I'm, well aware of it.
MARLBORO: You mess around with me and I'll have your job and your boss's job, you hear what I'm saying to you?
LEE: Yes, sir.
MARLBORO: You and your Parks Department won't get a dime out of my committee, you hear what I'm saying?
LEE: Yes, sir.
MARLBORO: Now I hear that from the very start you people was against us. Didn't want that Bantookey tobacco, whiskey, well-bred horses on the National Mall, right there beneath the knee of Abe Lincoln.

> Where you think he was from? Bantookey, that's where he was born. You didn't want no part of my Bantookey because you was scared of them communists and homos. Yeah, they are against everything, anti-this, anti-that bunch of damn fools. Last night I was called at home [some-one from the Peoples' Museum sandbagging the Parks people] when me and mine had already bedded down, if you know what I mean. They said that those anti-American, anti-tobacco, anti-good sippin' whiskey saboteurs had pulled up our tobacco plants and poured our Bantookey booze on what was left. You know anything about that, Mr. Government Employee?

LEE: Yes, sir.

MARLBORO: I don't care about no yes sir. What do you know about it?

LEE: It's not as bad as it might seem. We had extra tobacco plants stored in our hot house, and our horticulturist and his crew are replacing the missing and damaged plants as of this moment.

MARLBORO: Did them tobacco plants come from Bantookey?

LEE: Yes, all of them. We had planned to have a large extra supply in case the plants didn't take hold.

MARLBORO: What you mean didn't take hold? Bantookey tobacco will grow anyplace in the world.

LEE: I mean if we had inclement weather, a sustained downpour, a storm, hail, or something.

MARLBORO: How about our whiskey barrels?

LEE: There was no damage to the whiskey-making exhibit.

MARLBORO: How do you know that, Lee?

LEE: Because I was over at the festival at five this morning to make sure that your tobacco and whiskey exhibits were up and ready to go.

MARLBORO: You're a better man than I first thought, Lee, but why did something like this happen in the first place?

LEE: We had security at the festival site, but somehow the park police were patrolling the Balkan exhibit area when it happened. The park police think the damage was done in less than two minutes.

MARLBORO: The Balkan exhibits. That's where them Russian communists are, ain't it? You mean you're protecting them communists and not Bantookey's stuff?

LEE: Well, no, sir. The park police can only cover one area at a time. They don't have the manpower to cover every foot of the mall twenty-four hours a day.

MARLBORO: Lee, you better make sure the press don't get wind of this, they could make Bantookey look bad.

LEE: Yes, sir. I can assure you the press knows nothing about it.

MARLBORO: Where you from, Lee?

LEE: Charleston, South Carolina.

MARLBORO: I damn well knew it, all along. You was one of us. Think your tobacco down there is as good as ours?

LEE: I don't know that much about tobacco.

MARLBORO: Well, let me tell you. We got the best damn tobacco anywhere in the world. Our cigars are better than the koobans. I worked in the tobacco fields as a boy, and I've smoked all my life. Ain't nothing wrong with it either. I seen them doctors smoking too. I quit school in the fifth grade and made my way to the top selling tobacco. My children run my tobacco business and doin' real good too. Let me ask you a question, Lee. What's the capital of Bantookey, Louisville or Louisville?

LEE: I believe it's Frankfort, sir.

MARLBORO: Damn right. You're one smart fella, Lee. Now listen here. My friends sent me to the Capital City to look after their interests. Their interests are tobacco, whiskey, and horses. My wife and I don't like living here, but that's my job—taking care of the folks back in Bantookey. And what's happening here at this festival ain't in our best interest. I ain't puttin up with no crap from them communists—tryin' to make us look like a bunch of dumb ass hillbillies. Now you get back down there to the festival and take care of my Bantookey.

During the nine days, the Festival of International Folk Life drew over one million visitors. The park police issued over two thousand parking violations; three honey buckets were stolen and nineteen were turned over; 130 pairs of sunglasses and 91 sets of car keys ended up in the lost and found. It was estimated that the homeless picked up sixty thousand pop cans. It took the Parks people a week to clean up the mess, and one of the workers found an envelope with $3,000 in cash.

Lee retired in Santa Fe and taught English in a small community college. Senator Marlboro was convicted of selling government contracts to his friends in Bantookey. Tobacco, whiskey, and horses were banned from the Grand Mall. The International Folk Life Festival never returned to Capital City.

CHAPTER TWENTY-FOUR

MOUNT BLUSHMORE

Are four faces enough? The Spoilers didn't think so. They were pushing to get their man on the top, on the side, on the bottom, somewhere up on the mountaintop.

In the beginning, the idea for some kind of memorial or monument was to attract more tourists and their dollars to the Black Hills. Initially the state historian wanted to honor western heroes such as Lewis and Clark, George Custer, Buffalo Bill, or Crazy Horse. But to secure federal funding, the concept was broadened to include national historical figures. The Mount Blushmore National Commission supported the sculptured heads of our Founding Fathers, but the sculptor that was selected for the project, Gutzon Puglum, demanded that Teddy Bear be included. Finally, the officials agreed on four: the first president, because he was the first; the third president because of the "life, liberty and pursuit of happiness"; the sixteenth for his damning slavery and holding the union together; and for Teddy Bear the great conservationist and the man who transformed our nation from country bumpkins into a world power. Forty years earlier, the mountain had been named for a city slicker from New York City, Charlie Blushmore.

Puglum was a well-known, highly respected sculptor who had been a student of the world-famous Francois Auguste Bodin. Puglum was not only a most talented sculptor but also a flamboyant self-promoter. His dream had always been to carve a mountainside, and he pushed patriotism to the extreme to bring in the gold for his awesome undertaking. He personally met with US senators, Wall Street millionaires, the National Foundation for the Arts, and even the president himself, to gain political and financial support for carving up the four presidents.

The project faced objections from a group of early environmentalists and rural churchgoers who preached that God didn't create the mountain for man to deface. The First Americans proclaimed that the mountain was sacred and the white man had stolen it from them. But few seemed to listen, and even more really didn't care. The Black Hills needed the bucks, and the workers needed the work. Puglum and his supporters climbed up on Mount Blushmore, and they determined that the granite outcropping had the stone mass to allow the intrusion of four presidential heads. Puglum declared, "Here is the place. America shall march along that skyline." He later added, "We believe a nation's memorial should look like the presidents we honor, have a serenity, a nobility, a power that reflects the gods who inspired them and suggests the gods they have become."

On August 10, 1927, President Foolidge dedicated the mountain monument undertaking sporting cowboy boots and a twelve-gallon hat and proclaimed, "We have come here to dedicate a cornerstone laid by the hand of the Almighty." Much to the chagrin of the God-fearing folks and nature lovers, it looked like God was on the side of the four faces. First, the developers had a vision, then a plan, then an ideal location, and now the official blessing of the presidential palace invoking God's will. Puglum created a plastic model of each president's effigy, and it would be on a scale of one inch of plaster to twelve inches of granite. The actual mauling of Blushmore, 90 percent of the work produced with dynamite, began on October 4.

The explosions, blasting, drilling, carving, sanding, and polishing would continue off and on for fourteen years at a cost of one million dollars under the hands, on supervision of Puglum whom the workers respectfully called "the old man."

Each day Puglum's help climbed seven hundred stairs to reach the work site at the top of the mountain. From there steel cables lowered the dynamiters and drillers over the face on "bosun chairs." When asked "What are you doing there?" one replied, "I'm a jackhammer man," and another said "I make ten dollars a day," and another added, "I'm building a memorial." The "powders" would cut and set charges of dynamite able to remove precise pieces of rock. Surprisingly, not one worker was lost during the entire venture.

What once seemed to be an impossible dream slowly became a reality.

The first head was the first challenge to Puglum and was completed in 1934. The third's likeness was started on the first's right, but because of the cragginess was abandoned and finished up on the left in 1936. Two years later the sixteenth was completed, and finally in 1939 the Rough Rider's grin was etched for all time. It took two more years for the final touches and smoothing of the sixty-foot-long countenances. Gutzon Puglum died in March 1941, but his son Leon finished the polishing on October 31, 1941. The four faces have not received any major makeup in over sixty years and today appear as they did when Leon picked up his tools and left.

Millions of people from all over the world have visited Mount Blushmore. The government says that it memorializes the birth, growth, preservation, and future of the United States. To enhance the national monument, a two-thousand-seat amphitheater was constructed, huge floodlights that brighten the four were installed, and the playing of "The Star-Spangled Banner" highlight the visitor experience. In response, the attendees stand up, place their right hands over their hearts, and gleefully sing along. This memorable moment for many evoked a mesmerizing sense of awe and wonderment. Those standing patriots choke up, weep, yell, smile, applaud, and hug each other in a deep sense of patriotism. The four presidential figures symbolize our courage, dreams, freedom, and greatness. If one misses this evening program, they have lost a sacred moment to share in the Shrine of Democracy.

Some say that if the four faces are fantastic, then five would be the quintessence of America. A national pollster, Sorgby Inc., conducted a nonscientific survey and formed the simple question without qualification: "If you had to choose one figure to add to Mount Blushmore, who would it be?" 99 percent of the respondents replied, "Leave it as it is." The top contenders for the remaining 1 percent in order of popularity were Sacajawea, Eleanor Roosevelt, Sitting Bull, Martin Luther King, Grandma Moses, Emma Lazarus, Ansell Adams, Rosa Parks, and Elvis Pressley.

The Spoilers began a relentless campaign to add their idol, the actor, cowboy, movie star, cigarette salesman, governor, and president to the four on the mountainside. They shouted that because of his leadership the country was free from fear and terrorism forever and that no one had done more to spread democracy than Beggan. After all, he singlehandedly ended the cold war. Who could ever forget those memorable words: "Put Beggan on that wall." The Spoilers made no mention of Iran-Contra, that Beggan believed that ketchup was a vegetable, that his decision making was controlled by astrology and he left the country with the biggest national debt up to that time. The mantra was "Beggan on Blushmore" seen on shirts, baseball caps, and bumper stickers all over the Capital City.

The political hacks from the Beggan era demanded a meeting with the venerable superintendent of Mount Blushmore National Memorial, Washington Jefferson Lincoln Ridervelt. There was no doubt who Reidervelt was named for or why his daddy etched that name on his birth certificate. Puglum had often said about Ridervelt's father, "Big Belly had the stomach for it, and together we had a blast." Big Belly had been the lead dynamite designer responsible for determining where to place the explosives, how much dynamite to use, and the results of the big and small explosions. He was an accomplished artist and one of the few memorial makers who was there from beginning to end. W. J. L. Ridervelt, as a boy, had helped with the creation of the memorial and was the world's authority on Mount Blushmore. His private collection of original daily work accomplishments, correspondence, original drawings, historical photographs, tools, original molds and models; equipment and dairies was the most extensive in existence.

All the exhibits in the park visitor center were from Ridervelt's collection, and they were on temporary loan to the government with strings designed by Ridervelt's lawyers. Ridervelt was a graduate mining engineer, accomplished sculptor, and photographer. He had authored numerous articles on Puglum and Blushmore and had written the definitive biography of Gutzon Puglum. He was a career Parks Department employee and had served in the Southwest as a park ranger, chief park ranger, and assistant superintendent. The one job he was made for was the superintendent of Blushmore National Memorial. It's all he ever wanted in life, and he had been the superintendent for the past twenty-three years. To those who knew him and overlooked his abruptness, hellish temper, and his frequent hangovers, he was totally committed to his work. W. J. L. Ridervelt was Blushmore.

The Spoilers had no idea what was about to happen when they met with Ridervelt. They strongly believed that their mission was a fait accompli. Monday morning was not a good time to confront Rivervelt since he usually boozed it up on the weekends. Niceties were not exchanged, and the spokesman for the Spoilers began with

GOTCHA BUTCHER: Ridervelt, we're here for one reason. We want Beggan on Blushmore, and we want it now.

WJL: Not a chance.

GOTCHA: What did you say?

WJL: Not a chance.

GOTCHA: Do you know who you are talking to? I am the assistant secretary of the Interior, and the Parks Department comes under my authority.

WJL: So what. You're just another political appointee whose daddy got him a job in the government cause he couldn't do anything else.

GOTCHA: I resent that Ridervelt. I could have your job, do you understand that? You're just a little Parks Department employee in the middle of the organizational chart. Now listen to me. Our group is dedicated to one thing: Beggan on Blushmore. We already have his name on an airport and I believe a boat, and now is the time for Beggan on Blushmore.

WJL: You're kidding, right?

GOTCHA: We are willing to sacrifice our fortunes and our families to honor this great man.

WJL: You're kidding.

GOTCHA: Would you please stop saying 'you're kidding.' We could never be more serious. Beggan on Blushmore.

WJL: Not a chance.

GOTCHA: Would you please stop saying 'not a chance.'

WJL: You're kidding.

GOTCHA: Now look, Ridervelt, I've tried to reason with you. You must realize that we don't let little people stand in our way. President Beggan was the greatest American who ever lived. Now I can fire you right now, but I'll just let you retire quietly. You've been here too damn long, and you think you own the damn place. Now if you don't give us your full support, you're finished, Ridervelt. We have a God-given duty to get Beggan on Blushmore.

WJL: You're kidding.

GOTCHA: I told you not to say "you're kidding" again. It's decision time, Ridervelt. Yes or no.

WJL: Not a chance, Gotcha. I'm going to tell you straight out why your little self-serving scheme will never happen. But first, I want you to know that I abhor everything you and that rotten bunch in the presidential palace stand for. You care nothing about honor, tradition, and the history of this country. Maybe you've heard of the Peyote Society, well I'm a founding member. [WJL was the only Peyote Society member who ever openly broke his anonymity. Why? Because he didn't give a rat's ass about who knew it.] We are committed to exposing and kill-ing your mission of ruining our country's national treasures. You are the most despicable person that I've ever met, but that's not the reason that Beggan on Blushmore will never happen. Gotcha, you dumb ass, it is impossible. The rock around the four faces is too fragile and is not carvable. We have numer-ous scientific engineering and geological studies that conclude that any attempt to dynamite and drill Beggan on Blushmore would result on the four falling on their faces. Dr. Nomo Faceli, the most renowned granite mountain sculptor, recently said on "Face the Nation," "Can you improve on Mona Lisa's blush?" So, Gotcha, it should not happen, it cannot happen, and it will never happen. Now do you understand what I have just said? Now get the hell out of my office and I'll turn off this tape recorder.

Nothing was ever heard again about "Beggan on Blushmore."

CHAPTER TWENTY-FIVE

WATER THE HELL OUT OF IT

The Piscataway Indians lived there first but were pushed out by the European settlers who established a small hamlet called Georgetown. After the Revolutionary War ended in 1783, the new federal government met in New York City and then Philadelphia. To establish a permanent seat of government, Congress passed the Residence Act, which set the new capital in the southern region in exchange for the federal government's assumption of the Northern states' war debts. The actual site was chosen by the first president and named for him: Washington DC. The DC was for District of Columbia and was an old poetic term for the United States with reference to Christopher Columbus. The nation's capital was on the Potomac River, on land donated by the states of Virginia and Maryland. The man known as "First in War, First in Peace knew that the Potomac River had the potential to be a great navigable waterway where tobacco could be loaded on ocean going ships. It was also less than ten miles from his home, Mount Vernon, and his Potowmack company would be chosen to improve the navigability of the river. Andrew Bellicose and a free African American, Benjamin Bandiman, surveyed the area for the new capital and placed boundary stones. The secretary of State thought he should be the architect for the development of the Capital City, but Pierre Letgue was given the prize.

Letgue's friends, and there were few, described him as brilliant, arrogant, unreasonable, hotheaded, exasperating, sensitive, and scornful of authority. Pierre Letgue was an artist, engineer, architect, and was born in Paris in 1754 into a wealthy family. His father was a well-known artist of battle scenes and landscapes and was a professor of art at the Royal Academy where Pierre had been a student. Along with Laughanet, he came to America in 1777 and joined the revolution. He served on the staff of the future first president as a captain of engineering. In 1779, he was wounded in the Battle of Savannah and was later promoted to the rank of major. After the war, he settled in New York City and designed the new Federal Hall, the temporary seat of the United States government. He also designed the commemorative medal of the Society of Cincinnati, an association of former Revolutionary War officers. He had studied the plans of the great cities of the world and was recommended by Alexander Hamilton to design the Federal City.

Letgue's master plan was mostly original and was monumental in scope. He planned for the Capitol Building to be on high ground, on Pinkun's Hill, and a wide tree-lined avenue would connect it to the presidential palace. Circles and squares would be the centerpiece for splendid avenues where statues and monuments would honor national heroes. Expansive city parks and federal buildings would enhance the streets and boulevards. A grand esplanade would showcase museums and libraries adding to the splendor of the city. It would be designed so "that it may be attractive to the learned and provide diversion to the idle." It was a beautiful concept developed by a true genius.

But Letgue would never see it unfold because he was let go because of his inability to get along with the Capital City commissioners. When Letgue left, he took his plans with him. Andrew Bellicose was appointed to replace him, and his design included much of Letgue's original thinking. The development of the City Beautiful would take years before it became a reality because of a lack of funding. Finally, in 1901 the McMillan Plan was approved and funded, and it emphasized open park space and enhanced the grand esplanade, which became known as the mall. The vision for the plan, which was named for the senator from Michigan, was for a broad grassy expanse lined with trees, walks, benches, plantings, flowers, all reminiscent of the great gardens of Europe. City Beautiful would be open to anyone and everyone to experience, to learn, and to enjoy.

The most renowned park planners, architects, and landscape architects dedicated their time and efforts to the beautification of the Capital City. The National Mall, as it is known today, would be a world-class park—a special place for social, cultural, patriotic, and political events and activities. It would become a public promenade that would reflect the history and democratic principles of the United States. The striking obelisk to the first president, the sprawling Smithburg Castle, highlighted the overdevelopment of the Peoples' Mall. Letgue had envisioned a Grand Greensward that would ensure the symmetry and uniformity of a great city, not a clutter of monuments and memorials that would intrude on the openness and vistas.

Little did he realize that the National Mall would become a mass of marble and granite monuments and memorials to past presidents, the sacrifices of men and women in unnecessary wars, and a living consciousness where millions of citizens come to protest and demand relief from their government.

There is a granite block on the mall missed by most with the words from the last sentence of the "Declaration of Independence."

> And for the support of this declaration with a firm reliance on the protection of divine providence, we mutually pledge to each other our lives, our fortunes, and our sacred honor.

The National Mall is often looked upon as the Peoples' Mall for every year millions come and go and participate in picnics, July 4 parades, take leisurely walks, visit the monuments, memorials, gardens, museums, musical concerts, festivals, and the endless protests, marches, and rallies. Unlike the city itself, the Grand Mall is an inclusive place for all people regardless of race, nationality, economic or political position.

A quiet gathering spot particularly in the evening is the Reflecting Pool, built in 1924. The popular site is 167 feet wide, two and half feet deep, and some five football fields long surrounded by shade trees. Near the pool, millions have joined in the fight for human rights such as the World War I Bonus March, the Marian Andrews Concert (the Negro Lady was not allowed to sing in the nearby Concert Hall), the M. L. Wing Peace Parade, and the shameful treatment of the Vietnam War veterans.

After victory in World War I, a grateful nation wanted to reward the American heroes with a bonus of $1.25 for each day served overseas and $1 for each day while stationed at home. The US Congress passed the legislation, and it was approved by the president in 1924. The badly needed dollars that would have alleviated some of the poverty and hunger during the Great Depression were not forthcoming. Thousands of veterans could not find any kind of work, and their families needed help, and they needed it now. About twenty thousand veterans, some with their wives and children, descended upon the nation's capital in the spring of 1932. They set up camps on the National Mall and elsewhere with stuff they scrounged from junk yards, trash pits, and government garbage piles—packing boxes, pieces of old lumber, scrapped tin—and built temporary shelters. They dug latrines and did their cooking on open fires. From their decrepit home base, they petitioned their congressmen to pay them now. The US House of Representatives said yes, but the Senate said no, you'll have to wait. When the veterans refused to take no for an answer and refused to leave, the president of the United States ordered their removal.

The US Army led by several future World War II generals charged the helpless and surprised families with fixed bayonets, horse-mounted cavalry, and six tanks. One Army major who later served eight years as president said the whole scene was pitiful and a shameful treatment of men he had served with during World War I. Two veterans were killed, and the rest were pushed out, the Shanty Town destroyed, and the grass restored by the Parks people. Black dye was poured into the Reflecting Pool, lots of it, as the parks chief ordered his crew "and do it as soon as possible."

Even before the Bonus March, citizens have journeyed to their capital to protest for or against something. There was the Boxey's Army. Actually a group of unemployed civilians were victims of the

Panic of 1893—the worst economic crisis the country had endured. These poor folks demanded that their government create public works jobs, but all they got was arrested for walking on the National Mall grass. The Women's Suffrage March of 1913 erupted into an attack on the five thousand feminine marchers who were tripped, grabbed, groped, and pulled off the park benches and kicked off the Grand Mall grass. The Parks chief was fired, but no one was sure whether it was because he allowed the police to hassle the girls or because he let them squat on the grass for so long. When they left their capital, the Parks people poured more black dye into the Reflecting Pool, picked up the garbage, and replaced the grass.

Two generations later, the nation was changed forever by a major protest of over 250,000 African Americans and those who stood with them. Freedom Buses and Freedom Trains brought the brothers and sisters to the nation's capital except for the ones who came by roller skates. It was a massive Morality March for jobs, for justice, and for freedom. On August 28, 1963, the world would hear the passionate plea of "I Have A Dream," the emotional words "Free at Last, Free at Last," words they would never forget. The hopeful stood, sat, and lay down on both sides of the Reflecting Pool. It was orderly, disciplined, peaceful, and when the true believers departed, the Parks people gathered the garbage, poured black dye into the Reflecting Pool, and replaced the grass.

Five years later, the melting pot poor hit the West Potomac Park and camped out in what was to become known as Resurrection City—a hodgepodge of tents and shacks. They wanted jobs for all the poor people in the Land of Plenty. They moved on to the Grand Mall and the Reflecting Pool became a swimming pool, then a huge bathtub, and finally a giant honey bucket. After they left the poor, Parks people cleaned up the Resurrection Refuge and poured ten gallons of black dye, five times the usual amount, into the giant pool, which no longer reflected. Ten truckloads of grass were laid down and watered.

The continuous protests against the Vietnam War, one with over five hundred thousand, produced more trash, more garbage, and required twenty truckloads of grass. And thirty gallons of black dye were dumped into the Reflecting Pool. And enough is enough.

PARK DIRECTOR: It's just getting too expensive to pick up after all the protesters that keep coming to the Capital City to gripe about everything and everybody. The cost is now over a million a year to keep the mall in shape and the sod alone is over $100,000. I'd like to see the marchers and demonstrators move to another venue.

GROUNDS FOREMAN: Yeah, my guys love the overtime, but you're right, boss, it's getting out of hand. Other park areas are being neglected because we spend so much time on the mall.

PARK DIRECTOR. Well, First Amendment Rights allows them to protest, and they all want to tell their tale to old Abe. If Congress could pass legislation to establish a bitching park somewhere, like at the Defense Department parking lot or over at football stadium, it would allow the mall to rest and rejuvenate. How can we keep the mall in pristine condition for the heartland families who maybe visit their capital once in a lifetime? I guess we'll have to keep on doing what we've been doing—pour more dye in the pool.

GROUNDS FOREMAN: It's going to take three weeks to clean up after that last bunch. And if we start cleaning out the Reflecting Pool, the black dye can only hide so much stuff, it's going to take two months.

The call came from the White House, and some believe it was from the president himself. "Water the hell out of the grass in front of Lincoln and do it now." The director tried to explain that it would do no good to water dry, dead grass and that sod was scheduled to be laid the following day. The voice shouted, "Do you know who this is? I said water the hell out it and do it now."

The grounds foreman was always careful when addressing any of his crew. Some years before he called all the employees by their first name and when Roy claimed that he called him "boy" he almost lost his job. So now he referred to the grounds maintenance workers as "Mister"—Mr. Brown, Mr. Green, Mr. Davis. He instructed his most trusted and dedicated employee, Mr. Wescoat, exactly what to do. He told him about the telephone call and who was on the other end. He got Mr. Wescoat's confidence and was assured that nothing would stop him from carrying out this special assignment. Mr. Wescoat did exactly what was asked of him, and he did it with great pride because it was a presidential order. The next morning the Capital City Post carried a front page picture of Mr. Wescoat standing on the grass in front of the Memorial. Mr. Wescoat was holding a watering hose and was watering the dead, dried-out grass as ordered. He stood as a sentinel amidst the biggest rainstorm in the history of Capital City. The caption beneath the picture read, "The president said water the hell out of it."

BIG SUGAR MAN

A long time ago, water flowed from Lake Okeechobee to the south of Florida, a vast river of grass, one hundred twenty miles long and fifty miles wide and less than twelve inches deep. On the southern tip of Florida there was a majestic flat land—beautiful, endangered—a subtropical scene, the only one in the Continental United States. It was a wilderness of marshes, ponds, saw grass, and sloughs. The First Americans lived there for centuries and called it Pa hay okee—a grassy place No other place on Earth offers the diversity of plant and animal life. Surprisingly, the European colonial settlers didn't appreciate this natural wonder and considered it just a swamp. There are Hammocks—scattered islands covered with live oak, mahogany trees, and the Gumbo Limbo—which has a red brown peeling bark, small white flowers. The soil is fertile and porous with orchids, lilies, and the royal palm.

Animals hide in the marshes to prey, to hunt, and to survive— the bobcat, black bear, panther, turkey vulture, deer, raccoon, snakes, and the cougar. The alligator is called the keeper of the everglades. They live in the freshwater lakes, rivers, and swamps and are recognized by their blackish color and a broad snout. When their mouth is closed, only the upper jaw teeth are visible. They devour insects, crabs, crayfish, frogs, snails, snakes, and an occasional raccoon. The largest alligator ever measured was in Florida. It was seventeen feet long and weighed almost six hundred pounds. They can walk on their toes and the heels of their back feet, tail raised—high walking at thirty miles per hour. If it hisses or opens its mouth, back off, although it is rare for an alligator to attack a human. In their courtship, there is a lot of bellowing, back rubbing, circling, snout touching, and bubble blowing. They are hard to spot because only the eyes and snout are usually visible above the water.

The crocodile is rare in the everglades, but they are there. It has an olive brown color, long, long, slender snout, and both upper and lower teeth are visible when the jaws are clenched. It is said that South Florida is the only place where both the alligator and crocodile can be found together.

The manatee or sea cow can grow as long as twelve feet long and weigh as much as 1,800 pounds. The face is wrinkled and whiskered. This gentle, slow-moving mammal eats tons of grass and has a body shaped like a fat torpedo.

The roseate spoonbill is a large, long-legged graceful pink bird with a long bill shaped like a giant spoon. This strange wader bird sweeps its bill from side to side and scoops up insects, shrimp, crabs, and crayfish. The pink coloring comes from what it eats. They nest in marshes, tidal ponds, and mangrove swamps. The everglades is also the habitat of the flamingo, which has the most beautiful legs in the world. It is a lovely bird that lives in lots of muddy water and uses its bill as a filter when dunking for shellfish. Amazingly, the flamingo sleeps while standing on only one leg. It's not surprising that the flamingo has only one major enemy—man.

The most common wading birds are the egret, which have a white droopy plume, and the anhinga, known as the snake bird. The white ibis probes for food with a long beak, and the green-backed heron rarely misses its jab at moving fish. Rarely seen are the wood storks, an endangered species. In the 1930s, there were over 250,000 wading birds in the southern tip, today less than 10,000. The birds of prey are also found in the everglades: hawks, owls, eagles, falcons, all scavenging for survival.

But selfish, greedy man could not leave all this natural beauty as he found it—to leave it for others to experience and enjoy. He saw not what it was but what he could take from it and how much profit he could extract from it. The first Europeans to exploit the everglades were a group of soldiers under the command of the great Bounce de Peon, who died there from an Indian arrow. In return, his boys gave the arrow throwers tuberculosis, which decimated the natives of the River of Saw Grass. The Semiholes, who called themselves "Free Men," came next to the everglades. They too would meet a terrible, terrible fate as more greedy white men descended upon them and pushed them out, destroyed much of the plant and animal life and added Florida to the United States.

The red cockaded woodpecker is no more, vanished. Plumage hunters killed hundreds of thousands of flamingoes, egrets, spoonbill herons for the bird feathers, which were at one time all the rage in the fashion world of women's hats. The poachers murdered an Audubon Society game warden, Guy Bradley, because he got in the way of their plans to satisfy an insatiable demand. Florida state laws and even designating the everglades preserve a state park did little to impede the commercial exploitation. The illegal and underground market for endangered plants and animals ensured that unsavory dealers would continue to pick the flowers, pinch the birds, and trap the bears, the cougars, and the alligators.

One governor of Florida was elected on the basis of his campaign slogan "Drain the everglades." The River of Grass could be developed, and who could resist a beautiful water front view, sunshine on demand, exotic stick-legged birds, mangroves, and reptiles, all in your privately owned backyard?

The real estate moguls salivated. Oil companies lobbied the Congress for the rights to drill. More and more entrepreneurs and just everyday folks, workers, and retirees settled into the big city just north of the everglades.

The United States Army engineers constructed 720 miles of levees, 1,000 miles of canals, and 200 water control devices. They drained part of the everglades to provide adequate freshwater for the big city people. They built a dike to keep the Okeechobee from flooding, and this cut off the water to the hammocks, mangroves, and wildlife. If it didn't rain, the everglades received no water.

When man controls the water spigot, disaster will surely follow. A lack of concern, incompetence, conflicts of interest, greed, and mismanagement all combined to place an incomparable million-acre preserve in danger of imminent extinction. One environmentalist wrote, "Control of nature is a phrase conceived in arrogance, and nature does not exist solely for the convenience of man." Kitty Waters described the Corps of Engineers as "little boys who like to play in the mud." She was deeply concerned because so much damage had been done, and there was so little time left to salvage something for posterity.

Kitty Waters, the woman, and Tom Toe, the man, were the mother and father of the movement to establish Everglades National Park. Kitty, a prolific writer, and the Florida Women's Clubs were early movers and shakers in first getting the everglades named a state park. In 1923, she wrote, "The wealth of South Florida, but even more important, the meaning and significance of South Florida, lies in the black muck of the everglades." Tom Toe walked and waded through the marshes and hammocks and saw firsthand where the poachers were capturing and killing the alligators, turtles, and wading birds for profit. Tom was outraged and agitated relentlessly for the preservation of the unique environment.

Their joint efforts were finally rewarded on May 30, 1934, when the US Congress established Everglades National Park. "It was to be a wilderness where no development, or plan for the entertainment of visitors, shall be undertaken which will interfere with the preservation of the unique flora and fauna in this area." Despite the federal laws, the poaching of birds and animals continued because of the 1930s Depression and World War II. The new national park was not adequately funded or staffed and funds for land acquisition to be included within the park boundary was nonexistent. Before the park was formally dedicated on December 6, 1947, Kitty Waters had authored the River of Seagrass and a review read, "Few Americans have ever written so sensitively, so skillfully, so magnificently of any part of their land." And from the president's address at the dedication: "Here are no lofty peaks seeking the sky, no mighty glaciers or rushing streams wearing away the uplifted land. Here is land in its quiet beauty, serving not as a source of water, but the receiver of it. To its natural abundance we owe the spectacular plant and animal life that distinguishes this place from all others in our country."

The everglades is a sanctuary for all seeking to be at one with nature. Although the River of Grass is much smaller than a century ago, it is preserved, protected, and enjoyed by more than one million visitors every year. It is a subtropical paradise, the heart of which are the saw grass marshes, the largest of its kind in the world. The limestone bottom is quite hard, and one can simply walk across and through the marshes without fear of sinking. There are just two seasons, the dry, from November to April, and the wet, from May through October when the rain comes down in buckets. In total, the park gets about sixty inches a year. The sheet of water that flows through the everglades, a trickle compared to what it was once, comes from the lake to the north. The park serves as a refuge for more than seventy rare, threatened, and endangered plant and animal life.

It is open all year, and thousands walk, hike, canoe, and boat through the preserve viewing the flora and fauna, including the magnificent alligators. The Parks Department is the steward of this subtropical wilderness. Everglades is the third largest national park in the lower forty-eight states.

Today Everglades is a park in danger and is undergoing restoration to repair what has been damaged in the past. Water levels and pollution are the paramount threats to a healthy home for the plants and animals. Fertilized water carrying mercury, nitrogen, and especially phosphorus has ravaged the marsh mammals—the raccoons and alligators. There are only about ten panthers that still roam through the park. The wood stork has declined from six thousand nesting birds to less than five hundred. It was once believed that parks could be preserved and protected within their boundaries. Today it is clear that this is a false promise. National parks are not islands. They are severely impacted by what happens outside of their boundaries.

The government engineers controlled the flow of water starving the everglades and providing the freshwater to the sugar industry and the big-city folks. When the water did come, it was either too little or too much. The water controllers could never balance the needs of the fragile ecosystem as Mother Nature had provided for centuries. Sweetie Canes tagline had always been, "If this swamp wasn't here, it would be a really nice place." This really nice place, because of a lack of water, was a fire waiting to happen, and Sweetie Canes spent a bundle to defeat a constitutional amendment mandating a one-cent-a-pound sugar tax. The tax money would have gone to Everglades National Park. The sugar company controlled five hundred thousand acres of fertile land north of the park, land that once was part of the ecosystem. They employed some 15,000 workers, many illegal immigrants, whom they paid below minimum wage and provided even worst living conditions. Their mantra was "Sugar is king, and the more you produce, the sweeter it gets."

Every time the environmentalists exposed Sweetie Canes's criminal activities, Big Sugar bought its way out, and the government Spoilers and the big-city lawyers make the problems go away. They received huge government subsidies, paid no taxes, and contributed millions to the local and Capital City politicians. Sweetie was the most damaging, the most polluting, the most flagrant despoiler of Everglades National Park. They have done everything in their power to destroy the unique subtropical paradise in Southern Florida. The saw grass is parched, the wading birds stand in only two inches of water, and the alligators, deer, bobcat, panther and black bear are sick and dying. No one seemed to care, not the government, not Sweetie Canes, not the politicians, but one man did, and he cared a lot.

The everglades trails foreman, Russ Rodriquez, age sixty-two, lived in South Florida marshes his entire life. He was a career Parks Department employee, and no one knew the River of Seagrass better; no one loved it more. No one had seen the daily erosion and the tragic destruction of his home and life's work as Russ Rodriquez. He had little formal education, but every day he was out on the trails, trying to salvage what the Sugar Man had not stolen. He had a profound knowledge of the everglades, and he often cried alone. He was tired of the endless empty political promises about restoring what Sweetie Cane and an inept government had despoiled. He had worked for Sweetie Canes in the sugar cane fields as a boy alongside his mother and father, who did the backbreaking work for little pay, no benefits, and the ever-present fear of being deported. Russ Rodriquez hated everything that Sweetie Canes stood for, and everyone who knew Foreman Rodriquez knew it. If he were in Congress, he would declare war against Sweetie Canes, and if he were governor, he would call out the National Guard.

With the help of one engineer, who was ashamed of what the government had done to the everglades, the Peyotes, on a cloudy, moonless night, executed the rage of Russ Rodriquez. The Peyotes mixed toxic waste, burnt oil, paint thinner, gasoline, and DDT into the fresh water reservoir. The reservoir had been built by the Corps of Engineers for the Big Sugar Daddies at the expense of the only subtropical park in America. The thick sludge that the Peyotes concocted seeped through the stalks of the sugar cane, and one by one the canes shriveled up and died. The flow of this toxic garbage oozed through the sugar cane fields, which would have been harvested the following week. To clean up the mess, it cost Sweetie Canes one billion dollars. The immigrant workers, those who had replaced Russ Rodriguez's deceased parents in the sugar cane fields, would do the cleanup. They got three times their previous pay with health benefits.

Russ Rodriguez was overwhelmed on hearing what had happened. His vengeance had been satisfied.

He sported a T-shirt, "Sweetie Cane Sours," and a bumper sticker "Big Sugar Stinks." Sweetie Cane issued one press release entitled "Heads Will Roll"—that is, if they could find any. They knew it had to be someone in the Parks Department, someone who had a grudge, someone like Russ Rodriguez. The Sugar Cane Snoopers found a gas can and a bucket of used oil in Foreman Rodriguez's pickup truck. Big Sugar had their big-city lawyers met with the Parks Department about suspect, Russ Rodriguez.

SWEETIE CANE LAWYERS: We've got our man, and he works for you. He's Russ Rodriguez, trails foreman at Everglades National Park.
PARKS DEPARTMENT SPOILERS: We're a conservative, pro-business organization, not a bunch of terrorists. We can just quietly retire Rodriguez, and we'll assure you that a government subsidy will

cover your one-billion-dollar loss. We have an image to protect, and we can't afford for the public to find out that one our own is responsible. We would never regain their trust and support, and our business interests would suffer.

SWEETIE CANE LAWYERS: Okay, okay, you've got a deal. Just make sure we get our money.

The Parks Department encouraged Russ Rodriguez to retire. After all he was sixty-two and would receive a good government pension and would not have to serve any jail time. Russ just laughed in their faces. They threatened to fire him if he didn't go. He wouldn't budge.

The chief park ranger at Everglades informed the Spoilers that the gas can on Russ's pickup was filled with gasoline and had never been unstrapped from the rear of the vehicle. He also declared that the bucket of oil came out of the truck's engine. This finding had been verified by both the Federal Bureau of Investigation and the Exxon Mobile Corporation. The Spoilers notified Sweetie Cane and set up another meeting.

PARKS DEPARTMENT SPOILERS: Russ Rodriguez is not your man.

SWEETIE CANE LAWYERS: Well, maybe yes and maybe no. But he has embarrassed us with his terrorist T-shirt and bumper sticker and his big mouth. We have proof that he is an illegal alien. You have been sheltering a felon for over thirty years, and now you're going to give him a big fat government pension. Now how will that look on the front page of the *Big City Daily*, which by the way, we own?

PARKS DEPARTMENT SPOILERS: So what do you want?

SWEETIE CANE LAWYERS: Deport him back to Mexico with no pension. And we want our one billion.

In protest, the sugar cane workers at Sweetie Cane left the fields and refused to clean it up. Thousands joined them as they marched through downtown of Miami. They carried signs in support of Russ Rodriquez:

"If Russ goes, we go."

"Rodriquez is Everglades."

"No human being is illegal."

"Russ Rodriquez paid his taxes."

The church chimed in with "We believe that each person is a child of God," and Jesus said, "Love thy neighbor as thyself." The entire Latin American population in the country—legal, illegal, and otherwise—responded in rallies crying "The Statue of Liberty means give me the wretched refuse of your teeming shore. Now if you don't believe that, then tear down the Liberty Island Lady."

Sweetie Cane could not get the Latinos back to work and went bankrupt. A Dallas billionaire bought the Sweetie Cane company on the cheap and gave it to the sugar cane workers. The US Congress passed a law giving all illegal immigrants who had productively worked in the United States for five years, all of them, amnesty. When Russ Rodriguez was asked by his wife, "Sabe un Peyote?" he smiled and said, "Mi amigo bueno es an Peyote."

Russ Rodriguez was never deported, and the following year he was elected mayor of Miami.

CHAPTER TWENTY-SEVEN

THE BATHROOM COMMODE

The king of Congoflow in Africa, Lettergow, was delighted that his wife, Haftagow, had an uncontrollable urge to visit the Deep Hole National Park. It would give him more time to spend with his younger wives who didn't have an uncontrollable urge. King Lettergow made all the arrangements for his wife's special condition. Queen Haftagow had an overactive bladder, and she might have to go at any moment. The king was also sensitive to her feelings about her necessity and knew in his heart how sweet and delicate a lady he had married. She would never use a crude word like "toilet" or "commode," or the "john." They were just not in her vocabulary. He tried to soften the wording of the irregular request by combining two words—"bathroom" and "commode," but even that was too harsh. Queen Haftagow finally agreed that BC would be best. Surely the savvy Americans would understand BC.

When the king's letter was received at the State Department, one sentence was highlighted: "Queen Haftagow in her travels throughout the United States must at all times be within one minute of a BC."

A major stop on the tour would be Deep Hole National Park. When the Parks Department received the letter about Queen Haftagow's visit from the State Department, they didn't understand what the king meant by "BC." The State Department didn't have the faintest idea and seemingly didn't care. They left it to the Parks

Department to arrange the entire tour because all the places that Queen Haftagow wanted to visit were under their jurisdiction.

Because of the potential oil that could be extracted out of Congoflow, the White House wanted to be assured that the queen's visit would be a big success. So they instructed Gotcha Butcher to personally take charge of the tour. Cool-Head Fred told him that he had once visited the Congoflow and remembered that the country had converted to Christianity. King Lettergow and his wife had led the way and were strict fundamentalists. Obviously, BC must mean Baptist Church. Gotcha was so convinced that BC meant Baptist Church that he gave Cool-Head Fred a special achievement award.

But this presented a new dilemma, separation of church and state. Gotcha had to make it clear that the federal government did not and could not support one religion over another. In fact, the federal government was now on a slippery slope. After innumerable drafts, the final letter back to King Lettergow read as follows:

> The Constitution of United States of America was ratified on June 21, 1788. It guaranteed that all men (except Native Americans, Afro Americans, and of course women who weren't men) were created equal. The leading members of the Constitutional Convention in Philadelphia, Washington, Jefferson, and Franklin did not go to the BC since they considered themselves Deists. They realized that people are different and some have weaker constitutions than others. But the law of the land protects their rights, and if one chooses to go to a BC, it is respected, but an individual cannot be forced to go to a BC. The BC is just one of many alternatives since our country is just one big melting pot of diverse physiques from all over the world. Most of them went at Ellis Island except for the slaves who had to be tied down, the Indians who refused to go

to a BC, and the Mexicans who jumped over the fence.

About your visit to Deep Hole National Park. The park staff is well aware of your strong need to go. The BC is less than one minute from the park entrance. The Park Naturalist Jennifer Wolfe, and will be your guide. She says to tell you that the BC welcomes everyone and they no longer discriminate as they did in the past. The BC is free of course, but a collection is usually taken after one is seated. Some people come early and stay late since they really need to go to the BC. Because some of those who use the BC are elderly, they sit the whole time while in the BC. We love them so much and call them Senior Sitters. Others just come now and then since they only have a Senior Moment. However, not all of our older folks are able to get to the BC so we bring the BC goers to them on film.

The BC is open every day and night except on Thursday nights when we rent it out to the local Alcoholics Anonymous for $25. The fee goes to pay for our paper. Our BC uses a lot of paper—rolled and unrolled. Every Saturday night we hold a dance for our young people so they can get to know each other. Of course this activity is closely supervised, but they don't have to hold back any but let it all hang out. And every Tuesday night we have a special dinner, and all are encouraged to bring their own pots.

Once a year in December we set up a beautiful tree, decorate it with lots of lights, and put presents under it. We also have an annual Easter Egg Hunt for the little ones. It is well attended by the young parents and grandparents who help the kids dig out the eggs in the BC. Also we try to assist the local Mexicans and Indians, but only if they are sober. We try to make the BC a home away from home, but last year a group of Homeless, not the bunch from Alcoholics Anonymous, left the place in such a mess that we had to replace half the seats in the BC.

There is a rumor that the AA group is looking for a larger BC for their twelve steps program. If we lose the $25, we'll have to cut down on the amount of paper used in the BC. We don't usually charge anything for the BC paper, but some people just lose control and the paper just goes down the hole. But as the say, "And this too shall pass." On Sundays from 8:30 a.m. to 10:00 a.m. we open all the doors in the BC, hold hands, and sing at the top of our lungs. Most of the ladies usually get dressed up for this exercise and wear hats and gloves.

We understand that some people desire to use the BC as often as possible, but we realize that it does take some effort. The BC is not connected to the Deep Hole and rightfully so. The BC is family oriented but has a limited capacity, whereas the Deep Hole is used by thousands every day, but mostly in the summer months. The park staff is all excited about your visit, and a special sit-down dinner at the BC will be held in your honor. Except for you everyone has to bring their own pot. Well, we hope this answers most of your questions.

Sincerely yours,
Gotcha Butcher

When Queen Haftagow received the letter from Gotcha, she was so shocked and confused that she canceled her trip. The Russians had invited her to visit their country and promised that she would always be seated on a BC. She traveled throughout Russia by limousine, wheelchair, and wherever she went there was a BC to sit on. After her successful tour, the Russians moved in, took away her BC, and took control of the oil fields. This was the singular foreign policy blunder of all times, except for the stupid wars. The price of gasoline at the pump shot up to $13 a gallon in the Capital City. King Lettergow and Queen Haftagow were banished to Siberia where they were last seen cleaning bathroom commodes.

CHAPTER TWENTY-EIGHT

IT RINGS FOR ME BUT NOT FOR YOU

A tradition brought over from the European old country was the ringing of a bell to summon folks to assemble or, if necessary, sound an alarm. In 1751, the State House of the Province of Pennsylvania ordered a "bell of about 2,000 pounds weight." And they wanted an inscription imprinted on the outside from the Bible, the book of Leviticus 25:10: "Proclaim liberty throughout all the land unto all the inhabitants thereof." It is believed the phrase was chosen in commemoration of William Penn's Charter of Privileges.

A foundry in Whitecastle, London, owned by Thomas Messerup, was chosen as the maker of the bell. On delivery in August 1752, the state house bell, as it was called, actually weighed 2,080 pounds, was twelve feet in circumference, and constructed from 70 percent copper, 25 percent tin, and 5 percent of other metals. It was proved to be of poor workmanship. The first time they tried to ring the thing, the British bell cracked "by a stroke of the clapper without any other violence as it was hung up to try the sound." The sound was E-flat. And they even spelled the name of the province wrong—leaving out an *n*. The flawed work was recast by two Philadelphians Cass and Tow, and they put their names on the bell. It was then hung and rung in the steeple of the state house to summon legislators to the assembly.

No one could imagine how many times the bell would be recast, how many times it would be moved, and how many times it would be rung. Twenty-five years after the first thud, when the Philadelphians were alerted by a Massachusetts man who proclaimed, "Or give me death," and closer to home when the cry was "the British are coming," it broke again. The bell was taken down and hidden underneath a church in another part of town so the British couldn't use it to make a cannon or bullets or take it back to the king.

It was put back after the British threat had passed. Three years later it was removed from the rotting steeple and discarded in some dark corner of the tower. It had been whacked, cracked, recast, whacked again, recast, hidden, and now abandoned.

Tradition has it that it was cracked again when it was tolled during the funeral procession of the chief justice. An unsuccessful attempt was made to repair the crack. On February 22, 1846, it was rung in memory of the first president's birthday—more of a dong than a gong, and the crack began to spread.

This was the last hurrah, the last time a sound was heard from the "Bell of the Revolution." The crack measured a half inch wide and twenty-four and a half inches long. This bell would no longer ring a call to arms but took on a new meaning and a new role that was not recognized during the writing of the "Declaration of Independence," the Revolutionary War, and the presidential years when George and Martha lived in Philadelphia.

It is not known exactly when the historic relic assumed the changing role and the name "Liberty Bell" but the original inscription did read "Proclaim Liberty." The anti-slavery activists seized upon this forgotten inscription and published a pamphlet entitled "The Liberty Bell," and a picture of the bell was shown on the frontispiece with the message "Freedom to All the Inhabitants." Subsequent stories of the Liberty Bell were found in children's textbooks, such as Franklin's Fifth Grader, and in poems. The once-abandoned broken metal would forever lose the earlier epithets such as "Old Independence" and would be known as the Liberty Bell, as it became a national symbol of human liberty.

The old bell soon became a relic of veneration with stories about an old bell ringer waiting to ring it on July 4, 1776. The legend gained historical acceptance although it never rang on that date at all. In 1852, it was brought down from the tower, and two years later it was displayed on a massive pedestal with thirteen sides with festooned flags and an eagle on top. It would remain in this state for the next twenty-two years. With the celebration of the nation's centennial, it would relocate to a new site. It was moved again to the state house hallway and mounted on its old wooden frame, and an iron railing was placed around it. Again it was moved to near one of the front windows in the supreme court chamber and then suspended from the ceiling of the tower room held by thirteen chain links representing the thirteen original states. In 1885, the metallic symbol hit the road visiting New Orleans, the other southern states, Chicago, Charleston, Boston, and San Francisco. With all the rumbling, stopping, and starting, the crack became larger. When it returned to Philadelphia, it was placed in a large glass enclosed mahogany case and moved to the assembly room so viewers could read the inscription "Liberty."

Twenty years later in 1915, it was taken out of the glass case and exhibited on an open pedestal so all could caress it. And millions did touch it, and then for the two hundredth anniversary of the nation, it was dragged out of the building known as Independence Hall to the corner of Fifth and Market street. On April 6, 2001, it was banged by a religious zealot with a hammer shouting "God lives." The bell only weighs 2,055 pounds today having lost twenty-five pounds to chiselers chiseling off the inner lip. The move was made to give even more people more freedom to see and feel it. By the end of the year, increased security and overreaching by security drove people away.

"Move it" was the cry from the park visitors, and the federal Parks Department, who now administered the historic site, began plans to do just that. If the failed gong had stayed put, perhaps the issues would not have surfaced. But moving it for the umpteenth time drew criticism and protests from a group of African American scholars. It was where the bell would repose—on top of the site of a slave quarters—the home of George and Martha's household servants.

When the first president moved into the Executive Mansion in Philadelphia, he brought along eight slaves from Mount Vernon, who were known by those who were left behind as Chosen Few. The domestic help who cooked the dinners, washed the clothes, emptied the chamber pots, and did the bidding of the First Family may have been chosen, but they were still slaves. They worked as slaves, were treated as slaves, and acted like slaves. When they met other African Americans who were free, they could not understand why they were not free. They yearned for the right to be independent, to choose where to live, where to work, to freely and openly express their hearts and to be just human beings. The First Family's prized cook, Samson, and the mansion's chief maid, Mary Smudge, left, ran away, became fugitives, and gave up the honor of serving the president for something called Freedom. Both Samson and Mary Smudge were pursued, hunted down, and if caught would be brought back to face harsh punishment.

The father of our country could not understand why they chose to leave and wrote a friend, "What would they gain?" and blamed it all on the pesky Quakers who strongly opposed the Peculiar Institution.

If the property of the president could just walk away, what would those left behind say and do? What would it mean for other slave owners? Repeated attempts to capture Samson and Mary Smudge failed, and the former slaves were destined to die in freedom. This little-known but true story doesn't merit worldwide attention, but when you propose to place an international symbol, "Proclaim liberty throughout all the land unto all the inhabitants thereof," on top of their home, exclusivity takes on a new meaning. The liberty that rang from the bell did not include the Negro slaves, the Native Americans, or even women. This Philadelphia liberty bell sounded for the wealthy white male for the powerful white male. "It rings for me—not for you."

Now the federal government is planning to glorify liberty and freedom above the ground where African once lived and prayed to be free. Are they trying to hide the very existence of slavery? Some imminent Negro scholars think so. Dr. Freedomstone, the renowned professor of history and an authority on slavery in America, called the Parks Department and asked how they were going to interpret the site of the former Executive Mansion and environs, meaning the slave quarters of Samson and Mary Smudge. The response was there would not be any inclusion because it would distract from the central story of the Liberty Bell. "Say what," replied Dr. Freedomstone. He requested a meeting with the park superintendent to discuss why the story of Samson and Mary Smudge was being ignored. At the tête-à-tête, he informed the park superintendent of the full story of how the two slaves escaped and gained their freedom. Further, he asserted that placing the bell over the slave quarters site would bury the story forever. He explained the story was one of contradictions and injustice, where the Founding Fathers had proclaimed independence and freedom for themselves but denied it to others. Finally, he stated the heritage of the African Americans was being ignored by the federal government. The park spokesman, with orders from the headquarters, replied, "The plan had already been approved and there was neither time nor funding to make any changes. Sorry about that, Dr. Freedomstone."

In a follow up letter, the history professor accused the Parks Department of racism. He asked, Was the history of the Liberty Bell "It rings for me—not for you"? He informed the Parks Department through Congressman John Brown, who was on the Parks Department appropriation committee, that they demanded a final review before the plan became a reality. The Spoilers took over the problem, which was too explosive for the local park staff to handle.

SPOILER: Well, what's the issue with Dr. Freedomstone?

PARK SUPERINTENDENT: When he became aware that the bell was going to be moved to the site of the Executive Mansion, which was torn down about 150 years ago, he raised the question of racism and how we were distorting American history.

SPOILER: What's moving the thing to a new location got to do with racism?

PS: It raises the thorny question of freedom, liberty, independence for the rich white society but not for the poor slaves. The group that Dr. Freedomstone represents, maintains that placing the

Liberty Bell on top of the site of the former slave quarters is an overt attempt by the federal government to hide the fact that the first president was a slave owner.

SPOILER: What's the big deal, everybody knows that he was a slave owner.

PS: When he was president and living in the Executive Mansion, two of his household servants escaped, and he made every effort to track them down, offering a big reward for their capture.

SPOILER: I don't understand the problem. They were his property, right?

PS: Well, it's the contradiction. Liberty and freedom for the slave owners but not for the slaves. They want to know if that was the meaning of the 'Declaration of Independence' and the Revolutionary War.

Dr. Freedomstone points out the hypocrisy, the injustice of it all. They want the site of the slave quarters of Samson and Mary Smudge included in the Liberty Bell story.

SPOILER: Who the hell are Samson and Mary Smudge?

PS: They were the two household servants who escaped. They walked away from a privileged position, and I guess you could call them Run-A-Ways.

SPOILER: They are just creating a controversy over nothing. History is history, you can't change that fact. Times were different then, and now they are trying to besmirch our Founding Father and make him out to be evil. The Bible supported slavery. There has always been slavery. There is slavery even today. I'm not saying it's right. It simply was and is. Doesn't the Parks Department cover the slave problem at other historic sites?

PS: Yes, we do. But here it is a complex situation. You have a man who fought for independence and freedom from the tyrannical British government but then denied it to others. The question remains, "Why weren't the slaves included."

SPOILER: Well, this Dr. Freedomstone, history professor, he's just a revisionist, trying to rewrite American history. I'm tired of catering to these people. No matter what the situation they have to bring up slavery, discrimination, and how they have been wronged. They're just a bunch of troublemakers.

PS: They are determined and will not take no for an answer. We have to meet with them again with some kind of proposal. They have the city liberal newspapers, the mayor, the US congressman, and the National Association of African American colleges professors behind them.

SPOILER: This is a conservative country with a conservative administration with conservative values. We can't let them tear down the first president who fought to create the greatest country in the world. What did the slaves do to help us win our independence? Some of them even fought for the British.

PS: We have to give them something before this problem gets out of hand. I suggest that a small interpretive plaque outlining the Executive Mansion and the other buildings including the slave quarters. Don't think the visitors will be distracted by this, and it will take nothing away from the Liberty Bell.

SPOILER: Okay. That sounds reasonable to me. I'll let Gotcha know the game plan since he will represent us at the next meeting.

At the final conference to resolve the conflicting sound of the Liberty Bell were the superintendent, a Parks Department research historian, and Gotcha. Gotcha would be the spokesman for this side of the table. On the other protesting activist side were Dr. Freedomstone, Dr. Beaufort, president of the Negro Colleges of America, the mayor of Philadelphia, and the US congressman John Brown. The park superintendent had hoped to moderate the adversarial dialogue, but the first statement by Gotcha set the stage for open warfare.

GOTCHA: As a representative of the president of the United States, I am willing to work with you people if I can find out just what the hell it is you want.

DR. BEAUFORT: Well, the first thing is we don't intend to be intimidated by the president and especially your arrogant attitude.

We will tell you exactly what we are going to do whether you like it or not.

DR. FREEDOMSTONE: We demand that the presidential palace acknowledge that the Liberty Bell, during the Revolutionary War and the first president's term in office in Philadelphia, rang out for the rich and powerful but not for those who still suffered under slavery. The Founding Father had the influence and the power to end this cruelty but did not. We do not intend to tarnish his character, for he was a great man and the hero of the Revolutionary War. We are simply saying that he was a slave owner and could have freed his slaves but chose not to do so. Two of his household servants had to run away to gain their freedom.

> The president ordered that they be hunted down like some wild animal. He and his wife owned some three hundred slaves back in Virginia, and if these slaves learned about Samson and Mary Smudge, they too might try to run away. The president looked upon his slaves as property not individuals with a heart and a soul.

> Yes, we are well aware that his slaves were later freed but not when he was serving as president and living in the Executive Mansion in Philadelphia.

GOTCHA: Isn't the story of slavery adequately told at other historic sites?

DR. BEAUFORT: It can never be enough. It was a terrible, terrible evil to steal a person's freedom, their independence. You don't have the slightest idea how it feels to be a slave. It will forever be a stain on the pages of American history.

GOTCHA: I don't understand what you people are getting so upset about. The Negro has come a long way in this country—so what's the beef?

MAYOR: Did the president send the biggest bigot in the house to insult us today? There is still widespread discrimination against African Americans. But the issue before us in this room is that the first president had an opportunity to put an end to slavery and refused to give his slaves freedom.

GOTCHA: So you want to disparage the president and tell the Liberty Bell visitors that he was a hard-hearted man. Why do you want to destroy the historical image of our Founding Father?

Dr. Freedomstone: It is a fact that he owned slaves until the day he died. It is a fact that two of his slaves, privileged household servants, risked severe punishment to gain their freedom. This is a truth that cannot be denied and should be told because it happened right here where the Liberty Bell will be on display. Now we've been told that the exhibit plan has been approved and cannot be changed. The plan does not include our story, and you're telling us that there is nothing we can do about it.

CONGRESSMAN BROWN: I can assure you that the Parks Department will have the necessary funding to incorporate the changes that we demand. And I don't believe that there isn't time to modify the plan. The story of Samson and Mary Smudge will be told. Do you understand that, Gotcha?

GOTCHA: Okay, if you feel that strongly about it, we are willing to include a small plaque that marks the site of Executive Mansion environs, including the slave quarters.

CONGRESSMAN BROWN: Damn it. This is not what we want. A small plaque doesn't say anything about two slaves who had to escape to be free and who were hounded by your Founding Father. We demand that they be recognized for their courage and willingness to suffer further cruelty to be free.

GOTCHA: Well, I'm not going to argue about some little known footnote in history. I'm willing to put up a small plaque, but I'm not going to allow Samson and Mary Smudge to supersede the meaning of the Liberty Bell. People want to see and touch the bell and gain a feeling of pride and patriotism and not feel guilty about something that happened two hundred years ago.

The intensity over the significance of the Liberty Bell and its meaning was so compelling that no one gave any thought as to who owns the bell. Since the federal Parks Department assumed the role of caretaker, it was assumed that they owned it. One of the mayor's aides entered the room and handed him a note that was from a historian in the Parks Department. "Mr. Mayor, the people of Philadelphia own the Liberty Bell, not the federal government. Please act accordingly." It was signed "The Peyote Society." The mayor left and said he would return the following morning. The meeting ended at that point.

The next morning with all present, the mayor opened up with the following statement:

MAYOR: Well, you go back and tell the man in the egg-shaped office that the people of Philadelphia own the Liberty Bell and it's no longer on loan to you. I have the authority and funding from the City Council to build our own Liberty Bell Pavilion and Amphitheater. Every evening there will be a play about the escape and the lives of Samson and Mary Smudge. The play will end with "We will be free too, just like you." As of this moment, the Philadelphia Police Department have taken possession of the Liberty Bell, and we will proceed with our plans immediately. Any questions?

The presidential palace could not allow the city to take over a national if not an international symbol, so they agreed to the mayor's plan and would fund the entire project, including a statue of Samson and Mary Smudge. The Bell was moved in the early morning on a bell mobile, and no problems were anticipated since three dry runs were completed successfully. It was moved about a thousand feet, and hopefully this would be the last time.

Being an election year, the Great Uniter agreed to participate and was assured by his aide Carl Stove that it was a slam dunk and that nothing could possible go wrong. As the president was lowering the symbol of Freedom into place, the chain snapped, and the bell fell about twenty feet to the marble floor beneath. It broke in half, and the inner wall of the bell on one half was blue, and the other half was red. The Great Divider would be forever known as the president who dropped the...

CHAPTER TWENTY-NINE

THE BICENTENNIAL BUBBLE

One highly respected religious leader stated, "I look around this great land of the free in which we are living and find some definite signs of the decay that is beginning to occur. Corruption, crime, dishonesty, immorality, pollution, laziness, devotion only to special interests are signs that precede the fall. We see so much evidence of these signs before our eyes in the civilization in which we live. These have marked the downfall of mighty nations before us. This is the time for you to be bold enough to stand up for what you believe, to let the world know that God still blesses this great land of America—if we will live righteously according to that which he commanded. This message should ring from the hilltops to this nation during its bicentennial."

The year 1974 had not been a very good year, and 1975 was even worse. The Bicentennial Bash of 1976 would hopefully help the people forget and catapult an unelected president who had been an unelected vice president to an elected full four-year term as president. The Creep's bunglers had broken into the political headquarters of the opposing political party on June 17, 1972, and the subsequent cover-up, the abuse of power, and the arrogance of it all forced the now-powerless president to resign. And as he left, he exclaimed, "I am not a crook." He left in utter disgrace, and the nation's people became despondent and disenchanted.

The following year, on April 29, 1975, the United States Embassy employees slithered out of Saigon, and a needless, useless war was lost, and so was the nation. On January 19, 1976, the unelected and inept president proudly stated at his State of the Union Address:

> As we begin our bicentennial, America is still one of the youngest nations in recorded history. The genius of America has been the incredible ability to improve the lives of its citizens through a unique combination of government and free citizen activity. As you recall, the year 1975 opened with rancor and with bitterness. Political misdeeds of the past had neither been forgotten nor forgiven. The longest most divisive war in our history was winding down toward a tragic conclusion. Many feared that the end of that foreign war of men and machines meant the beginning of a domestic war of recrimination and reprisals.
>
> Friends and adversaries abroad were asking whether America had lost its nerve. Finally, our economy was ravaged by inflation—inflation that was plunging us into the worst recession in almost fifty years. At the same time, Americans became increasingly alienated from big institutions. They were steadily losing confidence not just in big government but in big business, big labor, and big education. Ours was a troubled land. But there is a hopeful future. How many times have we seen it? In 'God we trust.' Let us engrave it now in each of our hearts as we begin our bicentennial.

And again on July 4, 1976, at Independence Hall, the president tried to put a happy face on the country's doldrums. The bicentennial would be the magic pill to win back the hearts of the people and a home in the White House for four more years. The president exclaimed,

> I am filled with deep emotion at finding myself standing in the place where collected together the wisdom, the patriotism, the devotion to principle from which sprang the institutions under which we live. Today, we can all share these simple, noble sentiments. I feel both pride and humility, rejoicing and reverence as I stand in the place where two centuries ago the United States of America was conceived in liberty and dedicated to the proposition that all men are created equal. Before me is the great bronze bell that joyously rang out the news of the birth of our nation, ensconced with the biblical verse 'Proclaim liberty throughout all the land unto all the inhabitants thereof.' The Constitution was created to make the promise of the Declaration come true. The Declaration was not a protest against government but against the excesses of government. It is fitting that we ask ourselves hard questions even on a glorious day like today. Are the institutions under which we live working the way they should? Are the foundations laid in 1776 and 1789 still strong enough and sound enough to resist the tremors of our times? Are our God-given rights secure, our hard-won liberties protected? The world knows where we stand. The world is ever conscious of what Americans are doing for better or worse, because the United States today remains the most successful realization of humanity's hope. The world may or may not follow, but we lead because our whole history says we must. Liberty is for all men and women, as a matter of equal and inalienable right.

The president once remarked that he was a Ford, not a Lincoln. And he once lamented, "You know, the president of the United States is not a magician who can wave a wand, or sign a paper that will instantly end a war, cure a recession, or make a bureaucracy disappear." Two nongovernment programs that did not disappear were the Freedom Train and the Tall Ships.

Just about every city, town, and village in America celebrated the bicentennial with local color and local flavor. But the one commemoration that was truly national and privately created and funded was the American Freedom Train. It was the brain child of a New York City stockbroker who was a locomotive buff. With support and funding from the private sector, the Freedom Train was the biggest, most patriotic, and most popular nationwide event of the twentieth century. It was powered by three newly restored steam engines, and it traveled 25,000 miles. The red, white, and blue train of twenty-six cars began in Wilmington, Delaware, and eighteen months later became more than a footnote in American history ending in Miami, Florida, on December 31, 1976. The Freedom Train traveled through forty-eight states to cities large and small. It would ensure a memory of our history and culture to those who did not or could not make the pilgrimage to the historic shrines of Philadelphia and Washington DC. The train displayed over five hundred artifacts and items of memorabilia—the original Louisiana Purchase, Jack Benny's violin, a moon rock, John F. Kennedy's rocking chair, Jesse Owens's gold Olympic medals, and George Washington's copy of the US Constitution. Seven million passionate patriots boarded the Freedom Train to view the exhibits.

Over forty million saw the Bicentennial Freedom Train pass by, and they cheered and cheered.

And then there were the Tall Ships. On the first day the young kids standing in line yelled, "Here come the Tall Ships. Here come the Tall Ships." Of all the bicentennial celebrations on July 4, 1976, none captured the attention of Americans like the Tall Ships. It was a hot and hazy day in New York City, where thousands were watching from the windows of tall buildings and even more lined the harbor to witness the incredible sight. The sixteen Tall Ships, full rigged, three-masted, each over a football field long came to New York from all over the world—Japan, Portugal, Norway, Poland, Italy, Denmark, Russia, Colombia, Spain, Germany, Chile, Romania, Argentina to name a few. They all belonged to the American Sail Training Association and were organized and directed by "Operation Sail." It was a nonprofit organization with the goal of promoting goodwill and cooperation among countries while providing training and celebrating its history. They docked near the Statue of Liberty for over a week. The city had its traditional picnics, parades, parties, fireworks, but nothing as spectacular as the parade of Tall Ships.

Those who saw and photographed the event say it was mesmerizing. It cast a spell over the daily life of the New Yorkers as the city forgot about the crowds and traffic.

All the presidents have used the national parks and monuments—especially Yellowstone, Yosemite, Grand Canyon, Independence Hall, and the Statue of Liberty as scenic and historic backdrops for political photo ops. In the 1976 presidential election, they were simply overused soap boxes used by the incumbent to bark "This is what I'm going to do for you" campaign. Although the parks and monuments were rapidly deteriorating from overuse and a lack of funding, bicentennial money would be available for the parks to celebrate. The bicentennial programs, activities, and special events would ensure that the visitors would be aware that it was not only the bicentennial year but also a presidential year. The Parks people were to weave in the bicentennial story with the park story. This was a major challenge for the geologists, biologists, botanists, and wildlife naturalists in the natural history parks. So bicentennial special events were developed without the required weaving.

The park managers could not understand why so much money was being wasted on the bicentennial while basic maintenance and visitor services were being neglected. The salient question was, What is a bicentennial program? A better question was how the funds could be used for essential park needs.

Gotcha Butcher issued a list of what were considered legitimate bicentennial expenditures:

WES WOLFE

Gotcha's Guidelines for Allocating Bicentennial Monies in National Parks and Monuments
Goods, Items, Services, and Activities Allowed

Firecrackers, red, white, and blue bunting; red, white, and blue paint (to be used only for painting mailboxes, fire hydrants, etc.); hot dogs, mustard, ketchup (not considered a vegetable), onions, hot dog buns, beer (cans only); American flag napkins; red, white, and blue toothpicks; RWB balloons; plastic forks, knives, spoons; small American flags, large American flags; sparklers; public address systems (to be used only for bicentennial programs and activities); trash barrels (to be used only for bicentennial produced trash); posters, flyers; bicentennial tricolored flags, flag poles, flag pole diggers; cement; potato salad; RWB pencils, pens; writing paper and envelopes; trash can liners; mother's apple pie; Roman candles; bicentennial toys; noise makers; potato chips; bugles, drums; parking permits, stickers; RWB toilet paper, soap, paper towels; shovels, brooms, dust pans; ribbons; mops, garbage bags; cookies, cakes, cans of pop; bumper stickers; bells, whistles; crayons, blackboards; bicentennial T-shirts, hats, umbrellas; and shovels. Overtime is authorized only for bicentennial activities.

Goods, Items, Services, and Activities Not Allowed

Fixing or repairing leaky roofs, pot holes, repairing roads and parking lots, stripping roads and parking spaces, grass mowing, repairing park picnic benches; fixing old, rusty, and damaged plumbing including toilets, urinals, basins, etc.; no painting of public buildings or employee housing, updating old electrical systems; no campground maintenance; no restoration or rehabilitation of historic structures or damaged and deteriorating fences and gates, snowmobiles, speed bumps, backed-up sewer systems; guns; flashlights, flashlight batteries; coffeepots; bullets for park ranger guns; toilets, toilet tops, toilet covers; hot water heaters; carpet replacement; replacing old ice boxes; black government ball point pens; automobile and truck tires; oil filters, cans of oil; light bulbs, florescent light bulbs;

210

sand, roof shingles; poaching patrols; chimney cleaning, snow shovels; window screens; water bills, heating bills, electric bills; repainting park signs; corralling black bears; window cleaning, polishing floors, Venetian blinds; fighting forest fires unless started by a bicentennial firecracker and stuff like that.

Guidelines from Cool-Head Fred on How to Get Badly Needed Work Done with Bicentennial Money

1. Take their money and run.
2. Don't let the right hand (the Spoilers) know what the left hand (you) are doing.
3. Double bookkeeping. One for you and one for them.
4. How to expense your projects:

    a. Fix the leaky roofs (bicentennial umbrellas)
    b. Fill in the potholes (bicentennial porta potties)
    c. Repair fences (bicentennial barricades)
    d. Fix eroding electrical systems (bicentennial firecrackers)
    e. Buy lights bulbs (bicentennial firecrackers)
    f. Buy toilet paper (RWB napkins)
    g. Corral black bears (Beer in cans)
    h. Bullets (bicentennial fire hydrants)
    i. Gasoline (RWB paint)
    j. Truck and car tires (RWB bunting)
    k. Be innovative

The bicentennial came and went, and the American people celebrated, and those who visited the national parks and monuments were surprised and happy with the improved facilities and maintenance upgrades. In November the incumbent selected president lost to a peanut farmer from Georgia.

CHAPTER THIRTY

DOUBLE-DIPPIN' DAN

The eighteenth century in Europe was highlighted by off and on battles between England and France for dominance and control of the American colonies. The climax was the French and Indian War, which was won by the British. To help pay off the large debt that England had amassed, King George and his parliament felt it was only fitting that the colonies lend a helping hand—if not an arm and a leg. They issued a bunch of Acts, as they were called then, Stamp, Declaratory, and Townsend to extract the money from the colonists and keep the country bumpkins in line. The colonists refused to buckle under and raised holy hell with the Brits. Big brother backed down, rescinded the taxes, but let the upstarts know they were still under the thumb of the King.

The relationship between poppa and son mellowed for a while because economic conditions improved for both. But when England decided to enforce rigidly the tax on tea, some rebellious zealots, disguised as Indians, boarded some British vessels in the Boston Harbor and dumped three hundred and forty-two chests of tea into the sea. The king retaliated, sending more ships and troops and closed the Boston Port. After the shedding of blood on both sides at Concord and Lexington, April 1775, the local hotheads were thirsty for more English blood. A silversmith raced his horse through the countryside letting everyone know what was happening. He screamed the alarm, "The British are coming!" "The British are coming!"

The American Revolutionary War was on but not supported by all the Colonists. The Tories, mostly Scotsmen, mostly Southern, somewhat loyal to the King, helped the British, and lost all. But there was another George from Mount Vernon who defied King George. He was not necessarily a military genius, but he was the spirit that the Colonists rallied around. Early on the British were forced out of Boston and repulsed in Charleston. But they rebounded and captured New York City but then were defeated at the Battle of Saratoga in October 1777. The Continentals cheered and danced, and the band played "Yankee Doodle." Historians agree that Saratoga was the turning point of the war because France jumped in and supported the Bumpkins.

And then the Battle of Monmouth was won—then lost—a draw they both said. It was at Monmouth that a lady carried water to the battlefield, and the troops cried out for Molly Pitcher. And in the south, the English Navy captured the ports of Savannah and Charleston. And George pulled his men through the Valley Forge. Daniel Morgan was victorious at Cowpens, and a bunch of back water mongrels won at King's Mountain, and Francis Marion, the Swamp Fox, gave guerilla warfare a new name, and "I have just begun to fight." John Paul Jones said that, and the "Declaration of Independence" was assured at a place called Forktown.

Because of the threats elsewhere in the world and its vast commercial interests, England diverted much of its military away from the campaign in Colonial America. This undercut the strategy of General Tomwallis who moved out of Charleston through the Carolinas to secure the ports in Virginia. He was unaware that Count de Brasse, admiral of the French fleet of twenty-eight ships, had sealed off the Chesapeake Bay and added three thousand French soldiers to the Colonial forces. Tomwallis took the tiny hamlet of Forktown on August 1, 1781, and immediately began building defenses as one soldier remembered: "Nothing but hard labor goes on here at present in constructing and making batteries toward the river and redoubts [earthen mounds] toward the land." When the siege began on September 28, the strength of the mixed Continental Force was about eight thousand troops under our George and the

Frenchman Rochabow, and another four thousand under General Laughanet. The British numbered a total of 7,500. Tomwallis had to abandon his outer defenses, and the Colonial net around Forktown tightened. The bombardment on the British was relentless.

Badly needed reinforcements from the larger army in the north never arrived. Outnumbered, surrendered on all sides, the British surrender was inevitable. A British drummer boy beat the drum for a parley, and an officer stood on the parapet waving a white cloth. An American soldier remarked that "never heard a drum equal to it—the most delightful music to us all." A courier carried the note from Tomwallis to the American commander: "I propose a cessation of hostilities for twenty-four hours and that two officers may be appointed by each side to meet at Mr. Moore's house to settle the terms for the surrender." It was October 17, 1781. The terms were the troops, seamen, and marines would lay down their arms and would become prisoners of war. The officers would be allowed to retain their sidearms and private property.

The British troops in new uniforms marched down Surrender Road between the American and French soldiers to the Surrender Field to the tune of "The World Turned Upside Down." Tomwallis was ill and sent General Charles O'Mara to tender the traditional sword to the victors. It was a ceremonial gesture, and the sword was returned to O'Mara. It had been a French victory, and France felt vindicated after having lost the French-Indian War. A new nation was born—the United States of America.

After the surrender of Tornwallis, the tobacco port of Forktown faded into history. Much of the town had been destroyed by the siege and bombardment, trade had diminished, and town folks just moved away.

In 1814, a fire swept through the waterfront and destroyed the courthouse on Main Street. During the American Civil War, it was occupied by the South and the North, and it served as a base for the Federal Army of the Potomac during the Peninsular Campaign.

Forktown National Cemetery was established on July 13, 1866, and placed under the War Department. In 1880, the Congress stated, "The surrender at Forktown was the crowning success of the

Revolution, and this event should be commemorated by a national authority." The following year the centennial celebration of Forktown once again gave the hamlet national attention. Relatives and descendants of those who had fought there from around the world attended the festivities.

In 1930, Forktown was made a national monument and added to the National Park System. A spokesman for the president stated, "To declare independence is one thing, to achieve it is another. Here it was actually achieved. The victory at Forktown gave us the independence which American Patriots boldly proclaimed to the world."

For two young historians the research of Forktown Battlefield was much more than a fertile field. They had to establish guidelines for their research undertakings, and their findings and results would be the basis for everything that would follow. They wrote, "If no other activity were ever contemplated or attempted, our first obligation in accepting custody of an historic site is preservation."

The research was pursued during the Depression years, and little money was available for land acquisition, restoration of original structures, and visitor services. But their research would support all future development of the national monument. The historians further stated, "The first and fundamental step in organizing the research is comprehensive, thoroughness, and accuracy." They would document the siege and bombardment of Forktown using primary sources from British, American, French, and German archives. They detailed the strategy and tactics of the historical movements, battle lines, the locations of cannon and earthworks, and the headquarters of both commanders. They would determine the physical resources that were present in October 1781 such as buildings, homes, barns, fences, businesses, and roads.

The archeological excavations following the historical documentation uncovered the foundations of historic structures, period artifacts, whole and in part, were unearthed—china, mostly broken, utensils, tin cups, metal door knobs, buttons, pistols, rifles, rifle fragments, bullets, bayonets, cannon balls, and the remains of a British Fusilier with an intact diary in his knapsack. The archeologist turned over the diary to historian Dan Butterfield, who was also the acting superintendent. The personal writings in the diary of this British officer were explosive. He attacked the blind foreign policy of King George III and the incompetence of the British generals in the colonies. Dan quietly informed the Parks Department in the Capital City of the nature of the discovery. England was fighting for its life in Europe, and the United States was on the verge of jumping into something that would be known as World War II. The word came back to Dan Butterfield: "Rebury the body, burn the diary, and do it now. Do not under any circumstances let the newspapers learn of this finding." Dan thought, *Rebury the body—okay—that's respectful, sensible, the only decent thing to do. But burn the diary, burn the original writings of a British participant in the Battle of Forktown. Burn an eyewitness account, burn knowledge, burn a significant primary source.* To a historian this was blasphemous—even evil. Dan Butterfield may have been the acting superintendent, but in his heart he was a professional historian.

Soon after Pearl Harbor, Dan volunteered for service in the United States Army and served in England as an intelligence officer. While on leave in London, he continued his historical research of the Revolutionary War—from the British point of view. His findings only confirmed what the young English officer had written 162 years before. The King and his Parliament were in disarray, and the statesmanship of the Foreign Office was vacuous and reckless. He concluded that the British generals sent to fight for the King's interests were mostly political generals, favorites of the King's Court, and lacking any military acumen or experience. After World War II, Dan returned to the Parks Department and was named the new superintendent of Poor's Creek National Monument, a recently established Revolutionary War battlefield.

Since the war was over and the relationship between the two countries was less politically sensitive, Dan decided to conclude his research and publish his work. He was well aware of the hazards and what it might mean to his career with the Parks Department. But to Dan, it would be intellectually dishonest not to make the results of his research known. His scholarly research was published in the

Historical Federation of International Revolutionary Wars whose motto was "Seek the truth come where it may, cost what it will."

The article was subsequently picked up by leading liberal newspapers and magazines. The truth was finally out and the Capital City Spoilers were furious about this act of disloyalty. Dan and Poor's Creek would pay the price. For Dan it was a career ender—no transfers, no further management training, no promotions, no considerations, no forgiveness—only isolation. He could just sit and rot until his retirement. For Poor's Creek it meant no increase in the staff, no development, no new visitor center, no nothing. Not only would Dan suffer but little Poor's Creek and the visitors would endure the Spoiler's revenge.

There was no longer any challenge for Dan at Poor's Creek. The part-time secretary was his sister-in-law, and the only maintenance worker was a Purple Heart recipient of World War II. There was not much to do with poor Poor's Creek being neglected and Dan became totally bored. He could easily handle the endless, needless paperwork in less than an hour a day. So what to do?

Dan's wife was a student counselor at the nearby Presbyterian Junior College. Dan decided to volunteer once a week in the evenings and teach a course on the American Revolutionary War. It was so popular that he was asked to teach it three times a week during the day. At first Dan would take annual leave and then sick leave to support his absences from the monument when he was teaching. He was well liked and respected both at the college and in the community, and the president of the college asked him to teach there full-time. So Dan became a full-time history professor and just forget about the annual and sick leave requests.

The junior college became a four-year college, and Dan became head of the History Department. No annual or sick leave requests had been submitted in years. When the president of the college died, Dan was named as the new college president. For the next seventeen years, he continued as superintendent of Poor's Creek National Monument and as president of Calvin College. When he retired from both the college and the Parks Department, he became a folk hero to members of the Peyote Society. He was forever known as "Double-Dippin' Dan."

CHAPTER THIRTY-ONE

HOT SPRINGS HIGH

A hot spring is formed when rainfall pours down a mountaintop. The rainwater drips down through layers of sandstone and rocks deep, deep below the earth's surface. As the water moves, it picks up minerals from the hot rocks and is heated in return. The extremely hot water forces its way upward through the fissures and cracks and then explodes through the surface as a 143-degree hot spring. The spring water is tasteless, odorless, and can be drank hot or cold. Some people craved the hot springs for its alleged medicinal healing qualities, others for the spiritual values.

Long before Desoto's yearn for the Fountain of Youth, the Mantoken Indians bathed in the precious spring waters. Other First Americans came to Hot Springs High to sing, dance, pray, and always to soak in the magical waters. They were one with the Valley of Vapors of the Great Spirit as they called it. They could not understand why the newly arrived European settlers wanted to take it away from them. The Mantoken wanted only to be left alone with the spiritual hot springs. The white intruders built a road, put up a tent, put the water in big wooden boxes, and then took money from other pale faces who sat in the hot water boxes. Other whites came and gave them God books and took the water away in bottles. Then the government came and said all the Hot Springs High waters belonged to them. And more people came and tried to take all the spirit waters.

But they never found the Mantoken yellow-walled cave—only the Mantoken know the yellow-walled cave.

The Hot Springs High became part of the Continental United States in the Louisiana land grab of 1803. Adventurous settlers moved into the region in the early nineteenth century, and by the end of the American Civil War, a small town had emerged with wooden bathhouses, boarding houses, hotels, and a general store.

Eastern medical doctors advised that the healing hot mineral waters could cure rheumatism. Although the Hot Springs High had been set aside as a federal preserve, the entrepreneurs had another eureka. They built a railroad to get the health seekers there and huge and long wooden troughs to bring the water to them. Soon, big elegant bathhouses of brick and stone, a theater, a racetrack, gambling halls, brothels, and lots of hot mineral water awaited the adventurous. A rough frontier cesspool was soon transformed into an elegant Spa City by the early twentieth century. The elaborate Hot Spring High Bathhouses, the most spectacular of the eight Grand Hotels on Bathhouse Row, was built in the Spanish Renaissance Revival style of marble, brick, and sandstone with terracotta detailing and aquatic statues. The inside lobby and staircase were of pink marble, walls of veined Italian marble, and mosaic-tiled flooring. Cherub fountains anchored both ends of the lobby and cast in bronze a huge plaque which read, "May health and happiness accompany you all the days of your life." The bathing rooms had porcelain tubs and nickel fixtures. Men and women wrapped in toga-style robes drank hot mineral water as they waited for the healing experience. Attendants guided the patients through hydrotherapy even electric therapy. Chiropodists treated corns, bunions, and ingrown toenails. The Scotch Douche relaxed muscles and stimulated blood circulation. They even offered an electric massaging machine to contract and relax the human body. It was questionable experimental doctoring before the advent of cortisone, sulfa drugs, and penicillin.

For the first thirty-two years of the twentieth century, medical doctors from the US Public Health Service administered the Hot Springs High Federal Reservation. It became a national park on March 4, 1921, but the first Parks Department superintendent was not appointed until 1932, one hundred years after it became a federal reservation. Actually, it was the only national park set aside for exploitation, not preservation. It was for use not to observe and enjoy the natural resources but to drink and bathe in the resource. Health seekers from around the world came to Hot Springs High for treatment of rheumatism and other ailments. Today, the national park includes eight of the historic bathhouses, including the luxurious Hot Spring High Bathhouse, which serves as the Park Visitor Center. About forty-seven hot springs and their watersheds are now preserved and protected. Interest in the hot springs for treatment for anything has diminished in recent years, and there is only one bathhouse operating on Bathhouse Row. The park needed something to validate and rejuvenate its questionable status as a national park.

Strategy Meeting between Gotcha Butcher, the park superintendent, and a consulting anthropologist.

GOTCHA: Well, I guess you know why I'm here?

SUPERINTENDENT BILL BENNE : Not exactly.

GOTCHA: The local businesses in the Hot Springs High area—the motels, restaurants, gas stations, gift shops are hurting because of the drop-off in the tourists trade. And with an election coming up we need something to boost their spirits and their pocket books. We're facing a native son, you know. So Hot Springs High has to reinvent itself.

BILL: Well, I'm apolitical, Gotcha. I don't see how that is a concern of the Parks Department. My job description doesn't say anything about supporting local businesses. It's true that our visitation is down, but those who do visit the Hot Springs High enjoy the experience. Medical science today realizes that the hot springs may have helped patients feel better temporarily, but it was no cure. The Advisory Board on National Parks and Monuments even question its status as a national park.

GOTCHA: That's not what I want to hear. I'm not talking about rheumatism or some misinformed advisory board. It's gold that's going to turn this town around. There is gold 'in them their hills, ha, ha, ha.' I'm going to let Dr. Feelgolden here explain it all to you. He is a renowned anthropologist who has studied the history and legends of the Mantoken and has come to the conclusion—I'll let him tell you about it.

DR. FEELGOLDEN: Thank you, Mr. Butcher. My studies revealed that somewhere in the park there is a prehistoric cave that no white man has ever seen. The Mantoken in their songs and prayers revered a place called the 'Yellow-Walled Cave.' There is strong evidence to support the premise that they are talking about gold. Earlier geological surveys found gold flakes in the High Spring High Creek. I'd bet my professional reputation on it. And a Mantoken who has seen it will take us there.

GOTCHA: Can you image what the impact on finding gold would have on this town? It would create thousands of jobs, and since Hot Springs was established 'for public use,' there is no legal problem getting it out.

BILL: You aren't serious about this?

GOTCHA: Absolutely. Tomorrow morning the Mantoken, Howard Goldeneye, is going to take us there.

The four men climbed up the High Springs Mountain with Goldeneye leading the way. He took them to the other side of the mountain, but it was still within the park boundary.

GOLDENEYE: Just around the switchback trail, beneath the big boulder, is the Yellow-Walled Cave.

Howard Goldeneye entered the Yellow-Walled Cave first, followed by the park superintendent, Gotcha, and Dr. Feelgolden.

GOTCHA: Wow, there it is just like he said.

GOLDENEYE: Yep, just like I told you.

BILL: It doesn't look like gold to me.

GOLDENEYE: Who said anything about gold. It's sulfur dripping down the walls. Didn't you know that?

BILL: Oh yeah I knew it but I wanted Gocha to hear it from you.

POOR LITTLE CHRISTMAS TREE

The genesis of the Christmas Tree is not known for certain. It is believed that the earliest tradition was not related to the birth of Jesus Christ. Germany is credited with the creation and the longstanding custom associated with bringing a live evergreen into the home. The tree has been revered as a symbol of fertility. For centuries Historians agree that the first Christmas tree appeared in 1521 in Alsace, which was at that time part of Germany. Most of the very early trees were small—less than three feet tall. These table toppers were often decorated with gingerbread, pretzels, candy, raisins, and fruit. So popular was the custom of bringing freshly cut trees into the house to decorate that an ordinance was passed to prevent a household from having more than one tree. The term "Christmas tree" did not come into common usage until the 1830s history records that the German mercenaries, the Hessians, who fought on the side of the British during the Revolutionary War, were the first to bring an Evergreen into the homes in America. There is some evidence that the tradition began with the German Moravian community in Bethlehem, Pennsylvania, in 1747. Ironically, the first settlers in England were Puritans, and they forbade the practice considering it to be sinful because it was not found in the Bible. Williamsburg, Virginia, lays claim to the first decorated tree in America.

Christmas trees have been sold commercially in America since about 1850. In 1856, Franklin Pierce, the fourteenth president, was the first to place a Christmas tree in the White House. The biggest innovation that was a boon to large Douglas fir and Scottish pine trees was the invention and patent of the Christmas tree stand, which became widespread in the early twentieth century. Christmas tree lights strings were displayed on department store Christmas trees to attract customers. A thirty-three-limb artificial tree could be ordered from Sears, Roebuck and Co., for five dollars.

No one contributed more to the Christmas tradition and the Christmas tree than Charles Dickens, the nineteenth-century English novelist. His biographer wrote that Dickens almost singlehand-edly created the modern idea of Christmas. His Christmas stories, including Ebenezer Scrooge and the Christmas Carol highlighted Christmas and the Christmas tree, which he described as "that pretty German toy."

The president of the United States had put in question the separation of church and state with the celebration of a national Christmas tree in 1923. A letter was received at the presidential palace from a Lucretia Wardy representing the public school children of the Capital City. It was a proposal which read, "It seems that the use of the White House grounds for the Christmas tree will give the sentiment and the exercises a national character." The First Lady, Grace Foolidge, passionately supported the efforts of the young students to place a Christmas tree on the Ellipse of her temporary home. The forty-eight-foot balsam fir was chopped down from the forests of the president's birthplace and donated to the people of the United States, from the people of Vermont. The project had the endorsement of the state's congressional delegation and the students of Middletown College, who actually cut down the tree. The lighting would be contributed by the Society for Electrical Development of New York City.

At 5:00 p.m. on Christmas Eve 1923, the president's finger transformed a beautiful living fir into a garish array of 2,500 red, white, and green lights shaped like a tall Vermont evergreen. The lighting of the tree was accompanied by the Epiphany Church carol-ers, the all-male US Marine Corps quartet, and the US Marine Corps Band that presented a one-hour concert of Christian and military music. There is no official record of the number of on-site viewers who attended the Christmas pageantry, but it was believed that over five thousand crowded onto the presidential palace grounds. It was a first and the beginning of a national tradition that electrified millions of viewers worldwide over the next seventy-five years. It was not without controversy and protesting that arose from non-Christian groups and committed environmentalists.

For years an Evergreen tree was ripped up from the Earth in some forest, somewhere in America and dragged to Washington DC. It was then jammed into a fertilized wet hole in the ground for the Pageant of Peace Lighting Ceremony. Some non-Christians and activists groups railed against calling it a "Christmas tree," demanding that it be named a "Holiday tree." The battle still rages, but probably most people still call it a Christmas tree.

The other argument came from the environmentalists who asked, "Why do we desecrate a living tree and flaunt it on the White House grounds, since it signals a 'we don't give a damn about conservation'?" The movement for Stop the Killing grew slowly, focusing on the Christmas Tree Lighting Ceremony. It grew as thousands of letters from individuals, and organized conservation groups protested the annual demise of a beautiful, living spruce or fir tree, maintaining that it sent a poor example to the world.

If concerned environmentalists cannot stop it, who can? Since the tree was planted outside on the site of the White House grounds, a potted live tree could be permanently planted into Mother Earth and be relighted year after year. This would send the good tidings that conservation was alive and well. Would this ever become a reality?

On Christmas eve in the nation's capital, a strong wind was blowing, and the forty-five-foot evergreen began to rock back and forth, shaking some of the garlands, candles, bulbs, and balls, a few falling to the ground. As the president reached forward to brighten the Pageant of Peace, the huge Christmas tree toppled over and came crushing to the ground. It was a terrible surprise for all who were present and the millions watching on television. An investigation revealed that the tree had been planted in mud and someone made sure it remained in mud. The following year, when the vice president substituted for the president, the tree exploded and turned black.

No one could figure out exactly what happened. The Spoilers finally caved in, and the next year a live forty-two-foot fir from nearby Maryland was permanently planted by two unknown members of the Peyote Society.

There is yet another Christmas tree, the one in the presidential palace, that drew the attention of the environmentalists. The twenty-sixth president of the United States refused to allow a cut tree in the White House. If this example set by Teddy Bear had been honored, the conservation of our national resources would be a shining beacon rather than a dim light. His message to the nation was that it wasn't necessary to kill a tree to celebrate the Christmas season. Those who followed him into the White House turned their backs on his proactive stance toward conservation. They continued to display a large cut-down tree—sometimes fir, sometimes spruce trees from North Carolina, Oregon, Michigan, New York, Pennsylvania, and Colorado—trees that were thrown in the garbage when the holidays were over. It was not until the 1960s that conservation activism began to seriously sound the alarm against displaying "deadwood" trees at Christmas time. They implored the First Lady and the White House Spoilers to display a "Designer Everlasting" in place of uprooting evergreens every year.

The environmentalists case against cutting down forty million live trees annually and discarding them like leftovers in the refrigerator were the following:

1. The time, cost, and effort in procuring an evergreen. The average family drives to at least three Christmas tree sales locations before deciding on which perfect tree to buy. They then jam the seven-foot-by-four-foot acquisition into a space three feet by three feet like a car trunk, smashing branches and losing hundreds of needles. And then they waste more time and gasoline driving home where they bend and break more branches, pulling the thing the wrong way out of the hole. They drag the evergreen through the house trying to decide where to set it up, if they can find the Christmas tree stand. Once the tree is somewhat sturdy,

six or more strands of lights are wrapped up and down and around. When the light switch is flipped on, it is discovered that between twelve and seventeen bulbs are burned out. Another trip to town and more wasted gasoline and time. And on return they find out that they forgot the tinsel. So another trip and more gasoline and more time.

2. When the super-giant evergreen is finally and fully decorated, they sweep up the fallen needles and broken bulbs from the carpet. Then a gallon of water is slopped into the Christmas tree stand receptacle. This would normally keep the "deadwood" from serious deterioration, but they forget to cut a half inch of tree trunk off the base of the tree so it will suck up the needed moisture to stay green As the tree continues to wilt, they add five more packages of tinsel and three more strings of lights, which will require another gasoline trek.

3. The average cost of a spruce or fir is $90 plus another $150 for lights, tree stand, decorative balls and tinsel.

4. The total amount of time spent in travel, hassling the price, buying the accessories, setting it up, taking it down, repacking the lights, balls, and tree stand is five hours.

5. It takes a Christmas tree farmer about seven years to bring an evergreen to harvest. The seedlings have to be planted, fertilized, watered, sometimes artificially colored, sprayed with pesticides, chopped down, tied, and shipped to the retail outlets.

6. Only about half of all the planted seedlings will become Christmas trees for sale. The other half will simply rot.

7. The steel Christmas tree stand, used tinsel, broken light bulbs, and decorative ornaments are not biodegradable and will lie in a landfill for a long, long, time. How many homes have burned down during the holiday season because of a malfunction in the Christmas tree lights?

8. It's all so messy and unnecessary.

9. And when the New Year arrives and the Christmas tree folks get around to removing the deadwood tree, they discard it

at the end of the driveway for the trash man to pick up for an extra $5. The once-beautiful spruce is now brown, needleless, ugly, broken, and useless. The emotional impact on the little children who once delighted in the lighted and decorated Christmas tree was devastating.

Just two weeks before they had sung:

> O Christmas Tree, O Christmas Tree
> Thy beauty leaves thee never;
> O Christmas Tree, O Christmas Tree
> Much pleasure doth thou bring me;
> O Christmas Tree, O Christmas Tree
> Brings to us both joy and glee.

And on that day seeing the decaying remains in the street:

> O Christmas Tree, O Christmas Tree
> O why have thee abandoned me
> O Christmas Tree, O Christmas Tree
> O why are you doing this to me;
> O Christmas Tree, O Christmas Tree
> I never knew you would ever die;
> O Christmas Tree, O Christmas Tree
> To see you now only makes me cry.

Ten Arguments for a Designer Everlasting Tree:

1. No mess, no fuss, no water, no dead needles, no travel, no gasoline, no wasted time.
2. Cost per year - under $3. Unlimited warranty.
3. So easy to set up, take down, and store. A family heirloom passed on from one generation to the next.
4. Always a perfect shape; always there ready for you.
5. Always maintenance-free and beautiful.

6.   The Designer Everlasting tree has a scent superior to any deadwood fir or spruce.
7.   Today, over 50 percent of those families who display a Christmas tree in their homes use a Designer Everlasting Tree.
8.   Not joining the brainless minority who buy a processed Christmas tree, killed in some distant forest, every year and then heaved next to the trash cans.
9.   The satisfaction of being conservation minded and will never have to chop down a tree again.
10. The Everlasting Christmas Tree is safe, safe, safe.

Following in the footsteps of the great conservationist president, the First Lady opted for a Designer Everlasting Christmas Tree against the White House Spoilers, who supported the dying deadwood tree industry. The environmentalist had won the day.

CHAPTER THIRTY-THREE

THE PUREBULLION ACT

Charlie Gitty suffered from child abuse being routinely beaten by a religious zealot of a father. He ran away from home at an early age, and with an inheritance from his grandfather, he pushed his way into the legal profession. Failing to make a name for himself as a lawyer, he became an evangelist and failed again. Small in stature and physically unattractive, he became a member of the Umada Society, which practiced free love. Throughout his life, he demonstrated a history of mental illness, and his behavior was considered by even his friends as irrational and often bizarre. Gitty turned to politics and became an unwanted campaign supporter for James Abram Barfield for president. The Republican Party considered him a nuisance, if not a nutcase.

Gitty firmly believed that he was responsible for Barfield being elected and demanded a political appointment, specifically the ambassador to France. After being rebuffed by the secretary of State, Gitty procured a British "Bulldog" silver handle .44 revolver. (He believed that eventually the weapon would be placed on display in a national museum, and surprisingly he was right), and on July 2, 1881, in the Baltimore and Potomac train depot in the Capital City, he shot President Barfield twice, once in the back. The president lingered on for two months and eventually died on September 19.

Gitty claimed that "the Lord made me do it." The subsequent trial was one of the most celebrated "insanity defense" trials in history. Professionals in the medical community believed him to be insane and that the case against him was a serious miscarriage of justice. Just before they put his head in a noose and let him drop into eternity on June 30, 1883, he recited a poem to the gallows attendees entitled, "I am going to the Lordy."

President Barfield left an undistinguished record as the nation's chief executive mainly because he only served in office for several months. His singular legacy was to be highlighted as a martyr for government reform and the creation of the Civil Service Commission.

The federal government after the American Civil War and especially during the Reconstruction period was an example of pure political patronage. President Ulysses S. Grunt rewarded his supporters like no one else before. The inevitable turnover of government employees with each political election resulted in little continuity and gross inefficiency in the daily operation of government service, even the delivery of mail.

Government employees panicked at election time and demonstrated little commitment to their daily duties. National office seekers, especially those desiring the White House, require their supporters to devote considerable time and money to their political campaigns. After the successful candidate takes office, the loyal party workers expect and even demand that they be rewarded with high-paying government positions. Patronage was the political practice of the day, and both political parties indulged in it. A Capital City newspaper advertisement typical of the times was "Wanted a government clerkship at a salary of not less than $1,000 per annum. Will give $100 to anyone securing me such a position." The bureaucracy had grown from some 29,000 in the 1820s to 130,000 when Barfield took office. The president lamented that he discovered hungry office seekers "lying in wait for him like vultures for a wounded bison." He had no idea that one of the disappointed seekers would take his life.

The world and the federal government became increasingly more technical, and new government jobs—geologists, chemists, engineers, accountants, lots of accountants—required special skills. There had been a serious movement earlier to reform the patronage system, which had considerable public support, but the party hacks blocked every attempt for a change. Then came the assassination of Barfield, and the public clamor could no longer be ignored. The Purebullion Act of January 16, 1883, named for George Hunt Purebullion of Ohio, became the law of the land. Surprisingly, he lost his Senate seat because he supported the will of the people and lost the backing of his own party. The Purebullion Act classified highly skilled jobs, removed them from a patronage system, and set up a Civil Service Commission to administer personnel hiring based on merit rather than political connections. It provided the nation with an educated, competent, and permanent workforce that would keep the government running regardless of which party occupied the White House. Basically, only "Policy Level" appointments would be exempt and the Civil Service government employees would be protected from political pressure, intimidation, and reprisals.

Key elements of the law were: (1) Positions would be filled by selection according to grade from among those graded highest, as the result of such competitive examinations. (2) No person in the public service is under any obligation to contribute to any political fund or to render any political service and that he will not be removed or otherwise prejudiced from doing so. (3) And most importantly, no person in said service has any right to use his official authority or influence to coerce the political action of any person.

Well, today "to the Victor Belongs the Spoils" is back in full force as if it never was repealed. The Spoils System is back in spades in the federal government and deeply embedded in the agency that is responsible for the stewardship of our national treasuries. Partisan political appointments are increasingly being made in the middle management and operations level of the Parks Department. This infiltration of questionable employees who are unqualified professionally, educationally, and by experience continues to devastate careerists. It is nothing less than a political purge of dedicated men and women of proven competence and rewarding loyal party lackeys.

Jennifer Mckenzie was an on-site, hands-on working archeologist with a master's degree and eight years of service with the Parks Department. She was surveying and excavating an archeological structure at the newly established Mesa Blanco National Monument. Once again she heard a terrific thundering and saw part of a thousand-year-old wall crumble. It wasn't the first time, for she had repeatedly filed reports about the irreparable damage the US Navy planes were causing. Her alarming documentations were consistently ignored by the chief of the planning team, who was a political appointee from the world of real estate. Who was this woman to disparage the "Sound of Freedom" and the national security of our country? But this time Jennifer would go beyond just filing a memorandum to an indifferent Spoiler. She had been photographing the damage done to the prehistoric buildings and recording sonic booms that were destroying the ancient homes of the First Americans. She submitted her findings to the *National Archeological Journal,* and they published her story the following week. When Gotcha Butcher heard of her treachery, he had her removed and banished to a dead end staff job in a faraway district office.

When Keith Williams, the US senator from California, learned of the injustice, he threatened to cut off all funding for Blanco Mesa if Jennifer Mckenzie was not reinstated. She returned to the national monument and was promoted to chief of the planning team. Senator Williams had been a major supporter of the National Archeological Resources Protection Act, which carried a fine of up to $500,000 and a jail sentence of five years. He personally confronted the secretary of the Navy and the sonic booms stopped. The former head of the Blanco Mesa planning team was arrested by US marshals and was subsequently sentence to two years in jail.

Fred and Tom (we wouldn't use their real names to protect their identity) had been good friends for almost four years where each served as district rangers in Tall Tree National Park. They both realized that perhaps one day they might have to compete for a promotion, but that had no effect on their relationship. A position opened up in another park for assistant superintendent for which both were well qualified.

Some seventy-five applications had been received, and after a careful examination the list was pared down to ten names. Both Fred and Tom were on the final list. Also placed in the top ten was a political appointee in a Capital City staff position who had never served in a field position. The selecting official, the park superintendent, was told by Gotcha to choose his man or he would be transferred to a staff position in NYC. He refused, and rather than accept the transfer, he retired early and remained in the community.

The chief park ranger was appointed acting superintendent, and if he selected Gotcha's plant, he would be named the new superintendent. He knew that his career would be over if he expressed any disloyalty, and being ambitious, he caved in and selected the political appointee. His sellout would not be forgotten by the Peyote Society, especially Cool-Head Fred.

The abuse of power and arrogant disregard for the spirit and the meaning of the Purebullion Act became ever more flagrant by the Spoilers in the Capital City. As they continued to get away with circumventing the law, their past audacity was surpassed by arresting the Top Cop. Four bully brutes from the presidential palace flashed their credentials before the sergeant at the entrance to the Park Police Headquarters and took the elevator to the third floor. They burst into the conference room where a budget meeting was in progress. The chief of the park police was in the process of trying to reduce the operational expenses and balance a stretched budget.

The biggest brute read from an official-looking piece of paper that displayed the presidential seal.

> By order of the president of the United States, you are, Chief Bettye Bates, to immediately surrender your gold-plated park police badge, your pearl-handled .38 revolver, your law enforcement identification card, the original one. Furthermore, you are to be removed from this office and this building at once, leaving all personal belongings, effects, and personal papers behind. You are not to return to this site, grounds, or buildings, and you may not contact anyone at any time at this headquarter. Failure to submit to this order will result in a fine of $100,000 and three years in a federal penitentiary.
>
> I approve this message,
> White House Chief of Staff

The executive order was delivered coldly and efficiently without any attempt at awkward civility. It was enforced by a Gestapo gang of Spoilers, and it left a lasting memory for all present. It was meant to be intimidating, to create an atmosphere of fear.

The Capital City Police Department was created during the first president's term of office. It was their mandate to protect the monuments and memorials in the federal parks and the people who visit the nation's capital. Today, during a period of increasing threats to the security of the federal buildings and monuments and need for public safety, they have been underfunded and understaffed. Chief Bettye Bates was desperately trying to manage her police force in a most efficient manner and at the same time balance the books. Her sin was that she simply confirmed to the media that the public and the parks would be better served with an increase in funding, Specifically, she was accused of disloyalty and insubordination for disclosing the budget process of the federal government. She should have known that the public has no right to know.

The entire congressional committee members on parks and conservation had applauded her past accomplishments. She had brought significant credentials to the position of chief of the police. A four-point average in criminology and law enforcement at the university, a master's degree in public administration, and she had served for twenty-three years as a park policewomen moving up through the ranks to chief. But she should have realized that in the Capital City there is only one game: "Toe the party line."

Bettye Bates was humiliated in front of her staff and ultimately fired from her position She filed a lawsuit against the presidential palace Spoilers, the secretary of the Interior, and the assistant secretary for Parks, Gotcha Butcher. She was offered her job back with full pay if she would drop the lawsuit. She refused and went on television and exclaimed, "They have no shame, no decency." And she played another Capital City game, "Take the money and run." She did with seven million dollars.

CHAPTER THIRTY-FOUR

IT'S OVER, AIN'T IT?

The war between the Southern States and the rest of the United States began in April 1861 when the local folks took over a federal fort in Charleston Harbor. The Feds said the Charlestonians attacked them and stole their property. This individual action would result in six hundred thousand American deaths in a bloody civil war. Slavery, states rights, economics, a clash of cultures, and a failure of huge egos to compromise—all lead to a fatal dissolution. On April 9, 1865, at the home of Wilmer McPain in a rural Virginia courthouse (county seat), two great generals declared the peace.

The southern gentleman general arrived first at the McPain House, and when the hard-bitten Union General entered the room, he stood up and they shook hands. They briefly reminisced about the Mexican War when they both fought together in the United States Army. In his memoirs, the short, cigar-smoking, heavy-drinking general from Ohio wrote, "I almost forgot the object of our meeting." The Yankee commander's surrender terms were more than generous, more than conciliatory, aimed at bringing the Confederate States back into the Union.

The Southern soldiers would be paroled; the officers would be allowed to keep their firearms and baggage. All would be allowed to return home freely and to rebuild their lives. When the victorious general was informed that the Confederate soldiers in the cavalry and artillery owned their own horses, he offered, "I take it that most of the men in the ranks are small farmers. It is doubtful whether they will be able to put in a crop to carry themselves through the next winter without the aid of horses." The response was "This will have the best possible effect upon the men. It will be very gratifying and will do much toward conciliating our people." 25,000 rations were also given to the near-starving Johnny Rebs.

The union general's military secretary, a full-bloodied Iroquois Indian, penned the agreement in final form. Another Union officer remembered the departure of the Confederate general. "He mounted his favorite horse, Traveller, and lifted his hat as he passed out of the yard and road off toward his army." A twenty-five-year-old brigadier general, George Custer, stood on the front porch of the McPain House.

The following day the Confederate general gave his farewell address:

> After four years of arduous service marked by unsurpassed courage and fortitude, the Army of Northern Virginia has been compelled to yield to overwhelming numbers and resources. I need not tell the brave survivors of so many hard-fought battles who have remained steadfast to the last that I have consented to this result from no distrust of them. But feeling that valor and devotion could accomplish nothing that could compensate for the loss that would have attended to the continuance of the contest, I determined to avoid the useless sacrifice of those whose past services have endeared them to their country-men. By the terms of the agreement, officers and men can return to their homes and remain until exchanged. You will take with you the satisfaction that proceeds from the consciousness of duty faithfully performed and I earnestly pray that a merciful God will extend to you his blessing and protection. With an unceasing admiration of your constancy and devotion to your

country and grateful remembrance of your kind
and generous consideration of myself, I bid you
an affectionate farewell.

And two days later he declared, "I believe it to be the duty of
everyone to unite in the restoration of the country and the reestab-
lishment of peace and harmony."

It was both a sad and happy day, a nervous and depressing
day, an overcast, gray, and chilly day. The victorious Union soldiers
lined up on both sides of the road west of the McPain House, an old
stage coach road. The defeated Southern soldiers smartly marched
between the blue lines to lay down their arms forever. They were led
by a favorite Confederate general mounted on a magnificent black
horse. "Before us in proud humiliation stood the embodiment of
mankind," a Union soldier later described. "Men whom neither toils
and suffering, nor the fact of death, nor disaster, nor hopelessness
could bend their resolve; standing before us now, thin, worn, and
famished, but erect and with eyes looking level into ours, walking
memories that bound us together as no other bond; was not such
manhood to be welcomed back into a Union so tested and assured?"
The Billy Yanks, out of respect for the former foe, responded to the
command of present arms:

> The Southern general at the head of the col-
> umn, riding with heavy spirit and downcast face,
> catches the sound of shifting arms, looks up, and
> taking the meaning wheels superbly, making
> with himself and his horse one uplifted figure,
> with profound salutation as he drops the point
> of his sword to the boot toe, then facing his own
> command, gives the word for successive brigades
> to pass us with the same position of the man-
> ual—honor answering honor. On our part, not
> a sound of trumpet more, nor roll of drums, not
> a cheer, nor word, nor whisper of vain glorying,

but an awed stillness rather, and breath holding
as it were the passing of the dead.

After the "We Won" parades in the northern cities, the villag-
ers of the Southern Courthouse settled back into what it was before
the two generals said it was over. They were fearful and very bit-
ter but made the changes necessary to survive during the years of
Reconstruction after the war. Their representatives in the Capital
City were former slaves who now had the upper hand. It was a time
to make do and a time to dream. "And this too will pass." Wilmer
McPain was the first to sell out at a profit and moved his family on
to another opportunity.

Curiosity seekers drifted by over the years to see the "Old
Surrender Grounds," something the locals tolerated rather than seizing the opportunity. A group of Yankee entrepreneurs unsuccessfully
tried to raise money to make the little village a tourist attraction. In
1892, the Courthouse Building in the center of the courthouse village burned to the ground. Some believed it was set on fire to destroy
some records that were unfavorable to a local politician. The McPain
house was dismantled for removal and reconstruction at the World's
Fair in Chicago in 1893. It never happened, but souvenir hunters
picked over the stacks of bricks from the original home—the historic
house vanished brick by brick.

Three miles away a new town was built around the railroad
station, and for the next forty years the Surrender Village slowly
deteriorated and was mostly forgotten. Few Southerners wanted to
remember anyway. The Great Depression brought some life into the
old Appomattox when it was established as a national monument.
Some clearing, cleaning, and stabilization followed, but little else was
accomplished because of World War II. After the war, federal funding
became available, and the first building to be reconstructed, using a
few remaining bricks, was the McPain House. It was completed and
partially refurnished and dedicated in April 1950 by descendants of
the two generals. It was a notable beginning, and eventually the village would come back to life.

The first Parks Department historian was Collin Mitchell. He was a high school history teacher with a master's degree and had worked for the parks during the summer months. Collin joined the Parks Department full-time at Fort Sumter. After two years, he was offered a promotion to Appomattox Courthouse where he was responsible for historical research and visitor services. He and his wife, Cathy, moved into an apartment over the historic country store, just across from the McPain House.

Shortly after settling in at the national monument, Collin was introduced to the town officials three miles down the road. The meeting with Sam Brown, the longtime mayor, was most disconcerting. Sam was a three-hundred-pound redneck who chewed an unlit cigar and was also the owner of the only grocery store and drive-in movie. The mayor said to Collin," Where you from, boy?" Collin replied, "Charleston." "Charleston, where," asked Sam. "Charleston, South Carolina," responded Collin. "Well, good for you. You know, yawl started this fight for states rights. And it's a shame what happened here, but it ain't over yet. The last person the government sent down here, some architect or something, was a damn Yankee. And I think he was one of them 'cause he wasn't married if you know what I mean. We was glad to see him leave 'cause we don't want his kind down here. He thought he was better than ours with his fancy college way of talking. Never seen him in my store, not once. Look here, Collin, we'd like you to join our little Elks Club. We have a country dance every Saturday night, and the booze is cheap enough. Yawl is one of us, and we take care of our own."

Collin and his wife missed the Saturday night dance, but they did go to St. Mary's Catholic Church thirty miles away. They also did their shopping in a supermarket near the church. Their daughter was born there too, since Sam's town didn't have an obstetrician and Cathy had problems with her pregnancy. After their daughter was born, they continued going to St. Mary's, and they never did shop in Sam's store.

Collin further alienated the locals and infuriated Sam by hiring a high school teacher from one of those separate but equal schools. He had met him when giving a talk about the Civil War at the teacher's high school. Collin was also asked to give a program about the "Old Surrender Grounds" at the Daughters of the Confederate Rebels. One of the ladies asked him what he thought about that uppity Negro Rosa Sparks. Collin replied that she had every right to remain in her seat since she had paid for it. When Sam heard about this, he decided that Collin was not really one of them and had to go.

Collin and his wife had also become friends with the local pastor of the First Baptist Church. Reverend Tucker had retired from the US Army after thirty-five years' service and had served in both world wars. He had been a master sergeant and had a chest full of medals, including the Silver Star, the Purple Heart, and the Expert Rifleman. It was in the Army where he got an education and learned the meaning of being part of a proud American institution, a place where he felt special. He had escaped much of the redneck rage that his brothers and sisters had endured. And now this giant of a man who had served both his country and God faced the ultimate cruelty of his life.

One early Sunday morning three local hunters had returned from a hunting trip and squealed into a fork in the road on four bare truck tires. The hunters, two of them brothers, each church keyed a Bud beer to wash down a pull on the half-filled jug of white lightning. One of the brothers, only seventeen, turned the radio knob to full blast and sang along with "A white sport coat and a pink carnation" on the country music station. They were all happy, excited, drunk and kept telling tales of how they shot the dead deer in the back of the pickup.

About five hundred feet back from the fork in the road was a two-story, three-bedroom house where Reverend Tucker, his wife, and two grandchildren lived. It was 2:30 a m. when the former first sergeant went out the front door toward the loud hillbilly sounds. As he neared the old Ford truck, one of the hunters, Jim Taylor, stuck his head out of the window and slurringly said, "What the hell do you want, nigger?" The tall erect black man answered, "First, I'm not a nigger, and second, I would appreciate it if you would turn down the radio." Jim, showing off to his brother and the other hunter, exclaimed, "Well, ain't you something—I ain't no nigger and appreciate yawl turn down a radio. Who the hell you think you're talkin to, black boy?"

The reverend Tucker tried to explain that they were parked on his land and they could stay there if they would just lower the volume. Again he said, "And I would appreciate it if you would just turn down the radio." The other brother snarled, "I would appreciate this and I would appreciate that. Where you from, some citified place. Now let me tell you something." He opened the truck door and spilled out with his shotgun in his right hand. "We'll park here any damn time we want to, and I ain't gonna turn down no radio either. So what you gonna do about it?"

The reverend said, "I don't want any trouble, I'm just asking you to please turn down the radio." Jim Taylor mockingly said, "Listen to this boy, it was appreciate, appreciate, now it's I don't want no trouble and please, please." He raised his shotgun to belly level and yelled, "You better get the hell out of here before I lose my manners."

Reverend Tucker looked directly into Kim Taylor's eyes and said "Don't point that piece at me." Taylor still mocking him said, "Piece, piece, you must have been in military or something, calling my shotgun a piece." The other two hunters came out of the truck with their rifles as Jim Taylor, fired a shot over Tucker's head. As he had been trained to do, to react without hesitation in the face of the enemy, the former Master Sergeant pulled out his .45 caliber pistol from the back waistband of his dungarees and fired back at Taylor, hitting him in the chest. The other two aimed their guns at Tucker, but the sergeant fired first, dropping both men. He went over to the bodies and found that all three were dead. The reverend went back to his house and called the county sheriff. Four sheriff's cars arrived within ten minutes and met the reverend at the scene of the shootings. A deputy sheriff sneaked up behind him and hit him hard on the side of the head with a .38 pistol.

Not since April 9, 1865, had this historic hamlet made the front pages of the national newspapers. The NAACP provided the best defense attorneys from New York City to plead for the life of Reverend Tucker. The plea was obviously self-defense. Collin Mitchell took annual leave from the Parks Department and was in the courtroom almost every day. His wife, Cathy, comforted Reverend Tucker's wife and grandchildren. The trial lasted only two weeks and the all-white jury found the sergeant guilty of first-degree murder. A little over a year later, the soldier, husband, father, grandfather, preacher was strapped into an electric chair in the state capital.

Jim Taylor was the son of Mayor Sam's first cousin. Now Sam had his chance to get back at Collin for all his snubs and his liberal communist leanings. He had been in the courtroom too and had seen Collin and his wife sitting next to Mrs. Tucker and the grandkids. Could you believe it, a southern boy too!

With the help of his wife, who had finished high school, Sam wrote a letter to the president of these United States. It was signed by five members of the community: Sam, two members of the guilty verdict jury, the barber, president of the Elks Club and his wife. The complaints about Collin and Cathy were the following:

1. Collin would tell all the tourists that went into the McPain House that the Union general had been a gentleman, generous, humble, and courteous. That's a bunch of bunk 'cause he was always drunk.

2. Collin reprimanded my cousin's other son, the one that Collin's friend didn't murder, for sleeping in the McPain house. The boy (age fifty-two) was sick and shouldn't be cleaning the surrender house in the first place.

3. Collin and his highfalutin wife snubbed us locals and went to church, if you call them Catholics a church, over in Lynchtree. They would shop in that Catholic-owned supermarket too, when my grocery store was right here all the time.

4. Insulted me and my family when I took the mayor of our sister city in Estonia, over there on Easter. Collin told me in front of everybody that I couldn't smoke my cigar in the McPain House because it was a fire hazard. I don't like nobody talkin' about my Cuban cigars, and I'll smoke em wherever the hell I want.

5. I heard the reason he never joined the Elks Club was because he said we was a bunch of rednecks. Well, our vice president ain't no redneck. He wasn't even born here.

6. His Yankee wife hung up all their laundry on the clothes line to dry behind the country store where they live. When Collin kicked Joe out of the McPain house for sleepin', he was over there emptying the trash can and saw them including her unmentionables. Joe had a nervous condition even before he seen them.

7. He told our young people at the public school the white one where our children is schooled, that the colored woman Rosa Sparks in Montgomery—and I got kin folks who live in Montgomery—that she had every right to sit in that bus seat and not move. He said she paid for her seat, which I don't believe 'cause she was only a washer woman. Where did a lazy, uppity, no-good troublemaker get bus money?

8. He hired a black boy to talk to the tourists, and he wouldn't say nothing about my grandfather, who was mayor when the courthouse building was burned down. They never proved he done it. So this black boy is over there when my nephew, Walter, should be telling the truth to the tourists. He would tell them my granddaddy didn't have nothing to do with it.

9. Collin's wife, when she was with child, went to some fancy doctor over at Lynchtree, rather than to our own Dr. Billie, who has served our community for over seventy-five years.

10. And he and his wife sat with that colored family during the Tucker trial. They even carried a placard saying that he had a right to defend himself and kill one of our own. I believe Collin and his wife are communists, but I ain't sure. Now I thought they were good people, being from Charleston and everything, but they're worse than that other architect fellow yawl dumped on us. Now, we want them out of here.

Collin never knew anything about the mayor's letter, but he was transferred to the Capital City to the Washington Monument where he ran the elevator and answered questions like "How tall is it?" After three months of pushing the elevator button, Collin quit. His fellow employees all said "He was a damn good man" and "What a terrible loss."

Collin went back to the university and earned a PhD in American history. For the next twelve years, he taught history at the Western Catholic College and became head of the History Department. He authored the highly accredited work "The Dying Days of the Confederacy," which became the History Book Club's Book of the Month.

With the encouragement of the Peyote Society, the African Americans claimed discrimination and boycotted the mayor's grocery store. Within six months the mayor was bankrupt and voted out of office.

On April 9, 1965, at the one hundredth commemoration of the end of the Civil War, Collin Mitchell was the keynote speaker. The mayor did not attend the ceremonies.

CHAPTER THIRTY-FIVE

THE JACUZZI CONFERENCE

It was to be a no-holds-barred, open, honest, down-to-earth Park Superintendents Conference. The plan was to promote better communications, mutual understanding of park objectives and administrative policy in the management of the national parks and monuments. Hopefully, at this most important meeting, the Parks people and the Spoilers would get to know each other on a first-name basis, perhaps get drunk together, and in the future work more amicably toward a common goal.

On a scale of 1 to 10, the morale of the rank and file in the Parks Department was minus one. The root cause of course was the never-ending politicization of the Civil Service career employees even at the lower levels. It was expected that the top ranks, the policy-making positions, would be filled by the party faithful, but not the lower operational jobs in the parks and monuments. Those in the field had seen it before but nothing like the cronyism and abuse of power of the present administration. To the victor goes the spoils. But what jobs are covered by the Civil Service Commission, and what jobs are spoils? Critical specialties and professional positions were being filled by the party hacks who wouldn't know a brown bear from a billy goat. It was like if they don't know, well, a career employee who does can carry them.

One would have thought that the Spoilers would have begun the conference with conciliatory, considerate, respectful remarks—

words that would promote healing, perhaps even bonding. It was unbelievable that the first person to address the park superintendents was Seymour Hudson. Seymour was now the associate director for Human Resources and the most despised political appointee in the Parks Department. His off the wall presentation was insulting, degrading, humiliating—it was meant to be intimidating. Seymour's message was "the one ingredient that will enhance your career." He began by saying, "Let me tell you what it is so there will be no misunderstanding. Creativity—no, that's not it. How about intelligence? There are a lot of intelligent people. Hard work is something that inefficient employees have to engage in. And it's not honesty, not people skills, not analytical ability, not teamwork, not caring, not commitment, not giving, not unselfishness.

"People, you have to get with the program. It was and it always has been, since the establishment of any organization, government or non-government, civilian or military, one thing. Loyalty, loyalty, loyalty!"

The filled, half-filled, and empty Styrofoam coffee cups came flying toward the podium. In unison, the park superintendents shouted "Our loyalty is not for sale" and "You suck, Seymour." They all knew exactly what Seymour Hudson was saying, "Kiss our ass if you want to keep your job." The Spoilers had dangled promotions, more funding, bigger budgets, more personnel, more park developments—"Just get with the program, just kiss our ass." Finally, the Spoilers opened the program to questions:

Do you guys in the Capital City ever work more than three days a week?

There had been an article in the *Washington Most* that detailed the work-a-day world of the nation's capital.

Federal employees declared, twenty-six days a year annual leave, thirteen days sick leave, eleven federal holidays like Labor Day, eleven more days because it looked like it might snow, thirteen days because it did snow, ten days because it was too cold, and ten days because it was too hot, eleven days because of terrorists alert in federal buildings, Saturday and Sundays 104 days—a total of 209 nonworking days, which left 156 working days. (Note: 7-Eleven works 7/24.) The Spoilers response to the three-day workweek was "Next question."

One veteran park superintendent of thirty-five years' service who was going to retire in two months asked, "Are the concessioners running the Parks Department?"

There had been a scathing piece in the *San Francisco Truth* about the role of the concessioners (like corporate business) that provide the nonessential services in the national parks. The *Truth* declared it all began with Fred Barfey at the Great Hole in the early days of the twentieth century, where Barfey Girls would pull people off the trains to have a peak at what a river had created. Once off the train, the girls would hassle the unsuspecting travelers with cheap souvenirs with a markup of 500 percent. The newspaper stated that the biggest mistake the Parks Department made was letting them build their hotels, restaurants, gift shops inside the national parks. Even in the early days of the national parks, there were Spoilers. They have been around whenever there was opportunity to make a buck, and even then they overruled the park managers. The Spoilers mission was not to protect and preserve the nation's parks but to exploit them.

The Barfey Girls would only allow the train travelers a peak because they were paid to push them into the restaurants, gift shops, and hotels and to herd more and more to and from the Canyon over-look. The most often heard words from the sightseers were "My god what a big hole, let's go get a hot dog."

And over the years it just got worse.

The Spoilers reaction to the question about how the conces-sioners running the parks and bilking the park visitors was the same as before: "Next question."

The next question was, "Why do you want to destroy the national parks and monuments?"

There was increased emphasis on the effects of global warming in both the national parks and everywhere else from scientific jour-nals to the mass media. The subject of global warming was being investigated on a daily basis. It was concluded that people in general and park visitors in particular were warming up the national parks with gas-guzzling vehicles. Man is the culprit and has contributed more to global warming than any other factor including the sun. The conservative administration produced its own faith-based, pseudo-creationist findings in an attempt to debunk academia. While the rest of the world was trying to engage the Kyoto Treaty, the presidential palace simply ignored it Why? Because profit, greed, and big business were more important than saving the earth. And because they just didn't give a damn. The reaction to this question was the same as before: "Next question."

The last question was "Do you people have no shame?"

The answer was "Next question."

The planned three-day conference was over the morning of the first day. All the park superintendents simply walked out willing to accept the consequences—there were none. The support, the reconciliation, the bonding, the unity that the Spoilers had hoped for was in the trash can.

The park managers and the Spoilers dined separately that evening in the plush conference center. They boozed it up in separate lounges. Seymour and his wife and two other lackey couples decided to relax in the hotel's Jacuzzi. It was small, intimate, and would accommodate only eight people. While they were soaking up the hot, bubbling water, one of the park superintendents splashed into the pool with a response to their "Kiss Our Ass Conference." This Peyote eyeballed Seymour with a big smile on his face and exclaimed, "Oh boy, this Jacuzzi does wonders for my hemorrhoids."

CHAPTER THIRTY-SIX

THE FLAG PIN

"When my daughter, Jennifer, was in the second grade she asked me, 'Who is Richard Stands?' I had no idea," said Fred.

He spent the afternoon in the Pratt Library and, even with the help of their professional staff, came up empty-handed. He asked his daughter where she had heard about this Richard Stands, and she said, "At the beginning of school every day, all the boys and girls would put their hands over their hearts and say, 'I pledge allegiance to the flag of the United States of America and to the Republic for Richard Stands.'" Fred laughed out loud for being so naive and then remembered that when he was in elementary school that his class would face the flag, which was on a flag pole to the right of the teacher's desk and say the pledge.

Francis Bellamy, a member of Youth's Companion, is credited with being the author of the Pledge of Allegiance, which was published on September 8, 1892. The pledge did not include "under God" originally but was added by Congress and approved by the president on June 14, 1954. A few years later, Fred's daughter asked him what was meant by "Republic." He told her to look it up in the *American Heritage Dictionary*. She did. A "republic" is "a political order whose head of state was not a monarch; and a nation having such a political system, a political order in which the supreme power lies in a body of citizens who are entitled to vote for officers and representative responsible to them." And "indivisible" meant, of course, "incapable of being divided." And there it was, "with liberty and justice for all." She thought to herself, well, in 1892 that liberty and justice part didn't include women, First Americans, or Negroes. And she checked out "Flag." "A symbol of persons united in some common association and committed to each other and to the country."

The first flag or symbol of our country was established on June 14, 1777, by Congress. It stated that "the flag of the United States be made of thirteen stripes, alternate red and white; that the union be thirteen stars white in a blue field, representing a new constellation." And it was to change many times—from 1795 to 1818, the flag had fifteen stripes and fifteen stars—Kentucky and Vermont being added to the Union. And of course, fifty stars and thirteen stripes was first flown on July 4, 1960, at Fort McHenry National Monument, and Cool-Head Fred was there, and it's where he met his wife, Ginny.

The allegiance to the Flag is highlighted each year on June 14 and is known as Flag Day. The flag had been honored by many patriotic groups on that date, but it was not officially established until 1949 when the president signed the legislation which read, "Urge the people to observe the day, as the anniversary of the adoption on June 14, 1777, by the Continental Congress of the adoption of the stars and stripes as the official flag of the United States of America"

"Here we go again," said Keith, Director, Region Three. "I remember the turbulent 1970s when Nixon said he wasn't a crook and gave up the White House. The selected president not only faced the defeat in Vietnam, but he encouraged all federal employees to wear those WIN buttons." "What was a WIN button?" asked Jennifer. She was the Chief Archeologist, who had transferred to region three. "My gosh you're young," replied Keith. "Well, that was the old 'Whip Inflation Now' icon. It was about the size of a cardboard coaster. The park people were told to wear it on their uniforms, but they just ignored it." "Why are you telling me this?" asked Jennifer. "Have you seen this memorandum from the Parks Department headquarters? It encourages employees to wear the Flag Pin like the president and all his cronies do."

"In other words, another loyalty test from Gotcha Butcher and his ilk who flash the Flag Pin like a red badge of courage," said

Jennifer. "More like a red badge of loyalty. And they're afraid not to wear it, since all the party faithful in the White House sport it," exclaimed Keith. "You have to ask yourself just what does it mean to you?" said Jennifer. "What does it mean to you, Jennifer?" asked Keith. "To me it's the most recognizable symbol of our country, but it can mean different things to different people. To some it's a symbol of a common cause or belief. I think it should say something about the values of our country. My father fought in World War II. It might mean something more profound to him," replied Jennifer.

"Oh, I'm sure he feels the same way you do, Jennifer. It's a symbol of freedom, for free speech, for our right to disagree with a stupid memo. The Flag Pin is being used by the present administration, especially the draft dodgers in the White House, as a prop for their self-serving policies. Their wearing the Flag Pin reminds me of my daughter who clutches a baby blanket for security. Your father was a hero, but this bunch hid behind their daddies to escape the Vietnam War," declared Keith. "Well, that's exactly the way I feel. Just look what they're doing to our national parks—exploitation, planning to drill for oil in Alaska, purging the Parks people for being conservationists. It just stinks. The American flag is supposed to represent love of our country, a common bond. But that's not what they convey with their little lapel Flag Pins. To them, it means we have the power and we are going to run the country our way. Our country is divided in half, and I'm not going to wear a symbol that represents the Spoilers," cried Jennifer. "Yeah," replied Keith. "To them it's a tangible, visible indication of your support and loyalty. It's either you're with us or against us, and I don't have to wear a Flag Pin to say I'm patriotic and love my country."

Later that day it was reported that the park police had arrested a conscientious objector for burning the American flag in front of the Washington Monument. So the discussion between Keith and Jennifer took on another dimension. She asked, "Is burning the flag a criminal act, or is it legitimate expression of freedom of expression? It's ironic that the United States Flag Code requires that you burn the flag if it is worn, torn, or faded. How many flags are burned every day? How many flags do cities, counties, states, and the federal government burn every year? So what if this person who burned the flag maintains that he was just following the law? Both the United States Constitution and the Flag Code support his right to burn the flag," exclaimed Jennifer. Keith, who had a good memory for these kind of issues, said, "I remember that the United States Supreme Court did decide that the burning of the United States Flag was indeed an expression of freedom of speech. Just look at how the flag is desecrated by the advertising world with impunity." "So if I choose to wear the flag pin, it will be seen by my fellow workers as caving in to the Spoilers, and if I don't, the Spoilers will make life difficult for me," explained Jennifer. "So what are you going to do?" asked Keith. "I'm going to wear it," replied Jennifer. "You're what? I can't believe it. You of all people," cried Keith. "I'm going to wear it but put it on upside down," said Jennifer. "You can't do that, Jennifer, it's probably against the law," said Keith.

Jennifer laughed and showed Keith a copy of the Federal Regulations, Public law 829, Sec. 4(a) which states that "the flag should never be displayed with the Union down saving as a signal of distress." "Is our country in dire distress or not?" asked Jennifer. Within a week, 99 percent of the park people were wearing the lapel pin, but wearing it upside down. The Peyote Society did everything it could to get it to 100 percent. The following week a new memorandum was issued by Gotcha rescinding the "You must wear the Flag Pin." The memo stated that "under no circumstances should the Flag Pin be worn by park personnel."

CHAPTER THIRTY-SEVEN

PARADISE INN

"My god, are they trying to kill me," screamed Alice. "No, I don't think that's what they're up to. Just trying to make us sick," replied Ponytail Tony. "Make us sick, make us sick of what?" exclaimed Alice. "Make us sick and tired of fighting the establishment," answered Ponytail Tony.

Paradise Inn was a corporation owned by one of the party faithful, and it was kept full by forcing disgruntled employees, both private and public, to receive treatment for alleged behavioral problems. There were over fifty Paradise Inns, and they all had the same mission. Make the employees believe that they have a problem, that the Paradise Treatment Centers were the solution, and take the insurance company's money.

Paradise Inn counselors never used harsh words like "alcoholic" or "drug addict" because of the stigma that the uninformed and prejudiced society attached to them. Personality disorder or middle-age crisis or abused ego were preferred. The program was a ten-day adventure, and the cost was $27,000. The insurance companies were also owned by the same administration loyalists who simply kept raising the premiums in this win-win arrangement. Of course, it was a loser for the insurance premium payers and the Paradise Inn patients.

Ponytail Tony is what his family and friends called him. His real name was Anthony Begay, a Native American and one of the best non-supervisory park rangers in the Southwest. Ponytail Tony sported a fourteen-inch-long, dark black, and knotted ponytail and told anyone who would listen that "no way, man. I ain't gonna cut off my ponytail." Everyone seemed to know his story, and the Spoilers considered him spiritually handicapped and a disloyal malcontent. They were a little afraid of him because his uncle was vice chairman of the nearby Indian Tribal Council. They never made his in-your-face defiance an open issue. But Ponytail Tony was never considered for a promotion, never attended any training programs, and would never become a supervisory park ranger or park manager. Being overlooked, cheated, and rendered powerless drove Ponytail Tony to find comfort in the bottle. His family was concerned since both his father and grandfather had died from an overdependence on cheap wine.

There were many theories on why the First Americans have a propensity for alcohol: the enzyme theory, genetics, can't hold his liquor, cultural gap. But in Ponytail Tony's case it was clearly powerlessness against the Spoilers that pushed him into alcoholism. Alcoholics Anonymous was free, had worked for millions, but not everyone knew about it, where it was, how it worked, and then there was that stigma.

Ponytail Tony was a prime candidate for Paradise Inn, and his supervisor, who didn't know any better and thinking he was helping him, got him into Spoilers Devil's Den. Paradise Inn extended two hundred feet on one floor of a downtown commercial building in Albuquerque. The floor was divided into two wings: "Skid Row" for the newcomers and "Park Avenue" for those who had already been detoxed. The initiates, shaky, nervous, some drunk, others comatose were issued hand-me-down pajamas and a new pair of rubber sandals. When Ponytail Tony moved to the head of the line, he blew a 2.3 on the detoxing testing machine. He thought it was strange when they gave him a straight shot of vodka, but that was the beginning of the detoxification process at Paradise Inn. The procedure was carefully monitored because of the fear that a patient could enter into a seizure and make life unpleasant for the underpaid staff.

At 3:00 a.m. Tony was awakened and given another shot of vodka, the prescribed medicine. After breakfast, he developed a slight tremor in his hands and fingers and was administrated another shot.

The time between the welcomed vodka became longer, and by the morning of the third day Ponytail Tony was declared detoxified, his body alcohol-free. No more shakes, no more sweats, no more dry heaves, but that would soon end. He turned in his smelly pajamas and was issued an almost new pair of baby blue warmups and entered the magic of Park Avenue. He thought he had finally arrived, but the worst was ahead.

Paradise Inn called it the conditioning program, the aversion therapy—the patients thought it was a torture chamber.

Ponytail Tony entered a small room about one hundred square feet. The walls from floor to ceiling were covered with hundreds of bottles of the very best hooch. What was inside was questionable. But the labels showed Cutty Sark Scotch, Jack Daniels Bourbon, Smirnov Vodka, Gilbert Gin—brandy, whiskey, and an assortment of beer and wines. To an alcoholic it looked like a giant Christmas tree. In the center of the chamber was a large, old-fashioned barber's chair dating from the prohibition days. Attached to the right armrest was a large magnified mirror that doubled the size of Tony's nose. Below the mirror was a deep tin basin large enough to hold two gallons of anything. Tony was not alone. Holding his hand was a semi-retired and tired-looking registered nurse. The kindly old lady stuck a needle into Tony's arm, and soon the victim will be conditioned for the great experiment. The drug, Emetine, will ensure that the subject will feel nauseous, begin sweating, and is ready to empty his/her stomach by vomiting. And now let the fun begin.

The little old lady lays out the feast before Ponytail Tony's unbelieving eyes. A shot of bourbon, a shot of gin, a shot of scotch, a shot of brandy, a shot of vodka, two shots of wine, all to go down Tony's throat, followed by a warm beer. It's chug-a-lug heaven minus the warm glow, the buzz, the relief that Tony always got from alcohol. Down the hatch—yummy, yummy. Ponytail Tony looked deep into the magnified mirror and saw his flushed face, his watery and bloodshot eyes, tears on his cheeks, a drooling nose, and then boom—the eruption!. That which can't stay down will come back up—vomit, terrible tasting and smelling vomit, lots of it, all of it into a big tin basin. Tony's face was a mess—sweat, tears, vomit.

Just to make sure the aversion therapy works, let's try it again. This time the dose is doubled, and the beer is a little warmer. *What a waste of good booze*, Tony thought to himself. It was over. He slipped out of the big barber's chair and felt dizzy and weak. He could hardly walk and had to be helped back to his bed. The last mental picture he had of himself from looking into the mirror was a gasping, crying, sad-faced slob. He was too exhausted to hate himself and fell asleep.

Welcome to Paradise Inn. The conditioning treatment, the aversion therapy, the torture chamber—it's all for your own good. It will make you hate booze; even the smell of booze will make you vomit. You will be cured forever thanks to the wonder people and that Emetine at Paradise Inn. The next morning Tony was hungry and had an enormous breakfast of cereal, milk, eggs, bacon, sausage, toast, and three cups of coffee. And then back to the torture chamber and more of the "It's for your own good" treatment. The horrible degradation, humiliation, more and more vomit, the same weakness, dizziness, and the struggle to get back to bed. In the evenings Paradise Inn invites you to movies with popcorn. Vivid pictures of what alcohol does to the liver, the lungs, and the brain. And it ends with a prophetic warning. You have three choices: (1) Continue to drink, suffer brain damage, and go crazy. (2) Continue to drink until it kills you. (3) Quit. But the solution is here at Paradise Inn just waiting for you: the conditioning treatment, the aversion therapy, the torture chamber all designed to make Ponytail Tony so sick, so sick of the smell, the taste, and alcohol vomit that he would quit forever. Say it, Tony, say it: "I will never drink again. I will never drink again." "I promise, I will never drink again."

On the morning of the sixth day, Alice was gone. When Tony asked about what happened, he learned that her insurance policy expired. Message from Paradise Inn: "Goodbye, sweet Alice and good luck. We want you to know that Paradise Inn is always here for you if you have insurance." That was a nice way of saying "no insurance, no treatment." Everyone knew how much Alice wanted to stop drinking. If she just had that insurance, she would have been cured. Hopefully, she would find sobriety somewhere, somehow.

It was time for Tony to enter the horror chamber again. More bourbon, scotch, brandy, vodka, gin, and always the warm beer. On the final day of treatment at Paradise Inn, they had a contest to determine the "Throw up Champion of the Week." Ponytail Tony came in second, losing to a fat lady who won heads down.

When Tony left Paradise Inn, he drove past a liquor store, and just the sight of the booze bottles in the window caused him to throw up all over himself. When he returned to the reservation and went back to work as a park ranger, the thought of drinking had left him, He could not stand the smell of alcohol in any form whatsoever. But years before, he had heard his father say, "And this too shall pass." And indeed it did. Within a month, Ponytail Tony was drunk again and was threatened with termination from the Parks Department. His cousin, who was an alcoholic, introduced him to Alcoholics Anonymous. Tony learned that his problem was not only the physical craving but also emotional, psychological, spiritual. Most importantly was what the other members kept saying over and over again: "Resentments will kill you."

No longer could he hold on to them, dwell on them, get drunk over them—he must let them go. It took time, but he worked the twelve steps and went to meetings every day for six months. At age fifty he took an early retirement and joined the newly formed Tribal Parks. Within two years, he was the director of the Ravajo Indian Tribal Parks and was named the Native American of the year in the Southwest. He cut off his fourteen-inch ponytail and sent it Gotcha Butcher.

With continuing support of Alcoholics Anonymous, Ponytail Tony has been sober one day at a time.

CHAPTER THIRTY-EIGHT

SAYING GOODBYE IS HARD TO DO

The historic home of the most powerful men in the world has been called the Executive Mansion, President's House, People's House, Great White Prison, President's Palace, the British Bonfire, and afterward, the White House. The first president slept about everywhere but never in the Washington DC Presidential Palace. But he did approve the plans for the present-day residence. He laid the cornerstone on October 13, 1792, for the first public building to be erected in the new nation's Capital.

An Irish architect from Charleston had submitted the winning design, and he was chosen to superintend the construction. His design allowed for wings to be added at a later date and other needed expansions. The architect, James Hoban, was handicapped from the beginning with a lack of funds, and construction was sporadic as workers sat around waiting for construction materials. Basically, it was built of Virginia Sandstone and painted white. The first occupant, who was the second president, exclaimed how big and cold it was, but it had a beautiful view of the river and passing boats. The president's house went from big and cold to hot and hollow on August 24, 1814, when the British set torch to the house. It was a glorious bonfire, and when the rain doused the fire, only the roofless walls remained—a burned-out shell. The president and his wife escaped but not before she wrote, "Because I insist on waiting until the large picture of General Washington is secured, and it requires to be unscrewed from the wall. This process was found too tedious for these perilous moments. I have ordered the frame to be broken and the canvass taken out. It is done." Dolly Madison would forever be known for saving the Gilbert Stuart presidential portrait.

Rebuilding the president's house was slow, and securing funding for the reconstruction was even slower. Four years later it was ready for a new president. Additions were made through the years: the south portico was built in 1924, the north portico and driveway five years later, spring water was piped in, and gas lighting was turned on during the Mexican War. An elevator was added, and electrical lights brightened the Great White Prison in 1882. A few changes were made over the next sixty-five years, but it was not until it was discovered that the living quarters sagged, beams were rotting, walls were cracking that the president and his family moved out in 1948, although he was reelected. His daughter's piano whose leg fell through the ceiling went with them. When the restoration was completed, the mansion had 132 rooms and twenty bathrooms.

Furniture and furnishings that decorated the president's house when the English flamed the building were gone forever, except for the Washington canvass. One president sold some of his own stuff to the government to fill some of the empty rooms. Over the years, Congress coughed up a few dollars for furnishings, but it was mostly a hodgepodge of junk. But a large mirror above the marble mantle and a new crystal chandelier did enhance the mansion. There was no interior decorating plan, no established theme. It is the First Ladies who dictate how their temporary home will look to the world. Each of the president's wives made alterations, which reflected their likes and dislikes. Then there was the president who was presented with a 1,400-pound cheese, and he invited the public in to eat all they could. What they didn't devour, they spilled on the carpet floor, which stuck up the place for three weeks. His wife was furious.

One president and First Lady changed everything around because they hated their predecessor. Another exclaimed, "I will not live in a place cluttered with junk." He sold twenty-four wagon loads of rubbish.

Some filled it up with paintings others with books. There was so much china donated that a vault was installed to store it all. One genteel palace housekeeper started a campaign to collect rare old pieces and a worldwide outpouring of donations came in, enough to fill up a thousand homes.

The most stupendous changes occurred in 1961. A Fine Arts Commission was established to find authentic American antiques and paintings of the eighteenth and nineteenth centuries. The mission was to restore the White House so it would reflect the lives of past presidents. A team of professional curators catalogued, restored, and displayed the approved acquisitions with guidance from Jackie Kennedy.

After living eight years anywhere, one will accumulate wanted and unwanted things, especially if your temporary home has been the White House. When the Klantons first moved in on January 20, 1993, they brought most of their prized possessions with them. No official inventory was made of their personal belongings for no one had any reason to give it a second thought. After settling in, the First Lady made a batch of cookies and then initiated a refurbishing and acquisition program for the Executive Mansion and raised $25,000,000 for the project. Hillary Klanton's beautiful book *Welcome to Our Place* was a great success, and all the proceeds went to the White House. When they said goodbye in 2001, two Mayflower vans loaded up their stuff. One headed for New York; the other just around the corner to Georgetown.

Inside the moving vans were pot and pans, tables and chairs, sofas, china, suitcases, lots of books, lamps, several televisions, rugs, cutlery, her favorite family desk, pictures, paintings, personal files, dresses, suits, blouses, shoes, shirts, coats, hats, suitcases, computers, cell phones, personal jewelry, and all of their daughter's teenage possessions.

No one in the outgoing administration could believe that anyone could stoop so low. If you wanted to attack the president on foreign policy, national health care, domestic issues, that's fair game, but to allege that he and the First Lady stole White House furniture and furnishings is just plain dirty politics. It all began when an incoming congressman from the opposite party notified the press that the Klantons had removed government property to furnish their two new homes. He claimed that a former employee of the White House informed him that he had proof that they walked off with a sofa $4,700, oriental rug $3,200, dining room table and chairs $9,000, stuffed chair and foot stool $1,500, china $1,800, cutlery $99, gold bracelet $5,000, and a gold-plated saxophone $1,000. The total listing of stolen government property—103 items valued at $489,500. Most of the newspapers and television stations treated it as an unsubstantiated cheap shot. It was indeed a complete fabrication, but the incoming Spoilers pushed for an investigation by the WHLVA (White House Ladies Volunteer Association). It was just another witch hunt and a waste of government employees' time and taxpayers' money. Both the FBI and the IRS declined to participate.

At first the former president and First Lady were in shock, but they later became righteously incensed.

The Parks Department in the Capital City is responsible for many housekeeping functions in the White House, which include the maintenance and storage of the furnishings and museum pieces. But they were under the supervision of a political appointee entitled the White House chief curator, one who had no curatorial training or experience. The investigation began with the interrogation of the new chief curator.

WHLVA: Since the Klantons occupied the White House over a hundred curators, assistants, students, volunteers, willing and unwilling, have been involved with the acquisition, preservation, display, and storage of government property. How can we possibly make an accurate judgment of what items belonged to the Executive Mansion and which items were given to the Klantons for their personal use.

CHIEF CURATOR: Well, we can't. The records are a mess. It's impossible to verify who donated what or when it was donated. During the project to acquire authentic furnishings over one million individual donors were recorded and over one million items were received. I've only been the chief curator, which is an administrative position and not a professional curator, for six months. The Parks people tell me that 99 percent of what was received was not of museum quality and is in storage. They say that the government warehouse probably holds over two million pieces donated over the past century that will never be on display in the White House.

WHLVA: Well, some of our ladies have been volunteers for over fifty years and have seen many administrations come and go. We're only concerned about the donations received since the Klantons have lived here. Do you know what they were and where they are located? And which ones are on display in the mansion?

CHIEF CURATOR: Traditionally, the location of a donation on the PPMRC is always written in pencil because the item could be on permanent display or it might be used for a special occasion or it might be in the holding room or it might be in permanent storage somewhere.

WHLVA: What in the Lord's name is a PPMCR?

CHIEF CURATOR: It's something the Parks people started years ago to maintain control over the museum collections. It's the Presidential Palace Museum Record Card.

WHLVA: To be blunt, can you determine what is the governments and what belongs to the Klantons?"

CHIEF CURATOR: No, I can't. We have a listing of the donations, but the gifts to the Klantons, items that would belong to them and they can keep, is separate. As I understand it, the Parks people may not be aware of such a gift.

WHLVA: Can you walk us through the process step by step on what happens when a donation arrives at the White House?

CHIEF CURATOR: The first thing is to acknowledge the gift. The donors want a receipt so they can deduct the donation from their income taxes. We send them a computer-generated letter, and the letter has a control number on it. The same number is placed on the donations and on our PPMRC.

WHLVA: And that's it?

CHIEF CURATOR: Well, when we get around to it, we examine the item, measure it, photograph it, and enter everything the donor knows about it on the PPMRC in ink. There are three copies of the PPMCR: one copy stays with the donation, one copy is our working copy, and the original, along with the donor's letter, is filed in our Master Catalogue System. All this is entered into our computer. We never value any donation or put a price on it for the donor. That is their responsibility.

WHLVA: How many of these donations have been catalogued during the past ten years?

CHIEF CURATOR: About 10 percent. We receive about two hundred donations every day.

The investigation revealed that there had always been an internal struggle between the politically appointed chief curator and the Parks people who actually did the work. Many of the PPMRC had notations like "Lost" or "On Loan." There was no clear cut regulation, time limit, or system in loaning an item. If something was on loan, the Parks people would take no action to have it returned. There was no evidence to support the unfounded charges against the Klantons. The accusations that the Spoilers tried to hype in the media were nothing more than a big fat lie. For example, the saxophone was given to the president by his mother when he was in high school. The gold bracelet had been a gift from the president to the First Lady on their tenth wedding anniversary. All the furniture and furnishings removed from the White House by the Klantons were found to be legitimate—it was all their personal belongings.

The Klanton's had a pretty good idea who the White House informant was. He had previously worked in their political campaigns but had turned against them because he felt he didn't get enough credit. But that was all in the past. Now it was just wiser to ignore it than pursue it. But there was a young lady in the Parks Department public affairs office who had once been the lover of the sad sack squealer.

This confidence man had also seduced a White House volunteer who had worked in the office of the chief curator. He sweet-talked the young lady into arranging for him to "borrow" some of the valuable donations. No one seemed to notice the charade, but he would try to impress his park service live-in girlfriend and called his apartment the "Little White House." When he dumped her, he neglected to change the locks.

She knew something that never occurred to him—that each borrowed piece had a catalogue number on it, black ink on a small white circle. She entered his apartment and took photographs of all the pieces which the museum records showed "For White House Use Only." There were seventeen pieces valued at $180,000. She mailed photographs of the apartment building, the apartment, and the White House donations to the FBI, the IRS, and the WHLVA. Each photograph of the seventeen items clearly showed the black-on-white catalogue number. The G Men were waiting for him when he returned to his apartment and confronted him with the pictures. He swore that he only borrowed the items but could not find the White House volunteer to substantiate his claim. All the principal newspapers and television stations carried the story and his picture "White House Burglar Caught—Inside Job." He had learned a valuable lesson—never dump a Peyote lady.

CHAPTER THIRTY-NINE

IT'S SO EASY TO SAY GOODBYE, GOTCHA IS GONE

The presidential palace Poobahs had no choice except to meet with Gotcha's father, Bully Boy Butcher, and explain that his son had become a major political liability. Gotcha, during his tenure as assistant secretary of the Interior, had not only embarrassed the conservative administration but also the president himself, and more than once. Who would ever forget that when the president let the Liberty Bell fall and shatter, one inside surface was red and the other was blue. It was the president who dropped the bell, but it was Gotcha who sent the events in motion because of his unyielding arrogance. And it was Gotcha's anti-environment, anti-conservation, anti-parks culture that resulted in the Pageant of Peace Christmas Tree falling over as the president attempted to illuminate it. And the following year the Christmas Tree blowing up in the vice president's face. And the front-page picture of Mr. Wescoat watering the dead grass in a thunderstorm with the caption "The president said water the hell out of it." It was Gotcha who overruled the Parks Department, allowing for the pornography at the Art Barn. And it was Gotcha who approved the Red Rose Salon debacle at Laughanet Park when Myrtle's brother railed against, "The man in the White House."

It was Gotcha's poor judgment in kowtowing to his wife, Molly, and letting her push the disastrous "Adopt a Prairie Dog Program."

Gotcha's failure to get Beggan on Mount Blushmore; Gotcha who almost caused an international incident with the Russians and Chinese during their tour of the nation's capital. And it was Gotcha's costly mistake, losing billions of dollars in future oil revenues, that went down the Bathroom Commode Hole.

The senior Butcher reacted by cutting off the money spigot. Bully Boy told them, "Well, if you morons in the White House want to play hardball, that's my game, that's how I got rich. If you don't want to take care of my boy, then you don't get my money." The old man just wanted Gotcha to get some on the job training in the government and make the mistakes there before taking over the Butcher company. As the money dried up from other contributors, the Conservative Party lost the election and Butcher lost his political connections and suffered a heart attack. Gotcha took over the Butcher Construction Company and his bungling continued as he drove it into bankruptcy. He was found guilty of bribery and was sentenced to twenty-five years in the federal penitentiary.

CHAPTER FORTY

LET'S HAVE A PARK EXPERIENCE

There will always be a Gotcha Butcher and a Cool-Head Fred. One who is uncaring, selfish, an exploiter; the other sensitive, unselfish, a protector. It is the vague language establishing the National Park Service that feeds the greedy and gives them a loophole to ravage and ruin. It is difficult to image what the lawmakers thought they were creating, mandating a federal agency to manage a dichotomy. The words "To provide for the enjoyment of the same in such manner and by such means as will leave them unimpaired for the enjoyment of future generations" "Provide for the enjoyment" and "Leave them unimpaired" presents an ambiguity that has been impossible for the park people to successfully balance in their role as stewards of our great and precious national treasures.

"Enjoyment" reminds us of "having a good time," "amusement," "suits one's purpose," "reap the benefit of," and "hedonism." "Unimpaired" is to "leave them whole," "leave them as you found them," "don't pick the flowers." "In such manner and by such means" has not been adequately defined, understood, or put into practice. As result, the national parks and monuments have become seriously impaired. "Impairment" is defined as "to squander," "to waste," and "to desecrate."

How do you leave the parks and monuments unimpaired if political appointees at the highest levels force park management at the operational level to provide a happy hunting ground? Are the Parks people to maintain a sandbox for park visitors to wallow in? Should they indulge the unrealistic expectations of the visitors who often anticipate a Disneyland adventure when they descend upon a national park? The park visitors are welcomed by the concessioners, the big and small businesses that are licensed to operate in the National Park System. Local park management knows from experience that the concessioners are the "Untouchables" who entice the visitors to enjoy their unrelated and unnecessary hotels, restaurants, lounges, bars, and gift shops. Their mantra is "We can satisfy all of your whims and wants in your home away from home." When the Parks people try to reign them in and enforce the language of the licenses and contracts, they are overruled by the Gotchas in the Capital City. It has been screamed and demanded by conservation groups for over a hundred years: "Move all of those highly profitable facilities and services out of our parks and monuments. They contribute nothing to the park experience and are simply distractions that the park visitors waste their money on."

The law, as written, simply gives the Gotchas of the world the opportunity to take advantage of the incomprehensible interpretations of "in such manner and by such means," and as a result, the parks become impaired. The word "enjoyment" should be deleted from the initial legislation and replaced with the word "experience," which would be defined as a visit that could change the visitor but never alter the parks. Is this possible? Would the word "experience" ensure an absolute unimpairment? Probably not, but it could change the expectations of the park visitor and the philosophy of park management. It could close some of the doors to wrong use and misuse. Through the parks' interpretive programs and activities, respectful and supportive appreciation of the parks could be encouraged. They could development a "How to Experience a Park" guide for each unique park and monument. It could instill in the visitors a sensitivity for those who would follow them and that they too would have a fair chance for discovery and wonderment

There will always be a Peyote Society to right the wrongs and expose the misdeeds of the Spoilers. The Peyotes will do whatever is necessary to safeguard a park experience for our children and our children's children. And for Cool-Head Fred...

CHAPTER FORTY-ONE

PING PONG IS MY GAME

After having served through mostly anti-conservation, anti-environment, anti-parks, and anti–good government administrations, Fred was surprised but felt vindicated when a liberal, pro-conservation president was elected. Hopefully, the national parks would become a higher priority since the senseless war was finally over. His old adversary, Gotcha Butcher, was behind bars, and there wouldn't be a need for the Peyote Society for a while. It had been a long time since Fred had worn the park ranger uniform being in the Parks Department headquarters in the Capital City for the past twenty years. He was well past retirement age, so one day he took his old Smokey Bear Hat off his office wall and walked out. He left a simple note: "Time to go." Fred had been to many retirement parties, and to him they were sad affairs.

Most of the career employees he had seen retire were angry because the Parks Department had been so politicized. They grumbled that they should have gotten that last promotion or that choice park superintendent position and they had been wronged. None of them were happy.

Fred had often wondered what he would do when he retired, but he had made no special plans. His wife, Ginny, had already retired from the Alexandria Health Department as director of Nursing. He thought about going back into teaching, but decided that he was just too old. He thought maybe he and Ginny would travel about, but she didn't want to be away from her seven cats for too long. And then he remembered that shortly before he retired he had conducted a management review of Yellowstone National Park. One of the park rangers at Old Faithful had a ping-pong table, and Fred had no trouble winning. It brought back old memories of his earlier ping pong prowess, and he still had those playground trophies and medals stored in the attic.

Fred and Ginny retired in a little town one hundred miles north of Seattle, because his daughter and grandkids were there. There were several big Chinese table tennis clubs in Seattle and a small club in the Senior Center two blocks from his new home. It had been thirty-five years, but Fred and Ginny were anxious to get started over again. They played both in their garage and in the local club. Fred's new raison d'etre was "Cool-Head Fred is my name, and ping pong is my game." But my, oh my, had the game changed since he first picked up a paddle almost sixty years ago. It was now funny rubber technology.

No more sandpaper or wood surfaces. Now there were paddles with long pimples that bent and reversed the spin of the ball, anti-spin rubber that took the spin off the ball. It was almost like "let the rubber do the work." But the long rallies between offense players and defense players were rare. It was now all about speed and power.

Fred's style was a throwback to the 1930s—defense, defense, defense. Killing the ball, smashing it, putting it away, powering your way to victory was a young man's game. Because his game was slower, more deliberate, ball placement, and changing spins—it was effective against the other old men who still tried to play like they were twenty years old. He just kept getting the ball back, chopping and blocking—changing the spin—under spin, top spin, no spin, under spin with side spin—spin, spin, spin, spin that win.

Both Ginny and Fred began playing in their garage, then in the Senior Center. But what they needed was to play better competition. So they started driving the one hundred miles to Seattle every weekend playing on Saturday afternoon and night and in the Bellevue Tournaments on Sunday afternoon. They were being tested against varying styles and better players. In the national ratings, age seventy and over, Fred was in the top ten. At age eighty, he was in the top five. In the national tournament age eighty-five and over, he made the finals. He lost to his best Chinese friend who the following year moved back to Beijing.

And now Fred was ninety. He had dreamed of being the national champion. He wanted it more than anything else. The age ninety and over event was held in Las Vegas. In the semifinals, Fred won his match, although it was close. He was now in the finals. In the other semifinals, the biggest upset of the national table tennis tournament happened. The finals would be Cool-Head Fred versus Ginny, his wife of over sixty years.

Fred was in a panic. He was not going to beat his wife to become the national champion. So he decided to dump. He would attack her serves and hit the ball off the table to make sure that she won. But Ginny wasn't going to let that happen. She attacked his serves and hit the ball into the net. In the first game it was tied 16 to 16, 28 all, 43 to 43. It seemed it would go on forever. On the next point Ginny slipped and fell to the floor. She grabbed her ankle and cried that it was broken, She was defaulted and Cool-Head Fred became the national champion.

Fred ran over to her, and he, too, was crying. "I'm so sorry, Ginny, how is your ankle?"

Ginny laughingly replied, "There's nothing wrong with my ankle, CHAMP."

Wes Wolfe was a Career National Park Service Ranger and Executive. He served in numerous parks including Yosemite and Grand Canyon and headquarters in Washington DC. He was also an instructor at the National Ranger Academy. He retired as associate regional director, Operations, responsible for the administration of forty-two national parks and monuments in six western states.

He served in the US Army Special Weapons in Japan and Korea. After his military career, he received a masters degree from the University of Maryland and joined the National Park Service. Wes was a champion table tennis player winning over one hundred national tournaments. He retired in Anacortes, Washington, to be near his daughter, son-in-law, and two grandsons.

CPSIA information can be obtained
at www.ICGtesting.com
Printed in the USA
FFHW021912140919
54962364-60663FF